To Hunt an Heiress

To Hunt an Heiress

MARTHA KEYES

To Hunt an Heiress © 2025 by Martha Keyes. All Rights Reserved.
All rights reserved. No part of this book may be reproduced in any form or by any electronic or mechanical means including information storage and retrieval systems, without permission in writing from the author. The only exception is by a reviewer, who may quote short excerpts in a review.

This book is a work of fiction. Names, characters, places, and incidents are either products of the author's imagination or are used fictitiously. Any resemblance to actual persons, living or dead, events, or locales, is entirely coincidental.
http://www.marthakeyes.com

To Marc and Jane
who read everything I write—even when it's as questionable as
Sebastian's poetry

Chapter One
Sebastian

"Did you hear me, Miss Fernside?" Sebastian Drake stared at the back of Miss Fernside's straw bonnet in mixed aggravation and disbelief until she finally—and reluctantly—turned toward him.

"Hmm?" she asked, even as her gaze flitted back to the trees.

Sebastian had managed to guide her away from her uncle long enough—and far enough—to ask his burning question, but their privacy would not last. It was Hyde Park, after all, not the Dark Walk at Vauxhall Gardens.

"Did you hear me?" he repeated, more to prove a point than due to any doubt about the answer to the question.

Her pale brows rose, making it evident she had not, in fact, heard a word he had said. "Did you say something? You must forgive me"—she turned again and stretched her neck from side to side, craning to see something in the distance—"I am nearly certain I saw a yellow-throated wood warbler." After a moment, she seemed to accept that she had not, in fact, witnessed the desired miracle, and she returned her gaze to him, all polite interest. "What did you say?"

Sebastian forced his smile to remain intact even as his teeth gritted against each other. To be obliged to repeat himself was not only humiliating; it was annoying. But it was necessary.

"I asked," he said with every bit of sunny patience he could muster, "whether you would do me the honor of becoming my wife."

Miss Fernside's pleasant expression hovered on her face as though frozen, her eyes unblinking. The only evidence she was not a statue was a slight flaring of her nostrils.

She was still smiling, but Sebastian knew an impulse to draw back, for there was a forbidding look about her. The Miss Fernside he had come to know over the past seven days was well-mannered and pretty and amiable. While she *did* have an odd preoccupation with birds—which was proving aggravating at the moment—it was nothing compared to her most important attribute.

Miss Fernside was eye-wateringly wealthy.

Repeating his offer of marriage because she was too busy admiring sprinkle-crested twig garblers was a price he was willing to pay to gain access to that wealth. He would be able to pay *any* price once they were married.

Quite suddenly, her head tipped back, and she began to laugh. It was not the musical laugh of delight from a woman who has just received the offer of marriage she wishes for, but rather an almost mad sound. A few nearby sparrows took flight as it continued.

Sebastian considered following their example, for the eyes of Miss Fernside's uncle, Mr. Haskett, swept to them from his place in conversation on the nearby path.

But Sebastian had to see this through. Everything depended upon it.

He waited for Miss Fernside's amusement to expend itself, at which time she gave a little sigh as her focus returned to him. She silently surveyed him for a moment, then opened the ever-present notebook she carried and began to sketch with maddening calm.

Sebastian watched for a moment, battling consternation and

incredulity, then opened his mouth to speak, only to be interrupted.

"I heard you this time, Mr. Drake," Miss Fernside said. "Or rather, I heard the question you *meant* to ask me."

Sebastian's brows drew together. "What do you mean?"

She continued to sketch, her head tilting to the side as she did so—no doubt adding detail to the feathers of the butter-chested borbler she wished she had seen. "Your true question was whether, after but a week of knowing you, I would give my fortune into your greedy hands."

"Miss Fernside," Sebastian began awkwardly, "that was not—"

"Spare yourself, Mr. Drake." She closed the notebook and regarded him frankly, her eyes colder than he had thought possible. "The answer to both questions is the same." After a short pause, she spun on her heel and left to rejoin her aunt and uncle.

She took her eye-watering wealth along with her.

Chapter Two
Sebastian

Three weeks later

Sebastian gripped the sides of the dressing table and stared hard into the mirror of his bedchamber in St. James's. His brown hair was carefully coiffed, as always. He wore a neat suit of blue superfine, shirt points starched into oblivion, and a fashionable knot at his throat—for a well-tied cravat covered a multitude of sins. By all accounts, he *looked* like someone capable of providing.

The world responded to the appearance of wealth.

"Drake!" A fist banged on the bedchamber door. "Stop staring in the mirror and come down."

"Never!" Sebastian called back.

The door opened slightly, revealing Frederick Yorke, whose face screwed up. "Gads, you really *are* staring in the mirror. I was only joking."

Sebastian offered a roguish half-smile to his friend and fellow lodger. "Can you blame me?"

"Quite easily." Yorke opened the door more widely and leaned his shoulder against the frame. He was handsome, with light brown hair, a square jaw, and a lively sense of humor. "But if you need further incentive, every minute you spend admiring yourself is a minute lost with the young women at the ball."

"Ah." Sebastian gave himself another look in the mirror, smoothed the hair at his temples with his hands, then stood straight. "It would be wrong of me to deprive them, wouldn't it?"

Yorke rolled his eyes good-naturedly and led the way downstairs, where their friend Benedict Fairchild was waiting in the entry hall, hat and gloves on. Fairchild was the last of the three lodgers who shared the St. James's townhouse that belonged to Fairchild's ailing uncle. He was shorter and stockier than either of his housemates and generally followed Yorke's lead in everything from fashion to politics. The two of them had political ambitions, while Sebastian's ambition was...whatever would saddle him with as much money as possible.

He was determined to take a step forward in that plan tonight.

He had spent the last three weeks reflecting upon what had gone wrong with Miss Fernside and had come to a firm conclusion. He had been too impatient to charm Miss Fernside the way women wished to be courted. More subtlety and artfulness would be required for his next attempt.

"You are wiser than we, Drake," Fairchild said after he and Yorke had unburdened themselves of their most recent political woes.

"I am, aren't I?" Sebastian agreed. "What has brought you to this vital realization?"

"You are not obliged to wade into the murky and thankless waters of politics."

Sebastian chuckled and peered through the chaise's side window, thinking of the letter in his dressing table. "I have no shortage of murky waters to wade through, I assure you."

"Do you?" Yorke asked curiously.

"The waters of being the firstborn and inheritor of an estate," Fairchild teased.

Sebastian did not respond immediately, tugging at the base of his gloves as he considered what to say. Fairchild and Yorke might be his closest friends, but he had not acquainted them with the particulars of his situation. He could use their intimate knowledge of the *ton*, though. "I must marry."

The two men stared at him, one of Yorke's brows cocking.

"Let me rephrase," Sebastian said. "I must marry *money*. A great deal of it, preferably."

"Why?" Yorke asked.

"I shan't bore you with the details, but I assure you, it is a necessity."

Yorke sat back against the squabs, looking at him curiously. "What I heard is true, then."

"You cannot possibly expect me to confirm without more information, Yorke."

"I heard," he said significantly, "that you asked Miss Fernside to marry you after knowing her but a week. I heard that you were swiftly rebuffed. And I heard that you were blackballed from White's because of it." There was a pause. "Is any of it true?"

Sebastian took a moment to seriously consider the allegations against him. "All of it."

A laugh burst from Yorke just as the carriage rolled to a stop in front of Lord Markston's estate on the outskirts of London. "And here I have been defending you! Though, I confess, I had been wondering how you came to be a member of Blackstone's."

"Haskett," Sebastian replied as they stepped out of the carriage and onto the pavement. "He is Miss Fernside's uncle, and I am certain it was he who blackballed me from White's."

Being offered membership into Lord Blackstone's club of misfit gentlemen had been a questionable balm to Sebastian's spirits after having been barred from the domain of London's elite. He had hoped to make valuable connections at White's that would aid him in his quest. But alas.

Blackstone's would have to do.

Lord Blackstone was a viscount, at least, but he was also an oddity. The man collected an inordinate amount of taxidermy, with which he littered his club, then surrounded himself with gentlemen who had been blackballed like himself. Dead animals and dead reputations—those seemed to be his domain.

Lord Markston's house towered over the three of them, a beacon of wealth and grandeur, with its creamy stone façade, imposing columns, and pristine windows alight. They were not destined to see whether the interior matched the exterior, however, as guests were being shepherded around the house and toward the back.

Markston had certainly spared no expense to make the grounds magnificent, however. An expansive manicured lawn spread out before them, a ballroom floor at its center. Gauzy silks were draped around the edges while small lanterns had been strung above, making the polished wood gleam. Liveried servants balanced glinting silver platters on their hands, offering champagne and delicate pastries to anyone needing something to revive them after spirited dancing.

Small, tented alcoves created the outer boundary of the lawn, with plush seating beneath for those who wished to observe without participating—or perhaps pretend they were not waiting for an invitation to dance.

"Well, gentlemen," Sebastian said as they admired the scene. "Why not put all of that political knowledge to use and tell me where I should focus my attention this evening?"

"You wish for us to point out the heiresses?" Yorke said with a hint of amusement.

Sebastian gave a little bow. "If you please."

"Marriage is a life sentence, Drake," Fairchild said. "Are you certain you wish for money to be the primary factor determining your wife's identity?"

"Miss Potts is a prime candidate," Yorke offered with an air of innocence. "Only look at her." He nodded toward one of the alcoves, where a woman who must have been sixty if she was a day sat with a small white dog cradled in her arms. "Never married. Inherited her father's enormous fortune."

"Loves dancing," Fairchild added. "But only with her dog in her arms. A very endearing trait, you must admit."

The dog in question yapped at an innocent passerby.

"I have no liking for animals," Sebastian said. He was already obliged to look at more than his fair share at Blackstone's. At least those were silent.

"No liking for them *yet*." Yorke cocked a brow. "I feel certain the beast would win your affection if you only gave him a chance."

"After all," Fairchild added, "what is a dislike for animals when the Potts fortune is ripe for the plucking?"

He and Yorke shared a chuckle.

"I take your point," Sebastian said with his own acknowledging smile. "I suppose wealth is not the *only* requirement, but it is certainly foremost."

"Let us have the other requirements, then," Yorke said. "Preferably over a drink."

Sebastian followed Yorke toward the nearest footman holding a platter and let his gaze run over the array of ball guests. What *did* he wish for in his heiress? He supposed he could sacrifice his dignity and marry someone like Miss Potts if needed. But was it necessary?

London had plenty of heiresses.

If Sebastian had not been in such dire need of wealth, he would have approached courtship very differently, indeed. He would have found a woman with a kind but keen eye, one with wit and a ready laugh.

But he *was* in dire need of wealth, and his own selfish wishes had no place in a decision that would affect far more than himself.

"Would Miss Dillamond meet your requirements?" Fairchild took champagne from a platter and offered it to Drake. "She is dancing now—the one with the yellow feather in her hair. I made her acquaintance just last week. This is her first Season."

Yorke accepted a glass from Fairchild. "Seventeen. Fresh from the schoolroom."

"Impressionable," Fairchild added.

Sebastian pulled a face. "I have no desire to prey on the innocent." He took a sip of champagne. "Someone with a bit more experience, if you please. But without one foot in the grave," he hurried to add, anticipating the direction of their minds.

"A widow, perhaps?" Yorke nudged Fairchild. "What wealthy widows do we know of?"

They surveyed the scene, shoulder to shoulder, offering up options, only for Sebastian to dismiss them for reasons that sounded increasingly spurious, even to him. Fairchild's comment about marriage being a life sentence had niggled its way into his mind. He might gain access to his wife's money almost instantly upon marriage, but there was nothing instantaneous about the lifetime he would spend with her afterward.

Yorke snapped. "That's the ticket!"

"A perfect fit," Fairchild agreed.

"What, now?" Sebastian asked, less hopeful than their excitement suggested he be.

"Mrs. Lawrence." Yorke leaned toward him and spoke more softly. "See her over there? I had forgotten about her, for she rarely comes to Town."

"Only here playing chaperone to a relative, I believe," Fairchild said.

Sebastian tried and failed to locate Mrs. Lawrence amongst those near the entrance, for he hadn't the slightest idea who she was or what to look for. "Where is she?"

"Just coming in," Yorke said. "Pink gown. Her companion is wearing virginal white, of course."

Sebastian searched for the two women described, fully prepared to find a squat, middle-aged woman guiding her wide-eyed charge with tight-lipped vigilance.

Perhaps that was why it took longer than it should have for his gaze to lock on Mrs. Lawrence.

Petite she was, but squat she was not. Nor was she middle-aged. At first, he felt certain she was near his own eight-and-twenty years, but after watching her for a moment, he realized it was the confidence with which she held herself that gave the impression.

Her mouth was not pulled into tight-lipped vigilance, either. In fact, she whispered something to her charge, then drew away with a laugh that made Sebastian's stomach somersault.

She was captivating—honey-colored hair that gleamed under the lights, rosy lips to match her gown, and eyes that glittered with amusement.

He refocused himself on the goal at hand. Beauty was not one of his requirements, but he certainly would not object to it. "What is her situation?"

"Husband died several years ago," Fairchild said. "Lawrence was obscenely wealthy, and he left everything to her, for he doted on her. She has been living very high indeed in her widowhood."

Sebastian's eyes locked on her, watching her progress through the crowd as she took a drink from the nearest servant and led her charge toward one of the alcoves, the smile still on her face. "Came from money of her own, I assume?"

He could not take his eyes away from her. For all her youth, there was a confidence borne of experience in her bearing—or perhaps it was wealth that granted such a thing.

"No," Yorke said. "Everyone was surprised when Lawrence chose her for a bride, weren't they, Fairchild? Positively showered her with attention and gifts, they say. Bowled over by her beauty, no doubt."

Sebastian let this sink in, his heart beating at a quicker pace than usual. A striking young widow who had only come by her wealth through marriage? She had sought a fortune, just as he was. Could a more perfect candidate exist?

"What do you say, Drake?" Yorke asked. "Will she do?"

He watched Mrs. Lawrence and her ward take seats in an empty alcove. "Will you introduce me?"

"Happy to," Yorke replied genially, "if I were acquainted with her."

Sebastian pulled his eyes away from her and looked at Yorke to see whether he was teasing. He was not. "Where, pray, does all this knowledge of her come from?"

Yorke put a hand on his shoulder and squeezed. "When women discuss people, they call it gossip. When men do it, it's called politics."

Sebastian pondered his predicament. Mrs. Lawrence's acquaintances must overlap with his *somehow*, but he did not have the time to devote to discovering precisely where. If she did not often come to Town, there was no saying how long she would remain. Time was of the essence.

"Well, then"—he tossed off his glass—"I shall have to arrange an opportunity myself, shan't I?"

Chapter Three
Selina

Selina Lawrence's eyes surveyed each young man on the ballroom floor like a huntress evaluating her prey. She noted appearance, bearing, and comportment toward their partners.

The exercise was not for her own benefit, however, but for the benefit of the young woman beside her. Phoebe Grant was Selina's responsibility, and she was determined that her charge enjoy a Season full of dances with a bevy of kind, young gentlemen—something Selina herself had never enjoyed.

"And that"—Selina Lawrence pointed out a young, strapping man with blond hair on the outdoor ballroom floor—"is Henry Vaughan."

A cough that sounded suspiciously like a laugh met this pronouncement, so she turned to the young woman who sat beside Phoebe.

Miss Winser met her gaze with a twinkle in her eye.

"Am I wrong?" Selina asked.

"It is *Horatio* Vaughan," Miss Winser corrected with good-natured amusement.

Of course Miss Winser would know the name of every

Vaughan in England. Her mother was an accomplished gossip, and the apple had fallen very close to the tree indeed.

Selina had introduced Miss Winser to Phoebe in an effort to help Phoebe become acquainted with other young, unmarried women, but so far, all it had served to do was put on display Selina's glaring lack of knowledge about the Season's most eligible bachelors.

"Ah," Phoebe said in her kind voice. "You were not so *very* wrong, then, for he *is* a Vaughan."

"It is no wonder I *was* wrong," Selina said, "for there are a dozen of them."

Miss Winser's amusement heightened at this liberal estimate of the Vaughan siblings. "Give or take a few, yes."

Selina sat back on the velvety squabs of the sofa. It was beautiful, with tufted deep crimson fabric and ornately carved mahogany, but it was more of a comfort to the eyes than to the body. "Poor Phoebe! You have been saddled with a far from ideal chaperone this evening. I have not set foot in London in more than three years and am woefully ignorant, mistaking Horatios for Henrys and heaven only knows what else."

"Unforgivable," Phoebe teased.

"You would be better off allowing Miss Winser to take you under her wing."

"Heaven forbid!" Miss Winser said. "I cannot keep track of my gloves, much less another person. But I *am* a reliable resource when it comes to the identities of the gentlemen worth knowing. I simply cannot make the introduction should you want one."

"That is where I *can* help," Selina said. "Together, we shall ensure Phoebe's evening is a success."

She had kept away from London since George's death and, as a result, lacked familiarity with the faces and names of the most eligible gentlemen. She had plenty of connections despite that, however, and could easily foster whatever acquaintance Phoebe wished to pursue.

Selina's sister-in-law, Jane, had intended to chaperone her own sister this Season, but two circumstances had prevented this: firstly, Jane was occupied with caring for her four young and spirited children; and secondly, she simply did not have the money or influence Selina did.

That was what it always came to: money and influence.

Selina had not always had them. She had been raised in a genteel household with very little of either. So when Mr. Lawrence had taken notice of her and had begun to court her and spoil her with all manner of flowers and jewelry and gifts, she had been gratified beyond expression. She had convinced herself that this feeling of gratification was love.

She let her eyes return to the dancers, thinking how different her own experience had been at Phoebe's age. She had never enjoyed a night of dancing with handsome young gentlemen, engaged in harmless flirtation, or admired the evening's prospective partners while laughing with a friend.

She had been married off to a man of middle age before she had even understood what it meant to be out in Society, and the sight of what she had missed stirred a familiar pinch of resentment.

And yet, for all that, she was grateful not to be bound by the strict expectations of the young, unmarried women present. As a widow, she was at liberty to do and say things that would have shocked the *ton* as a debutante—and shocked her late husband as his wife, for that matter.

"What of you?" Miss Winser asked Selina. "Do you not care to dance? Perhaps there is someone to whom *you* wish to be introduced."

Selina merely laughed.

"Mrs. Lawrence claims she has no desire to marry again," Phoebe explained.

"It is not a *claim*, Phoebe," Selina replied with amusement. "It is a plain and simple truth."

Phoebe and Miss Winser shared a quick, incredulous glance.

Selina was inclined to assure them further but decided against it. She and Phoebe were but five years apart in age, but in life experience, there were worlds between them. Phoebe was innocent and bright-eyed, while Selina was tested and perhaps a bit cynical. There were things Phoebe simply could not yet understand—and hopefully never would.

While Jane and Richard appreciated Selina's power to help Phoebe make connections, what they had failed to account for was that Selina was far from the best person to encourage Phoebe toward marriage. The greatest benefit of marrying George was that she now had no need to enter into the contract of marriage again.

She had everything she needed.

As a result, the sort of wisdom she possessed was not in the vein of how to identify and attract promising young gentlemen but rather how to appear a docile wife while chafing at the bit for more freedom.

Well, she had all the freedom she desired now. If she had wished to, she could have flirted outrageously with any man present—married or otherwise—without fear of ruining her future. Indeed, she could have done more than flirt with them. To be a wealthy widow was to be above reproach.

Across the floor, a man stood watching them. He was handsome, with dark brown hair, an angular jaw, and intent, considering eyes.

Selina pulled her gaze away and spoke in a low voice to Miss Winser. "Do not look just yet, but do you know the gentleman over there? Black coat. Blue waistcoat. Dark hair. This is the third time I have caught him staring at the two of you."

Miss Winser waited before casually letting her gaze veer toward the man in question, where it lingered on him but a moment before moving on.

"You are again mistaken, Mrs. Lawrence," Miss Winser said.

"Mistaken in what?" Selina asked, prepared to defend her assessment. She might not know names, but she knew a stare when she saw it.

"Mr. Drake—the man you have pointed out—is not staring at Miss Grant or at me. He is staring at you."

Selina couldn't keep her gaze from sweeping toward Mr. Drake again. Sure enough, their eyes locked, and her heart skipped in a way she found both unfamiliar and unpleasant.

He smiled slightly, as though he sensed her internal reaction.

She turned away, thoroughly discomfited. "He knows of my fortune, I imagine."

"Oh, come now," Phoebe exclaimed. "You assume a great deal—and unfairly, I think."

Selina smiled at her and tweaked the ring on her left hand. George had given it to her as a gift during their first year of marriage. *For my most beautiful diamond*, the tiny inscription on the inside said.

"An heiress must doubt the sincerity of *every* man's affection," she said.

George had not even been in his grave when men had begun showing a marked interest in her. It was why she had stayed away from London until now. She had been chosen for her beauty before; she had no wish to be chosen for it—or her fortune—again.

"Surely not every man's," Phoebe said. "You must be the easiest woman in the world to love, Mrs. Lawrence! With or without a fortune."

Selina smiled at her kindness, undeniable evidence of her naivety though it was. Selina felt a duty to both guard that naivety and break it down. "Call me Selina, if you please. Mrs. Lawrence makes me feel so very old." She rose to her feet, feeling suddenly restless. "Come, the set is ending, and both of you have yet to dance."

She led them through the crowds and performed introductions to two young gentlemen whose fathers she had hosted at Chesleigh House the year before George's death. When both young ladies had partners secured, she smiled and stepped back, aware of eyes on her again.

It was the man who had been staring earlier, and she cast him only a passing glance before making her way elsewhere to while away the time until Phoebe required her again. She disliked how the man's gaze affected her, making her heart beat more quickly and sending a feeling racing within her veins, though whether it was fear or excitement, she could not determine.

Whatever it was, it could not be indulged.

Selina's tranquil observation of Phoebe dancing was interrupted by Mr. Tolliver, an old acquaintance of George's who had sought Selina out shortly after her arrival in London, showing all the subtlety of a battering ram about his intentions toward her. He was far more self-assured than he deserved to be, and when she politely declined the invitation to dance, he insisted on fetching her a drink.

When another gentleman came to request the honor of Selina as a partner, Mr. Tolliver spoke before she could. "Mrs. Lawrence does not intend to dance this evening, good fellow. If she did, I can assure you, you would not find us here but rather on the ballroom floor."

Phoebe's return was thus very welcome indeed. Her smile was wide and her cheeks pink with the joy of happy exertion, and Selina felt a sting of jealousy.

She handed a drink to Phoebe, who sipped from it gratefully as she caught her breath.

"Shall I find you another partner?" Selina asked. "The Gilbert boy is a skilled dancer."

"Perhaps for the set after this one," Phoebe replied, still breathless. "May we sit again?"

"Of course." Selina led the way back to the small alcove where they had taken refuge before. Miss Winser had returned to her mother and did not join them.

"Well?" Selina asked. "How was your first set of the evening?"

"Everything I had hoped it would be!" Phoebe gushed. "He was patient with my mistakes and quick to poke fun at his own. And he had such a kind smile."

Selina's memory flashed back to her own first dance. It had been a tedious minuet with George, and they had already been engaged. There had been no other partners. In retrospect, Selina wondered if her parents had insisted on that due to a fear her eyes or heart might wander.

So, Selina had never felt the exhilaration of standing across the set from a young gentleman, wondering how he regarded her, excited at the prospect of their hands touching. She had been promised before she had been permitted to dream.

"He is still staring," Phoebe said after catching her breath.

"Hm?" Selina pulled herself back to the present.

"Mr. Drake," Phoebe said. "He seems quite taken with you."

Selina forced herself not to look at Mr. Drake, though it took all her willpower. Was he as handsome as she had thought him before? What would it feel like to dance with him? "With my fortune, you mean."

"It is possible," she granted, though with a great deal of skepticism. "But is it not *also* possible that he is simply struck by your beauty? What if he knows nothing of your fortune?"

Selina opened her mouth to reply, only to shut it again. Phoebe was generous to a fault; it was unlikely that explaining the ways of the world to her would convince her.

"Might you not dance with him, Selina?" Phoebe pleaded. "Just once! It seems a terrible shame for you to spend the entire evening in such a beautiful, idyllic place without dancing at all—particularly when you have eager partners like Mr. Drake."

It *was* an idyllic place. No doubt, that was why Selina's mind insisted on conjuring up an idyllic, alternative past to match—one in which she danced all evening, each set with a different partner, wondering when she would be able to continue the acquaintances.

"I can hardly dance with a gentleman I do not know," Selina teased. "And I am quite content as I am, Phoebe. But thank you for being so attentive to my enjoyment. I am far more interested in *yours*, however."

"Do you mean to say that, if you were acquainted with Mr. Drake, you would agree to dance with him?"

Selina laughed at her persistence, sliding her ring up and down her finger to adjust it.

"Do you not find him handsome?" Phoebe pressed.

Selina's eyes stole to him, where he was laughing with the gentleman beside him. Her heart fluttered, and she pulled her eyes away.

"Of course you do," Phoebe said. "Anyone would."

"I will allow that he is handsome," Selina granted, "but what odds does that make? I meant what I said, my dear: I have no intention of marrying again."

"But it is not as though dancing with a gentleman will lead directly to a marriage with him," Phoebe argued.

"True, but—"

"And who is to say you might not find a friend in him? Surely, you do not mean to claim you have no desire for friendship."

Selina's mouth stretched wide. "I welcome friends, Phoebe, but all of this is purely hypothetical and, thus, a grand waste of precious time you might be spending on the ballroom floor. Come. Allow me to introduce you to Mr. Gilbert. I think you will find him every bit as amiable as your last partner."

Phoebe looked as though she might press the matter, but when Selina rose from their place, she followed. Soon, she was happily engaged, dancing an energetic reel, which Selina watched with a smile from a distance.

She could not keep her gaze from veering toward Mr. Drake for long, but he was not where he had been. Her gaze traveled down the set and around the immediate area, but she did not find him. Had he left?

Why did that thought elicit a little prick of disappointment? She did not know Mr. Drake even a whit. All this dwelling on the past was addling her brain.

She reached for her ring, and her stomach dropped. Her gloved finger was bare.

Her heart raced as she picked up her skirts, her eyes searching the grass near her feet. There was no telling glint, though. She squeezed her eyes shut, trying to remember when she had last felt the ring on her finger. She should not have worn gloves of silk mesh—they were far thinner than the ones she generally favored.

She glanced at Phoebe, still dancing merrily, then began to retrace her steps, her gaze fixed on the grass.

It was strange to feel so anxious about losing it, for though she wore it always, she had come to hate it. It was a reminder that she had been George's favorite accessory, much like the expensive and extremely bright waistcoats he had favored. She had taken to wearing the ring as a reminder not to allow herself to become anyone else's diamond—something to be polished and flaunted and discarded at will.

"Excuse me."

She turned and sucked in a breath of surprise to find Mr. Drake addressing her. She was obliged to lift her chin to look at him, for he was taller than she had expected.

Taller and more handsome. His striking brown eyes were intelligent and warm, and his smile...well, his smile was nothing short of charming.

"Does this belong to you, ma'am?" He held out his palm, and her diamond ring sparkled from its place in the center.

She let out a sigh of relief. "Yes, thank heaven!" She reached for it, but his fingers suddenly closed around the ring. Her eyes flew to his, her relief replaced with confusion.

"How can I be certain?" he asked with a brow cocked, though his eyes teased.

She suppressed a smile. He had come to *her*, after all. He must have seen her searching for it—perhaps he even saw her drop it. "Is my frantic examination of the lawn insufficient evidence?"

He seemed to consider this. "Intriguing but insufficient, I fear."

"Given the shockingly high number of other people here doing the same thing," she said.

He smiled. "Precisely."

"And, pray tell, sir, what *would* constitute sufficient evidence? Perhaps this indentation on my glove where it was worn?" She held up her hand for him to see. "Or my knowledge of the inscription on the inside of the ring?"

Curiosity flashed in his eyes, and her cheeks infused with heat.

She had mentioned the inscription without thinking. What if he asked her what it said? Or looked at it for himself?

"You make a convincing case, ma'am." He unfurled his fingers again and allowed her to take it.

"Thank you, Mr...."

"Sebastian Drake." He offered a well-executed bow. "At your service." His mouth quirked up at one edge. "Will you think poorly of me if I admit that I already know your name? I was brazen enough to ask it of one of my friends when I saw you arrive. I could not help myself."

Selina could not decide how to respond, for there were two ways to interpret what he said: she might choose to be flattered that he had gone to the trouble of discovering her name—or she might realize that if he had inquired about her, he would know of her fortune.

"Well, you have spared me a great deal of worry," she said as she replaced the ring on her finger, "not to mention saving me quite the walk. I was retracing my steps, of which there were far more than I realized." She glanced behind her at the ground she had covered before Mr. Drake had found her. "There are certainly worse places to do such a thing."

"Indeed, there are. In fact...perhaps we should take a turn about the gardens—to ensure you did not lose anything else, of course." His eyes twinkled.

"But I have not ventured into the gardens," she pointed out, again torn between flattery and wariness. He was inarguably charming—which made him all the more dangerous.

Not every charming gentleman is a fortune hunter. Selina could almost hear Phoebe's rejoinder in her mind.

"Who is to say you might not find something of value there despite that?" Mr. Drake countered. "I myself happened upon a diamond this evening."

Selina couldn't help but laugh just as Mr. Gilbert returned with Phoebe. He deposited her into Selina's care, then made his excuses and left to take his mother home.

Once he had gone, Phoebe's gaze turned to Mr. Drake, then to Selina, unabashedly expectant—and just a little amused, as though despite all Selina's words against Mr. Drake, she had arranged to meet him.

"Allow me to introduce you to Mr. Drake," Selina said. "Mr. Drake, this is Miss Grant, the sister of my sister-in-law."

"A sister two times, then. A pleasure to make your acquaintance, Miss Grant." Mr. Drake bowed, and Phoebe made her curtsy.

"I misplaced my ring at some point during the evening," Selina explained, "and Mr. Drake was good enough to return it to me."

"How very kind of him," Phoebe said, shooting a glance at Selina that she purposefully ignored. Did Phoebe truly think this proved anything about his character?

"Anyone would have done as much," Mr. Drake replied meekly.

"I think not," Phoebe said. "Regardless, we are glad to add such a noble spirit to those we call friends. Are we not?" She turned to Selina, looking at her expectantly.

"Of course," Selina replied politely. She did not wish to be rude to Mr. Drake, but neither did she wish to encourage Phoebe. Though, clearly, she required no such thing in order to think very highly indeed of Mr. Drake. Perhaps *she* would fall in love with him.

"Ah, look," Phoebe said. "The next set is about to form." She smiled at Mr. Drake, then Selina, her meaning clear.

Selina would box her ears the moment they were alone in the carriage. She had not known Phoebe could be so...managing.

"So it is," Mr. Drake replied with slight amusement. "Might I request the honor of a dance, Mrs. Lawrence?"

For all her determination to decline, Selina hesitated momentarily. George had been the first gentleman she had ever danced with and the *only* one she had danced with before marriage. Of course, she had later danced with his friends at parties and gatherings, but then no one at all since his death. Some part of her wondered what it would feel like to dance with a handsome, charming gentleman outside of the confines of marriage.

She grasped the ring tightly. Was she truly considering the notion of dancing with a suspected fortune hunter to satisfy some years-old, childish curiosity?

"I am not at liberty to dance this evening," she said. "I have important duties." She smiled at Phoebe.

It occurred to her that the result of this comment might be for Mr. Drake to ask Phoebe to dance. It would hardly be responsible for her to allow her charge to dance with a man she feared to harbor ulterior motives.

"I promised to introduce you to Lord Essop, did I not?" Selina added quickly. "And he appears to be at liberty now."

Phoebe shook her head. "I would not for the world have you refuse a dance on my account. I can stay with Miss Winser—"

Selina grabbed her hand, mouth arranged in a determined smile. "On no account will I abandon you. My duty to you happens to be both important and enjoyable. I thank you for the offer, Mr. Drake, but I must refuse."

Phoebe's returning grasp was every bit as laden with meaning, and for a moment, they communicated and fought in the language of forceful squeezes.

"I would not wish to deprive Miss Grant," Mr. Drake said. "Or Lord Essop, for that matter."

"You might call upon us tomorrow," Phoebe suggested, abandoning the silent war with Selina and adopting more direct tactics.

Selina forced a laugh. "My dear Phoebe"—Selina emphasized

the word *dear*—"we cannot possibly trouble Mr. Drake in such a way."

"It would be no trouble at all," he said. "I would be most happy to call upon you tomorrow. If it is convenient, of course."

Phoebe's hand found Selina's and squeezed it meaningfully.

Selina squeezed it back with more force than was necessary. She considered fabricating an excuse that would preclude them from receiving Mr. Drake the following day, but if she did so, Phoebe would undoubtedly suggest the next day, then the day after, and so on until Selina was forced to choose between unforgivable rudeness or accepting his call.

"Certainly," Selina replied.

She provided him with their direction, and he graciously excused himself to ensure Phoebe was able to secure her partner for the set.

"Do you mean to ship me back to my parents first thing tomorrow morning?" Phoebe asked as Selina guided them toward Lord Essop.

"Certainly not," Selina replied genially. "I shan't be done boxing your ears until at *least* tomorrow evening."

"Oh, Selina," Phoebe said with amusement, "I think you should have danced with him! I saw no evidence that he is a fortune hunter."

"Are you so familiar with the signs? Perhaps you underestimate him."

"Perhaps *you* do."

Selina regarded her with amusement and affection. "You are determined to think the best of Mr. Drake."

"While you seem determined to think the worst of him."

Selina pressed her lips together, unable to counter this. "You think me heartless and cynical."

"I could never think such awful things of you! I merely think you too quick to dismiss a charming man who has plenty of reason other than your fortune for wishing to become better acquainted with you."

They reached Lord Essop, preventing further debate. Selina made the appropriate introductions, and his lordship invited Phoebe to join him on the ballroom floor.

Selina sought out the refreshments, reflecting on Phoebe's words. *Was* she dismissing Mr. Drake too quickly?

Perhaps.

The truth was that she was not altogether upset at the prospect of his promised call. She could not deny her own curiosity over his intentions, which she trusted would become clear.

Chapter Four
Sebastian

Could it be? Was fortune finally beginning to smile upon Sebastian?

His interaction with Mrs. Lawrence could not have gone more swimmingly. Of course, she had declined his invitation to dance and Miss Grant had extended the one for him to call, but those distinctions mattered little.

He would have the opportunity to continue their acquaintance. That was the most important thing.

The rush of success, the blinding light of hope after the darkness that had followed his rejection by Miss Fernside, made his blood rush pleasantly.

Yorke, who had been in a long conversation with one of various members of Parliament present, came up beside him. "Well? Did you manage it?"

"I did," Sebastian replied, unable to keep from smiling. "I am to call upon her tomorrow in Berkeley Square."

Yorke raised his brows, visibly impressed. "You made quick work of that! How did you manage an introduction?"

"There was very little managing about it," Sebastian said. "I was fortunate enough to see her drop something—a ring."

"Did you really?" Yorke said incredulously.

Sebastian shot him a look. "Yes, Yorke. Do you suppose I stole it from her hand without her knowledge?" Finding a diamond ring was a windfall in and of itself, but he never truly considered keeping it, for Mrs. Lawrence's gratitude was far more valuable to him than her ring.

"No, nothing like that." Yorke smiled curiously. "It is only that my brother met his wife the same way. He dropped his signet ring, and she brought it to him."

Sebastian considered this coincidence for a moment. "Well, let us hope for a similarly happy result in my case."

<hr />

Was there ever an ill that could not have been prevented—or cured—with money?

Sebastian defied anyone to claim otherwise.

Indeed, it was money—or the lack of it, rather—that had stopped his celebrations after the very welcome opening sentence of the letter from his solicitor.

Your petition to the Court of Chancery regarding the guardianship of Miss Margaret, Master Hugo, and Master Felix Hollis has been formally accepted for review.

Sebastian paced the worn wooden floors of his bedchamber in St. James's, rubbing a hand over his chin while the words from the letter he held pinched in his chest. The news certainly merited celebration, but the phrase that followed it nipped it in the bud.

The Court has acknowledged your standing as their half-brother and has directed that notice be sent to their current guardian, Mr. Edward Hollis, who will be given due opportunity to respond.

As certain as he knew his own name, Sebastian knew Edward Hollis would fight a transfer of guardianship. Hollis had no liking for his charges—indeed, he seemed to despise them as much as he had despised, in life, the brother who had fathered them—but the money he had access to as their guardian? His affection for that ran deep.

The question was which between the two of them had the greater claim to guardianship over the children: their half-brother or their uncle?

That was what the Court of Chancery would have to decide, and it was why a phrase farther down in the letter sent a chill through Sebastian.

> *You will be required to demonstrate your ability to provide adequately for the children—both financially and with respect to their moral and physical well-being.*

Sebastian blew out a breath and set the letter down on his dressing table.

He could hardly provide for *himself*, much less three other bodies requiring food, clothing, and a roof over their heads, to say nothing of education or opportunity.

He opened the drawer of the dressing table and took out the letter he had received from Margaret two days ago. At fourteen years of age and as the eldest of his half-siblings, she was his steady and trusted correspondent, though he suspected she tried to shield him from many of the deprivations they experienced.

Felix has become more defiant of late, she had written, *going so far as to hide Mr. Hollis's liquor bottles in the privy last week. Hugo insisted on taking the blame. He fancies himself our protector these days, you know, be he ever so slight of stature.*

Sebastian's knuckles tightened, wrinkling the paper at his fingertips. Noticeably absent was the description of Hugo's punishment. Sebastian could only imagine what a drunkard like

Hollis would have chosen as retribution. The description of Hugo as "ever so slight of stature" was hardly confidence-inspiring, either. No doubt, Hollis preferred to use whatever money he had on spirits rather than on nourishing his wards.

Sebastian folded the letter and placed it back in the drawer, along with the one from his solicitor. Circumstances were quickly growing more dire for his siblings. It was why Mrs. Lawrence's appearance in his life was so very welcome.

All the letter from his solicitor and the letter from Margaret served to do was emphasize that his plan had to succeed. His attempt with Miss Fernside had been not only amateur but highly damaging. Though Haskett had blackballed him, he seemed to have declined to spread word of Sebastian's crime against his niece far and wide. There were whispers about the *ton*, however.

Sebastian would have to tread carefully.

Some thirty minutes later, he slipped a letter with Margaret's name written across the front onto the salver on the entry hall table, then snatched his top hat from the rack near the door.

He had waited to respond to her until he could offer hope. Now that he could do so, he was reluctant to make too much of it. Hope could be a costly virtue. The lack of it could be equally so, however, so he had settled on informing her that he had a promising avenue he was pursuing.

What she would make of this was unclear, for he had been hopeful in the past, as well, even before Miss Fernside. His attempts to make a living in the church had come to nothing, however. Piety only paid when one had the connections to make it so, he had discovered. And Sebastian had no connections.

He made the walk to Berkeley Square with swift strides, slowing only to consider a bouquet of flowers at a shop en route. He decided against them, however. A more subtle approach was warranted until he had a better sense of what Mrs. Lawrence liked and disliked.

The beating of his heart outstripped the pace of his feet,

thrumming with building nerves as he approached her residence, a distinguished townhouse in a location that spoke to her wealth.

He ascended the three steps, reached for the knocker, then paused.

Was this madness, what he was doing? Or worse, was it callous? Mrs. Lawrence seemed an intelligent and amiable woman, not someone deserving to be duped. But the sort of woman who *did* deserve such a thing was not the type of woman he wished to be tied to for the rest of his life.

It was a conundrum indeed.

He stared at his hovering, indecisive hand. If he did not pursue Mrs. Lawrence, what of Margaret, Hugo, and Felix?

His gaze moved to the knocker, waiting for his grasp. It was shaped like a lion, the bronze glinting in the morning sun. The door behind it was red—freshly painted, it appeared—while the surrounding creamy stone was devoid of any dirt or grime.

All of it spoke to the good fortune of the woman who lived within.

His siblings had done nothing to deserve their *mis*fortune; what had Mrs. Lawrence done to deserve her *good* fortune?

She had married someone with money. That was all.

Was that not precisely what Sebastian intended to do? It was not as though he meant to *take* the money from her, either. He simply needed to prove to the Court of Chancery that he was a fit guardian.

"This is for Margaret, Hugo, and Felix," he whispered, then he grasped the knocker and gave a decisive knock.

Contrary to his fears, he was not refused admittance, neither was he told the ladies were not at home to visitors. He was instead led through a fine entry hall with a carpeted staircase that wound around the walls to an upper floor. The walls were wainscoted below, then papered above, and the wide door carved intricately. Sebastian could only imagine what Mrs. Lawrence's country estate must look like. Perhaps she had more than one.

He was left to wait beside the wide door while the footman announced him.

"Mr. Sebastian Drake," the footman announced, then he made way for Sebastian to enter the sitting room.

Mrs. Lawrence and Miss Grant rose to their feet in front of a long, champagne-colored settee with dusky blue pillows that matched the curtains at the long windows.

Though Sebastian's eyes insisted on settling upon Mrs. Lawrence, he forced them to spend an equal amount of time on Miss Grant before smiling and bowing. "I am glad to find you at home to visitors."

"Did I not tell you we would be?" Mrs. Lawrence asked with a hint of amusement.

"I am ashamed for doubting you, but I can only imagine the number of invitations the two of you must receive every day. I would not have blamed you if you had chosen to indulge in one of them rather than staying at home for my call."

"Selina loves nothing more than being at home," Miss Grant said.

Mrs. Lawrence laughed, but her cheeks tinged with pink. "*Nothing* might be a bit of an overstatement. And now that you are here, Phoebe, I have changed my ways." She gestured to the chair across from them. "Do have a seat, Mr. Drake. Would you care for tea?"

"Thank you," he said as he sat down, "but I shan't stay long."

He had decided in advance that he would keep his visit short, hopefully leaving them wanting more rather than overstaying his welcome. His main aim today was to ensure he did not leave without a plan to see Mrs. Lawrence again.

"I trust you had an enjoyable time at the garden ball, Miss Grant?" he asked politely. Her presence gave him an easy excuse not to focus too much attention on Mrs. Lawrence at the risk of overwhelming her or making his intentions too obvious.

He would not soon forget the sound of Miss Fernside laughing at his offer of marriage.

"Oh, yes," she replied with enthusiasm. "I have never enjoyed dancing so much."

"Far more pleasant to do so outdoors than cooped up in a hot ballroom, is it not?"

"Decidedly," she agreed.

He turned to Mrs. Lawrence. "And what of you? I trust the ring was not foolish enough to attempt a second escape."

Mrs. Lawrence had been mindlessly spinning the object on her finger, but she stopped and smiled, displaying it. "After a severe talking to, I believe the two of us have come to an understanding."

"I am glad to hear it, though if the problem occurs again, a sound thrashing may be in order."

"Let us hope that it does not come to that," she said, her gaze meeting his with the glitter of shared amusement.

It sparked something in his chest—a thread of kinship, perhaps.

Instinct told him to grasp onto it and test its strength.

There was a knock on the door, and it opened to reveal a dignified servant with gray hair. The butler, no doubt.

"Forgive me for disturbing you, ma'am," he said deferentially, "but you instructed me to come to you with any questions."

Mrs. Lawrence nodded kindly, prompting him to go on.

"We have found a collection of hunting rifles and other such equipment, and I wondered if you wished it to be sent to Chesleigh House."

Mrs. Lawrence's eyes widened. "*More* hunting equipment? There is an entire room at Chesleigh already."

The butler had no satisfactory response for this.

"In any case, what purpose could there be for such things in Town?" she asked, more rhetorically than for an answer.

The butler cleared his throat. "Mr. Lawrence preferred to be prepared for hunting whenever and *wherever* the possibility presented itself, ma'am. And as you know, he always insisted on using his own equipment."

"Well, we certainly do not need to send it all to Chesleigh." She paused, her brows knitting pensively. "I will think on it, Bramley, and let you know my decision presently."

He bowed, then left the room.

Mrs. Lawrence let out a sigh, then turned back to Sebastian. "Forgive the interruption. We are sorting through my late husband's affairs, and I greatly underestimated the number of decisions it would require."

Sebastian hesitated before responding, trying to gauge whether it was the volume of decisions that overwhelmed her or the emotional toll they were taking due to the affection in which she held her husband. Both, he imagined.

It had not escaped his notice that she seemed to have a preoccupation with the diamond ring she wore. It stood to reason it had been a gift from her husband. She often touched and spun it on her finger, though whether consciously or not, he couldn't say. He had been sorely tempted to read the inscription upon it but had refrained from doing so.

He saw his opportunity and approached it warily. "I can imagine it must be overwhelming, particularly when the decisions comprise such things as hunting equipment."

"Hunting equipment, private correspondence, jewelry, snuff boxes, hundreds of books—many of them filled with the type of poetry I abhor...and the list goes on."

Sebastian's mouth quirked at one edge. "And what type of poetry might you *not* abhor?"

Her brow knit as she considered this. "I could not say, for I have yet to come across such a thing despite many years of forced study—and even a bit of imitation."

Sebastian laughed. "Well, happily for you, all hope is not lost. You may well find it as you sort through the books you mentioned."

"I am far more likely to force the task upon some poor, unsuspecting soul. Can I interest you, perhaps?"

"A generous offer," Sebastian said with feigned gratitude. "I would be more helpful with hunting equipment than poetry."

"Well, there is an idea," Phoebe said brightly. "*Would* you be willing to help, Mr. Drake?"

Sebastian was left speechless, for it was clear she did not understand his meaning. He had not meant to say that he knew a great deal about hunting. Quite the contrary.

Mrs. Lawrence let out an uneasy laugh. "Phoebe," she said with the smallest hint of censure in her tone, "I am certain that is the last thing Mr. Drake wishes to do with his time."

Sebastian's primary aim in calling upon her had been to leave with firm plans to see her again, and he was not about to let that opportunity slip through his fingers. He did not know the first thing about hunting. It was the sport of the wealthy, and thanks to his stepfather's efforts to spend his inheritance, he had never been wealthy. The one time he had joined a hunting party, he had narrowly missed shooting one of the hunting dogs.

But he would learn about hunting equipment if it would help his cause with Mrs. Lawrence.

"It would be my pleasure," he reassured her. "*If* it would be helpful. I am more than happy to do anything in my power to relieve the burden of decisions. Without wishing to boast, I *have* made a number of decisions over the course of my life."

Mrs. Lawrence fought a smile, but her eyes danced. "A veritable expert, I expect."

"Your words, not mine. Only tell me when you require me."

"Tomorrow?" Miss Grant suggested.

Sebastian glanced at her, feeling more and more certain that she was, for whatever reason, doing everything in her power to ensure his return. They were one in purpose in that regard, then.

"We have an engagement during the day," Mrs. Lawrence reminded her, "and Mr. Drake undoubtedly does too." She returned her gaze to him. "If it suits you, perhaps we could plan for this same time on Monday?"

Sebastian agreed to this, trying to suppress the sense of victory coursing through him. She wanted him back, and this time, he would be ready.

It would be no trial at all to spend more time with Mrs. Lawrence. The more he saw of her, the more he admired her, and he suspected his call had had a similar effect upon her.

Now, he just needed to learn about hunting equipment by eleven o'clock on Monday.

Chapter Five
Selina

The door of Hatchards shut behind Selina and Phoebe with a tinkling bell, nearly drowned out by the sounds of the bustling Town.

Selina was still reaccustoming herself to the din of Town after spending such a long time away. It almost felt as though London had grown sharper, faster in her absence. Society waited for no man—and certainly not for a woman trying to understand where she fit now that she was both widow and heiress.

She had returned to Town with every intention of keeping both her widowhood and her wealth intact, but Mr. Drake had put the merest sliver of doubt inside her. It was simple curiosity, though. A whisper of wondering whether she had been too swift to make such solid decisions about the long future before her.

"Well, that was a success, don't you think?" Selina said.

"Oh, most certainly." Phoebe resituated the two books she had bought, which were wrapped in brown paper and tied with twine, the Hatchards stamp pressed clearly onto the top. "Though, there was nothing so urgent about purchasing these that we could not have delayed doing so for another day or two."

Selina shot an amused glance at her, recognizing Phoebe's way of implying they might have welcomed Mr. Drake today rather than waiting until Monday.

The truth was, Selina too had found herself wishing she had not set their next meeting for so many days in the future. He had been so...amiable. He had not stayed long, either—something Phoebe had been quick to point out after his departure—and he had engaged Phoebe in conversation every bit as much as he had spoken with Selina. When Phoebe had latched onto Selina's facetious suggestion that he help with the task of sorting through George's poetry books, Selina had wanted to box her ears. Mr. Drake had responded with a gentle willingness, however, rather than the eagerness she would have expected from a man trying to weasel his way into her good graces.

She did not require assistance sorting through George's hunting equipment. She herself was an avid huntress, and George's dislike of that fact had been a constant cause of tension between them.

Selina had agreed to Mr. Drake's aid purely out of a desire to further the acquaintance and find an answer to the question of his intentions.

She could not deny the hope she felt that they were pure.

"Mrs. Lawrence!"

Selina turned at the sound of her name and found Mrs. Winser and her daughter hailing her from a dozen feet behind. A footman followed them, carrying a small object covered by a piece of cloth.

Mrs. Winser glanced at the package Phoebe held. "Hatchards?" she asked knowingly. "You will have less cause to regret your purchase than we, I trust. We have just come from the pet shop down the street."

"The pet shop?" Selina's gaze darted to the object the footman held.

Mrs. Winser nodded. "We are returning home for a few days, and the only way we could persuade little Johnny not to come to Town was to promise we would bring him a surprise when we returned." She motioned to the footman, who obediently stepped forward, held out the object, and removed the covering, revealing a cage.

Selina and Phoebe drew nearer to better see it and found themselves looking at a small, tawny rodent with a furry tail.

"What is it?" Phoebe asked with a hint of wonder in her voice.

"A dormouse," Miss Winser replied. "We nearly chose the flying squirrel, but Mama insisted this creature would be more suitable."

"The last thing we need is something that gives Johnny ideas about flight," Mrs. Winser said with a wide-eyed look. "He is forever jumping from trees and stairs. He was laid up nearly two weeks from his last adventure. He need never know of the flying squirrel, though, and will be quite content with this fellow."

The dormouse scrambled around the cage, then raised up on its hind legs, its whiskers twitching as its beady eyes darted around.

"Can you imagine how much Teddy and Lou would adore something like this?" Phoebe asked Selina, referring to two of their shared nephews and nieces.

"They would be in transports," Selina agreed. "Whether Richard and Jane would share their enthusiasm is the true question."

"Well, the shop is just around that corner." Mrs. Winser pointed to the street behind her. "Cutler's Emporium of Curious Creatures—or something to that effect. It is certainly worth exploring, even if you have no intention of buying anything. Prepare yourself for the smell, though."

After a few moments of discussion, Selina and Phoebe followed Mrs. Winser's directions and found themselves inside a dim shop. Cages and lanterns and a host of scents competed for their attention. Squawks and screeches and scurrying filled the room as the harried shopkeeper darted from cage to cage, looking much like the frantic dormouse.

He greeted them, but once they assured him they were merely

there to peruse, he excused himself to tend to a loudly squawking bird.

Selina pulled two handkerchiefs from her reticule and offered one to Phoebe. They put them to their noses as they began their exploration of the animals. The smell was overpowering, but the sights were too interesting to abandon: vibrant, talkative parrots, slow-moving iguanas, small wild cats who watched them with leering gazes, striped snakes, and an abundance of the tawny dormice Mrs. Winser had purchased.

They made their way toward the rear of the shop at a leisurely pace, always staying near one another but taking their time to admire the creatures that interested them most.

"Oh, Selina! Look at this!"

Selina joined Phoebe in front of one of the larger cages near the back of the shop. A delighted laugh escaped her when she reached it, for through the thin bars peeked the most curious gray creature with tufts of straight white fur sticking out of either side of its head. Its rich brown eyes were alert, flicking between her and Phoebe as its small fingers fiddled with its long, striped tail.

"What is this, if you please, sir?" Selina asked the shopkeeper, who was giving food to one of the nearby parrots.

He shuffled over in his brisk way. "Ah, that is a marmoset, madam. A small type of monkey. Would you like to see it?"

Selina glanced at Phoebe, who nodded eagerly.

The shopkeeper opened the cage and gently removed the marmoset from it, then stretched out the arm it sat upon so Phoebe could see the creature more closely.

"Its face is so very endearing." Phoebe tentatively stroked its back.

Selina took a step closer and followed suit, unable to stop a smile. "It *is* a difficult face to resist." She had heard of women who chose monkeys for pets, but never had she seen one herself. She could understand the appeal now. It was so soft and curious in its appearance.

"Would you care to hold it?" the shopkeeper asked.

Phoebe's eyes rounded, but she nodded, and Selina relieved her of the burden from Hatchards.

The shopkeeper transferred the monkey to Phoebe's arm, bringing a large smile to her face just as the bell rang.

He glanced at the shop door. "Just a moment, if you please." He hurried off to welcome the newcomer, leaving Phoebe and Selina with the monkey.

It reached a hand to the necklace Phoebe was wearing, and she laughed at the way it tipped its head inquisitively as it inspected it.

"Would you care for a turn?" Phoebe asked.

Selina hesitated, but there was something irresistibly charming about the creature and its wide, innocent gaze. "Very well. But only for a moment."

Phoebe set her arm next to Selina's, and the monkey obligingly moved over, apparently reciprocating her curiosity. But it did not sit still as it had done before. Instead, it crawled up her arm and around her shoulders as though she were a tree.

She laughed with surprise at the feel of its padded feet on the skin of her neck.

Holding to her shoulder, the monkey reached for the wrapped books in her hand and tugged at the string, undoing the tidy bow. He brought the twine to his mouth and chewed at it for a moment before discarding it.

He climbed down her arm, then took the package from her hand.

"Oh!" Selina said in surprise. She grasped the books to take them back, but the monkey would have none of it, evading her with ease by crawling up her arm again while unwrapping the package. The brown paper was tossed to the side, and he gave the two books a shake next to his ear. He dropped them to the floor with a large thud, apparently unsatisfied.

Trying to keep pace with the rapidity with which the creature jumped from task to task, Selina stooped to pick up the books and dust them off while balancing the monkey on her shoulder.

"Oh!" Phoebe cried out as he jumped and grabbed onto one of the cages.

Selina stood hurriedly, but the marmoset quickly scaled the wall, settling on one well out of their reach. In his hand was Phoebe's reticule. He uncinched the small sack and turned it upside down, shaking out the contents. Coins, a sachet of potpourri, and a fan fell to the floor of the shop.

"No, Pip!" The shopkeeper ran up and tried to reach for the monkey, which only climbed higher.

Selina blinked, still trying to grasp the change from the soft, docile creature who had first emerged from the cage to the busy and mischievous animal now fishing in Phoebe's reticule. He found a sugar lozenge and put it between his teeth.

The tight-lipped shopkeeper shook his head at the monkey. "He loves nothing more than sugar, but it makes him into a madman."

They watched as Pip worked out the best approach to ingest the lozenge, something he accomplished with astonishing rapidity. When he had finished, they were obliged to lure him back down with yet another sweet, which Selina provided from her own reticule.

Pip had to descend in order to take hold of the bonbon, and the shopkeeper snatched him while he was reaching for it, then put him swiftly in his cage.

Pip reached his arms through the cage slats for the bonbon Selina held, then screeched angrily. Gone was the wide, childlike gaze, replaced with intent, angry eyes and bared teeth, including two sharp incisors.

She backed away at the fearful image.

The shopkeeper let out a large breath of relief. "If there is one animal I have come to regret acquiring, it is *that* one."

"Is that you, Mrs. Lawrence?" The man who had entered the shop approached, smiling incredulously. He was a middle-aged man who had been friends with George for a number of years. "I had no notion you were in Town."

"Mr. Haskett," Selina replied kindly. "Of all the places to see you…" She introduced him to Phoebe, but the monkey continued to screech, so that they were obliged to move away to hear one another better. "Are *you* in Town for the Season as well, then?"

"Oh, no," he replied. "I am off on a little birding adventure with my wife and niece." His gaze shifted to Phoebe.

"Forgive me," Selina said. "This is Miss Phoebe Grant. She is the sister-in-law of my brother, and I have the pleasure of playing chaperone to her."

"Ah," Mr. Haskett said. "New to Town, then."

Phoebe nodded. "I have only been here a few days, sir."

"Still learning how to go on, are you?" he asked knowingly.

"Very much so," Phoebe said with her characteristic good nature.

"She is far better equipped than I was at her age," Selina said.

"Good, good," Mr. Haskett said with approval. "You mustn't let yourself be taken in, as some of these naive young women are."

Selina's cheeks warmed, despite the fact that she was fairly certain he was not referring to her. She had been both young and naive when she had married, and she certainly felt she had been taken in. She had been fighting resentment toward her parents for years as a result. They had not merely allowed her to be married to a man so much older than she when she had still been so wide-eyed and innocent—they had ensured it.

Mr. Haskett cocked a brow at Selina. "Nor must you let yourself be taken in, Mrs. Lawrence. The world can be a dangerous place for someone in your situation."

She smiled. "I have cut my eye teeth by now, you know."

"Hm," he said with skepticism. "Even so, it can be difficult to tell the wolves from the sheep at times. My own niece was nearly duped recently." He shook his head, his brows bunched together. "If Drake had not been so cow-handed, the situation might have become dire indeed. But there are fortune hunters who are *not* cow-handed. I urge you to be on the watch for them, Mrs. Lawrence."

Selina's entire body clenched. "Forgive me," she said, forcing calm into her voice. "Did you say Drake?"

He gave a curt nod. "Sebastian Drake. Tried to woo my little Lark into his web. Hadn't known her a week before he asked her to run away with him, the scoundrel!" He spat the last word.

Selina felt Phoebe's eyes on her, but her heart was beating too fast and her focus too fixed on Mr. Haskett for her to heed it. "I had the doubtful pleasure of making Mr. Drake's acquaintance recently, in fact."

Mr. Haskett let out a laughing scoff. "Of course you did! And here I had been hoping my revenge might have made him rethink his choices."

"Revenge?" Selina repeated, ignoring the sick feeling in her stomach and forcing her lips into a smile.

Mr. Haskett's mouth lifted at one edge. "Unfortunately for Mr. Drake, his application to be received into White's was... rejected. Last I heard, he had joined the misfits Lord Blackstone has acquired in his club."

Anger snaked through Selina's veins, threatening her increasingly weak smile. Anger at Mr. Drake for having skillfully dispelled some of her doubts, certainly, but also anger at herself for having been taken in by his lies. She should never have believed him to be anything other than a conniving fortune hunter.

How could she have been so foolish? Apparently, marriage had not managed to snuff out all the embers of her naivety.

All of his smiles, each of those moments she had felt a connection with him...they had all been fabricated for the purpose of winning her approval—no, her fortune.

Mr. Haskett had spoken of revenge, which had apparently not taught Mr. Drake anything.

Vengeance was certainly an appealing idea. Selina could not blackball Sebastian or thrust a duel upon him, but were there not other ways to teach a man a lesson?

Perhaps revenge was still within reach. He simply needed a

different teacher than Mr. Haskett—and a different lesson than the one he had been given.

Mr. Haskett regarded her thoughtfully. "Please tell me you have not entertained Drake's attentions, Mrs. Lawrence."

She gave a laugh that sounded unnatural even to her own ears. "You need not fear, Mr. Haskett. The only person I am interested in entertaining is myself."

Chapter Six
Sebastian

"Lock, stock, and barrel," Sebastian muttered as he walked to Number 14 Berkeley Square. "The lock being the flintlock, which includes the frizzen, flash pan, and...touch hole." He frowned. "Perhaps better to avoid that term. The stock"—he pictured the rifle Yorke had drawn to teach him the names of the different parts—"presses into the shoulder. And the barrel? That is the part of the rifle one hopes never to see down." He smiled to himself in satisfaction.

When in doubt, speak with confidence. That had been Yorke's main advice. He was an aspiring politician, after all. *She won't know a flintlock from a matchlock, so it makes no odds whether you* do.

Sebastian happened not to know the difference, despite Yorke having drawn multiple examples of both, for he had no real firearms in Town. But Sebastian knew a thing or two about confidence.

The strangest thing, however, was the realization he had come to over the past few days: he truly wanted to impress Mrs. Lawrence. He wanted her to like him, and not just because he needed her to. He genuinely admired her and enjoyed being with her. She was intelligent, witty, and engaging—and he had reason to hope that she reciprocated his admiration.

And if that was indeed the case, this could be a natural courting. And her fortune? Simply a result of the match. An acutely necessary result, but a result nonetheless.

When he reached Number 14, he was taken to the study, where he was surprised and gratified to be met by Mrs. Lawrence alone. Miss Grant was at Hyde Park with the Winsers.

Sebastian had not made a point of courting women over the past few years. He had been occupied doing everything in his power to seek financial solvency so that he could care for his siblings. Even the women with whom he *had* enjoyed some form of flirtation had never received him without a chaperone present. Such was the benefit of courting a widow.

The study had a formal air, being centered around a large desk, across which were spread a dozen firearms and various related equipment. The curtains of the window just behind the desk had been drawn open, allowing light into an otherwise dim room—Mr. Lawrence's past domain, it seemed.

"You did not change your mind after all," Mrs. Lawrence said with a smile, coming up and offering him her hand.

He masked his surprise at the familiar gesture and bowed over it. "Why would I have done such a thing?"

She lifted one shoulder. "You have no obligation to assist me with this task. I am sure you have better things to do with your time."

"Impossible." The fact that he was about to blunder through evaluating hunting equipment about which he knew not the first thing made it all the more impressive that he meant it.

Her eyes searched his for a moment, then she turned toward the desk abruptly. "Shall we begin?"

"By all means," Sebastian said with a distinct jolting of the heart as his gaze fell upon the hunting gear. His eyes ran over the lot while his mind grasped at the information he'd had from Yorke. While Yorke was a decent artist, however, it was a very different matter to study rude sketches rather than real, metal-and-wood firearms.

Mrs. Lawrence went to the edge of the desk. "You are an avid hunter, I take it?"

Sebastian opened his mouth to confirm, but he found it difficult to lie so blatantly and chose another route instead. He chuckled. "It would be very silly of me to offer my assistance if I were not."

She laughed softly. "Very silly indeed."

"And you are *not* an avid hunter, I take it?" It was a clumsy way to ensure she would not discover his ignorance.

She smiled widely at him. "It would be very silly of me to *ask* for your assistance if I were."

"Very silly indeed," he agreed with relief. He faced the first firearm. "Let us see what we have here." It was extremely long and wooden, with a single barrel and brass fittings at the top and sides. Thankfully, he remembered what Yorke had said about such things. "A beautiful fowling piece."

"Is it?" she asked, full of curiosity.

"Oh, yes." He picked it up with a confidence he was far from feeling. If he did not manage to blow his own head off today, it would be from sheer good fortune. "You can always tell the quality by the weight of the…uh…counterbalance."

"Ah." She tilted her head to the side curiously, as though looking for a part called the counterbalance.

Before she could ask about its location—for Sebastian had plucked the term from a discussion on swords—he ran a hand along the barrel, wishing he had the first notion whether it truly *was* a fine fowling piece that merited keeping. "I would not for the world give up such a piece."

"Then I would not dream of doing so, either. What of this one?" She moved to the next one, and Sebastian set down the firearm in his hands to follow her.

It was slightly shorter but, in most regards, nearly identical to the first. The brass was less polished, perhaps, and the ornamentation less detailed, but he could more easily have chosen between two bonnet ribbons than these.

He picked up the piece, then shook his head. "No, no."

She frowned. "What is it?"

Sebastian raised the fowling piece to his shoulder as though to practice shooting it. The last time he had discharged a weapon, a dog had nearly died. The memory was enough to cause him to lower it rapidly, set it on the table, and step away from it. "Far too long in the...mouth."

"The mouth," she repeated with uncertainty.

"You needn't bother your head about these silly terms we crack shots often use. But you may safely dispose of that piece—or sell it, *if* you can convince anyone to take it off your hands." He gave an incredulous chuckle.

"Thank heaven I have you to guide me, Mr. Drake."

And so, the blind guided the blind through the assortment of firearms on the desk, with Sebastian giving his entirely uninformed opinion about which ones merited keeping and which ones were fit only for a refuse pile. He found Mrs. Lawrence eager to learn and defer to his judgment, which fed his confidence.

He had plenty of opportunity to observe her over the course of the hour they spent in the study, and the more he saw, the more he felt certain that marriage to Mrs. Lawrence was the best possible outcome of an increasingly dire situation. It would be no trial at all to be married to her. Quite the reverse. He could easily envision a future with her smile, her laugh, and her wit as his constant companions.

As they looked over the last of the rifles—a double-barreled something-or-other—Sebastian felt confident enough to make a small but important step in his relationship with her.

He faced her and handed her the last rifle. "Feel it for yourself."

She took it warily, as though he was handing her a volatile bomb rather than an unloaded rifle.

At least, he *hoped* it was unloaded. Suddenly, he was not so certain. With the host of servants Mrs. Lawrence employed, surely the firearms would have been cleaned and unloaded after their last use?

"Note the perfect counterbalance of the...breech." He was fairly certain Yorke had used the word breech at some point. Or perhaps Sebastian was simply remembering how much he had admired the breeches Yorke had been wearing.

It made little difference as long as he spoke with certainty.

"I fear I am too stupid to take note of such details," Mrs. Lawrence said with a little laugh.

"Nonsense," he replied. "Here." He reached toward her to situate her hands around the rifle in the way he thought they should be. Whether that position had any relation to the proper way to handle a rifle was another matter.

His focus was not on such unimportant details but on watching her expression.

At the first touch of his hand, her body went still.

For a heart-thudding eternity, Sebastian waited for her to revolt or chastise him for his forwardness.

Instead, she relaxed, letting him guide her hold.

Success. Except now he was suddenly aware of the warmth of her hands beneath his and the delicate way her fingers curled around the wood of the rifle.

She glanced up at him through her lashes, and his heart stuttered.

Was she, too, conscious of the current running between them?

"So *that* is the way," she said.

"That is the way," he repeated, sincerely hoping she would have no occasion to soon encounter a man who truly knew the way to hold a double-barreled whatever-it-was.

"And then"—she raised the rifle slightly, and he reluctantly released her hands—"I do this?" She leveled the rifle so that it was aimed directly at Sebastian, her eyes fixed on him.

He cursed, covered his head, and darted to the side, his heart beating like a man who had just escaped the guillotine.

Mrs. Lawrence lowered the firearm, her eyes wide. "Oh, dear. Did I frighten you?"

Sebastian let out a nervous laugh and reached for the rifle. "No, no." He colored up at his dramatic response. "I was merely surprised to be staring down the barrels. Best not to aim it at people." He gently took the rifle from her, smiling as he did so to rob the action of offense.

"Forgive me," she said. "I fancied myself a true sporting woman for a moment there and was not thinking."

"No need for apologies." Sebastian set the rifle back in its place.

"Perhaps a respite is called for. Would you care for some tea?"

"I would welcome it." Apart from nearly having his head blown off, Sebastian's descriptions and evaluations were growing more and more desperate. Perhaps due to the term "muzzle" being shared between hunting and horses, he had fallen back on equine terminology, using words like "flank," "bridle," and "girth" when his memory had failed him.

Mrs. Lawrence led the way to the morning room, then excused herself to speak with the housekeeper.

Sebastian let out a long, slow breath once she was gone. All in all, it had gone better than he had anticipated. She had not rebuffed him when he had touched her, which was something indeed. And all in a day's work.

Of course, it was entirely possible that he had just instructed her to dispose of her late husband's most valuable firearms. He consoled himself with the fact that she had mentioned already having an entire room full of hunting equipment at her country estate.

Sebastian observed the room in which he found himself, noting the fineness of the furnishings and the simple elegance it all exuded, from the Axminster carpet at his feet to the vase of fresh tulips on the mantel. He admired such things, just as anyone would, but their importance was less due to his hope of possessing them and more for how the Court of Chancery would respond to such wealth. How could they possibly allow Hollis to retain guardianship of Margaret, Hugo, and Felix when this was the alternative?

The door opened, and Mrs. Lawrence came in, followed immediately by the housekeeper.

It was not until the door had been shut behind them that Sebastian noticed that the tea tray was not the only thing the housekeeper held. On her shoulder was perched a small and curious gray creature with a long tail that curled up into a small spiral at the end.

Chapter Seven
Sebastian

Mrs. Lawrence took a seat in the chair across from Sebastian as the housekeeper set down the tray, then handed the animal onto the arm of her mistress's chair as though it was part of every family's teatime routine.

"Do you require anything else, ma'am?" asked the housekeeper.

"No, thank you, Mrs. Beecham," Mrs. Lawrence said with a smile.

Sebastian stared with his mouth slightly agape as the housekeeper left them with the tea. And the animal.

"Ah!" said Mrs. Lawrence, apparently taking note of his surprise. "You must be wondering about Pip."

That was certainly a gentle way to put it.

She offered a piece of cheese to the creature, then poured two cups of tea while he munched. "He belonged to George and has become used to taking tea with me each day."

"Has he?"

She nodded and shot an affectionate glance at Pip.

"And what...*is* Pip?"

She gave a little laugh and handed Sebastian his tea. "He is a marmoset—a type of monkey."

As though he had heard his name, in one fluid motion, Pip leaped over the table that held the tea tray and landed on Sebastian's chair.

Sebastian reared back, nearly spilling the hot tea in his lap.

The creature faced him, staring at him with curiosity. Once his surprise abated, Sebastian reciprocated, noting the large, attentive eyes and the fur that fanned out from both sides of the monkey's head. "He reminds me of my uncle."

"Oh," Mrs. Lawrence said, a tremor of amusement in her voice. "And do you like your uncle?"

"I did," Sebastian said. "He had the longest, whitest whiskers I have ever seen. There was no taming them."

Mrs. Lawrence smiled, then set down her tea. "Here. Give him one of these." She lifted the lid of a small pot and took out a little bonbon. "He will take to you immediately."

Sebastian was uncertain he wished for such a result, but he was not about to admit it, so he took the sweet from her hands.

Pip must have had a special sense for the bonbon, for he stared at it with rapt attention as it was transferred, then tried to wrest it from Sebastian's grip.

Sebastian laughed and relented as Mrs. Lawrence looked on with an appreciative smile.

Content with his loot, Pip settled on Sebastian's lap.

Sebastian watched with amusement as the monkey worked at the bonbon determinedly. "He must keep teatime interesting."

"He certainly does that."

Pip finished the bonbon and looked at him expectantly.

Sebastian put up his hands to show they were empty.

Pip apparently understood, for he began peering into every pocket he could find on Sebastian's coat.

"There is nothing to find there, my friend," Sebastian said with amusement. "I suspect you would easily find them even if I *had* hid them, though."

"By all means, make the attempt," Mrs. Lawrence said, gesturing at the small pot that contained the sweets.

Sebastian took Pip and set him on the arm of the chair, gave him one bonbon to suck on, then took advantage of his occupation to hide others in different places around the room: behind the tulip vase, on top of the case clock, and beneath a candlestick.

He had barely hidden the third when the monkey finished and looked around. Spotting Sebastian, he galloped over.

Within three minutes, he had found all of Sebastian's hiding places and was in possession of three bonbons.

"Intelligent thing, isn't he?" Sebastian said.

"Very. And since arriving in London, he has been even more energetic than usual. I admit to feeling overwhelmed, for he has been a bit unruly."

Sebastian glanced at her as she watched Pip with an expression of mixed appreciation and something he could only describe as fatigue.

"George was the one who cared for him," she explained, "so I find myself out of my depth at times, and never more so than recently. He has made the process of sorting through George's belongings far more difficult."

"Perhaps you could give the task of sorting through the poetry to him."

Mrs. Lawrence laughed, and the sound was a new sort of pleasure to Sebastian. "He would undoubtedly enjoy it more than I, though the mess he would inevitably leave would put me in the black books of all my servants. We are all at our wits' end as is."

An idea occurred to Sebastian. He had told her he wished to be of help, had he not? And he needed a way to ensure their continued acquaintance. "Perhaps I could take Pip for a time."

Mrs. Lawrence's gaze shot to his, her brows drawing together. "You cannot mean that, surely."

"Surely I can," he said with a broad smile.

There was a pause as she stared at him. "Why would you make such a generous offer?"

With one bonbon between his teeth and the others clutched in a hand, Pip darted over to Sebastian using only three legs.

Sebastian welcomed him onto his lap again. "My friends and I could use a bit of excitement, and I can only imagine the delight this fellow would bring to our dull St. James's townhouse. We even have an empty bedchamber he could use. What do you say, Pip? Would you like to come join the bachelors?"

So long as Pip had bonbons, Sebastian doubted he cared where he was.

※

PIP WAS CLIMBING DOWN THE RAILING OF THE staircase at the townhouse when Yorke and Fairchild returned from their club. Happily for Sebastian, they were every bit as amused by the monkey as Sebastian had been.

"How did you fare?" Yorke asked, pouring three drinks in the drawing room.

"What?" Sebastian asked distractedly as he tried to keep Pip's claws from tearing his coat. The monkey was persuaded every nook and cranny of his clothing contained sweets.

"With the hunting equipment," Yorke said impatiently.

"Very well," Sebastian said, taking a seat on the chaise longue as Pip climbed across his outstretched arm and around his neck. "I forgot most of what you taught me, but she was nevertheless impressed. Confidence was the key, just as you said."

Yorke came and offered one of the drinks to Fairchild, who was lounging in the sole wingback chair in the room. As it was his uncle's house, the nicest chair was considered his.

Yorke brought a drink over to Sebastian, but as Pip tried to snatch it, he thought better of this.

"The last thing we need is Pip drunk," Sebastian said grimly.

Yorke laughed and sat down on the chair across from Sebastian, stretching out his legs and crossing them at the ankles, two drinks in hand. "You mean I might have spared myself the trouble of all those drawings and all the vocabulary I spent three entire hours teaching you?"

"Afraid so," Sebastian replied. "It all went clean out of my head the moment I found myself facing a dozen firearms. But I managed well enough using horse terminology for any gaps in my vocabulary."

"Horse terminology?" Yorke repeated blankly.

"What sort of terminology?" Fairchild asked, for he was a bit horse-mad.

Sebastian shrugged and fished in the one pocket Pip had not found and pulled out a small bit of cheese. "I think I mentioned something about the bridle at one point. I most definitely referred to the girth at least once." He frowned in an effort to recall his time with Mrs. Lawrence. "I am nearly certain I called one piece too long in the mouth."

Yorke covered his face with a hand while Fairchild laughed heartily.

Sebastian grinned. "You mustn't be angry with me, Yorke. I nearly died more than once." He frowned. "The firearms all would have been unloaded, would they not?"

"Of course," Yorke said, hardly concealing a scoff.

Sebastian let out a relieved breath. "Mrs. Lawrence pointed a double-barreled what's-it at me at one point."

"Pointed it at you?" Fairchild asked incredulously.

"A double-barreled what's-it?" Yorke repeated. "Please tell me you did not say that to her."

"I am not a fool, Yorke." Sebastian paused. "At least, not that much of one. I cannot be certain, but I believe I referred to it as twin-barreled musketoon."

Yorke shut his eyes.

Fairchild grimaced, then nodded at Pip. "And how do you come to have this fellow?"

Sebastian explained the situation, then left Pip with them so he could fetch the jar of bonbons Mrs. Lawrence had sent over. Sebastian had been obliged to go to great lengths to hide it from the monkey.

He gave a bonbon to Yorke and one to Fairchild. "Conceal

these wherever you wish. He will find them almost as quickly as you hide them."

"I accept your challenge," Yorke said, intrigued. "And I wish *you* the best of luck, little man!" He chucked the monkey under the chin. "You will certainly need it."

Pip grasped his hand, trying to wrest the bonbon from him, and Sebastian was obliged to distract the monkey so that the game could begin.

Pip won handily, but not before he had relieved himself on the rug in the entry hall.

That was something Sebastian had not considered: the monkey's bodily necessities.

The mess was cleaned by the servants, but Sebastian quickly found that the monkey's physiological needs were nearly all he *could* consider, whether it was food—or the cleaning up of that food—or Pip relieving himself—or the cleaning up of Pip having relieved himself.

The monkey might look like Sebastian's uncle, but Uncle James had been far better behaved.

As for Yorke and Fairchild, their amusement and awe at the monkey's intelligence lasted less than twenty-four hours. Pocket watches and brushes went missing, and the kitchen was raided during the night.

"I will pay for it," Sebastian promised when they found the monkey's bedchamber in utter disorder in the morning, the curtains ripped from climbing, the drawers open and turned out. How Sebastian would manage to pay for it, he had no notion. He was not particularly plump in the pocket, and the money he did have needed to be spent wisely.

Mrs. Lawrence sent over a note on the second day, asking how Pip was getting on.

Yorke took a paper out of the nearest desk and snatched the quill. "I will happily let her know what we think of her husband's dear Pip!"

Sebastian stole the quill from his hand.

"Whatever the size of her fortune," Yorke said upon reluctantly surrendering it, "it is not enough to make up for the devil's own pet."

Sebastian sighed and sat down to write his response. He hesitated over it for some time, but the word he chose in the end to describe how Pip was faring with his bachelor friends was *famously*.

Infamously would have been more accurate.

"It will all be worth it in the end," he reassured himself as he sealed the note with a wafer.

The following morning, the monkey managed to get ahold of the enormous sugarloaf in the kitchens, an event that was followed by unmatched chaos and then a period of dangerous lethargy that had Sebastian on the verge of rushing to Berkeley Square to apologize profusely for killing Mrs. Lawrence's dead husband's beloved pet.

He wrapped the listless marmoset in a cravat cloth and rocked him like a baby, attempting to offer Pip everything from water and coffee to brandy to revive him.

Thankfully, the monkey regained his energy after a prolonged nap, and the danger passed. But Sebastian soon found himself considering feeding the creature another sugarloaf, if only for a respite from the resumed chaos.

He chased the monkey out of the drawing room, and he could have sworn Pip was smiling as he did. He might be able to replace curtains in a bedchamber, but affording the destruction of the most elegant room in the house was simply not to be considered.

"You remind me of Felix," Sebastian said, shutting the door soundly behind them.

He had vivid memories of chasing Felix out of various rooms when he had been a small boy. The remedy he had found for Felix's penchant for mischief had been to take him out on the back lawn and allow him to run around like a madman for an hour.

That was when it occurred to him that perhaps something similar would benefit Pip. The garden attached to the townhouse was too small to be of use, however. They needed somewhere expansive if Pip's energy was to be depleted. There was nowhere quite so expansive as Hyde Park.

For the first half hour, he could not relax for fear Pip might disappear into the trees and never return. He did not imagine Mrs. Lawrence would be impressed if he was obliged to convey such news to her.

Apparently, the monkey's affection for Sebastian was strong enough to bring him back, however.

Sebastian felt exhausted thinking of even another twenty-four hours like the last twenty-four. He and Mrs. Lawrence had not specified how long he would keep Pip, after all, which was a terrifying thought.

That was when he remembered Lord Blackstone's affinity for animals. Of course, Blackstone collected *dead* animals, but it was only natural that someone who memorialized beasts was fond of the living versions.

And Blackstone did not merely memorialize them as most taxidermists would. He insisted on adding hats and spectacles and scarves to them. Sebastian had still not determined whether this was an intent to humanize them further or if Blackstone had simply found this an effective way of having his own accessories on hand throughout the club.

The viscount's club was located inside a Palladian building at the intersection of St. James's and Mayfair, making it a quick walk with Pip on Sebastian's shoulder—fortunate, as the monkey's curiosity led him to hop out of Sebastian's arms and onto the pavement more than once. Sebastian was obliged to chase after the creature and offer him a small piece of cheese. One of these days, he was likely to forget a piece in his pocket, which would lead to his arriving at some *ton* event smelling like a cheesemonger's apprentice.

Even with that formidable risk, better cheese than sugar for the monkey. Sugar, he was coming to find, was foe, not friend.

The doorman, Plockton, admitted Sebastian to Blackstone's, raising his brows at the sight of Pip.

Sebastian caught a glimpse into the drawing room and noted one of the men he had become acquainted with recently, John Aubin. Sebastian was not familiar with the particulars of Aubin's situation, but from what he had gathered, the man had been somewhat of a rake in the past. Whatever his history, he had easy conversation and manners.

Under normal circumstances, Sebastian would have gone over to greet him, but Aubin was nursing a drink and looking black-browed, as though he had perhaps been thwarted in love. Something told him that an introduction to a mischievous marmoset would not be welcome at this precise moment.

"Is his lordship here?" Sebastian narrowly prevented Pip from touching the ram's head mounted on the wall.

The doorman watched the monkey warily. "He is upstairs, Mr. Drake."

Sebastian nodded. "I will see myself to him."

He took the stairs, ignoring the glassy eyes of the myriad creatures that lined the wall.

Pip, however, seemed to be in awe at the assortment and remained perched on Sebastian's shoulder obediently. Perhaps in his animal fellows he saw the threat of predation.

"Just you wait," Sebastian said, for they had not yet passed through the *corridor of horrors*. That was the name he had privately assigned the walk that led to Blackstone's office. It was lined with cases full of every creature imaginable. Unlike most galleries full of preserved animals, these cases did not have glass, which gave them a more menacing feel.

Pip's little claws clutched at Sebastian's shoulder nervously as they passed by snakes and hawks and large felines.

Sebastian smiled. The monkey could use a bit of healthy fear to remind him that he was not, as he seemed to believe, at liberty to execute whatever madcap ideas occurred to him.

Lord Blackstone was in his study, seated behind his desk. He had an amiable if somewhat common face, with slightly unkempt gray hair. The pipe that was his frequent companion hung out of the side of his mouth.

Sebastian had been reluctant at first when Lord Blackstone had invited him to join his club. Belonging to a club exclusively filled with other gentlemen who had been blackballed hardly seemed conducive to his goal of appealing to the *haut-ton*, after all. But Lord Blackstone was a viscount and a respected member of Society, and he seemed to take care that those he invited to the club were not disreputable but rather unlucky or misunderstood.

The fact that Sebastian could dine well there instead of relying on the questionable meals at the townhouse had been an undeniable draw, as well.

"Drake!" Blackstone said, the greeting garbled thanks to the pipe, which he pulled from his mouth when his eyes landed upon Pip. "Zounds, boy!" He retreated into the wingback chair in which he sat. "What have you there?"

"This is Pip." Sebastian lifted his shoulder to display him. "He is a marmoset."

Pip climbed down his arm, and Blackstone retreated farther into his chair, a wary look in his eye. "Yes, yes. I see that. But what is he doing here?"

Not the most promising reaction.

"Do you mislike him?" Sebastian asked.

Blackstone forced a nervous laugh. "No, no! It is just that...I am accustomed to *still* creatures, you know." He jumped slightly as Pip hopped from Sebastian's shoulder to the floor. "It is easy to forget how fast they move."

"Pip is certainly quick on his feet." He frowned. "Or are they hands?"

"Two hands and two feet, just like yours and mine, Drake. Though *his* feet are prehensile, of course."

"Just so," Drake said, not having the smallest notion what this meant. If it signified that Pip was twice as likely to get into mischief, then he had to disagree. He was at least fifty times more so. "You know much about these things, my lord. I, on the other hand, am terribly ignorant. That is why I thought I would see whether you have any interest in taking dear Pip in for a few days. For your research and investigation, you know. He is quite charming."

Pip chose this moment to notice and take serious exception to the admittedly strange portrait behind Blackstone—a badger wearing a tailcoat. Pip opened his mouth wide, baring his teeth at the badger.

Blackstone's chair grated against the wood as he attempted to distance himself from the terrifying image Pip presented.

Sebastian suppressed a grimace and forced a laugh. "Silly creature, isn't he?"

Blackstone also laughed, but the nervousness of it and the way his eyes watched Pip spoke volumes of how he truly felt. "I wish I could, Drake, but, unfortunately, I cannot take the marmoset."

Sebastian did not betray his disappointment, though he felt it keenly. "I understand, my lord. Do you have any recommendations for me, then? Or advice on how to control it, perhaps?"

"Control it? Dear boy, one does not *control* living creatures."

"Hence the reason you surround yourself with dead ones," Sebastian commented, unable to stop himself from thinking just a bit wistfully of how much more manageable Pip would be if he was in one of Blackstone's display cases. With glass, preferably.

The monkey took to exploring the outer rim of the room, while Sebastian chased after him, taking away books and a small globe and a quill, in turn.

"You might try training it," Blackstone suggested, looking on with constant vigilance.

"Training it," Sebastian repeated, replacing a book on the nearest shelf. "To do what, precisely?"

Blackstone shrugged. "That remains to be tested. If you have something the creature wants, you might be able to use it to elicit a behavior you desire—or stop a behavior you dislike. "I might know a man who could help."

"By all means, supply me with his name and direction," Sebastian said. He was feeling desperate at this point.

Eyes flitting frequently to Pip, Blackstone scribbled with his quill upon a scrap of paper, then handed it to Sebastian from behind the desk.

Curiosity piqued, Pip drew nearer. Blackstone shot to his feet and quickly made his way around the desk. "I must be going now, Drake." He glanced warily over his shoulder once he reached the door. Pip was busy inspecting his pipe. "I wish you every success with the marmoset. Good day to you both."

The door shut with a resounding thud behind him.

Sebastian heaved a great sigh, folding his arms and watching the monkey put the pipe in his mouth. "Well, Pip. It is just you and me again."

He stood in silence, lost in thought as he watched the monkey and considered Blackstone's suggestion.

Could Pip be trained? Could life with him be less chaotic? It could hardly be more so.

With enough bonbons and the help of the man whose name he now held, perhaps there was hope yet.

Chapter Eight
Selina

Selina smiled to herself as she surveyed the attendees at the musical evening at Lord Plimpton's in Town. There were no empty seats in the drawing room, which hummed with chatter after the music finished. The musicians tended to their instruments while footmen bearing trays emerged into the room to refresh their master's guests.

Mr. Drake was not among those guests. No doubt he was occupied with...other things.

"And so he simply *pretended* to know about hunting equipment?" Phoebe whispered with a curious knit to her brow. Selina had recounted the events of the preceding day on their way to the musical evening, but Phoebe was evidently still trying to comprehend.

"Not just pretended," Selina said. "Spoke with unassailable confidence on a topic he knew nothing about. I would not be surprised if he had never held a rifle or a fowling piece before." She rose and took two glasses of sherry from the passing footman, privately and reluctantly admiring Mr. Drake's audacity.

"What happened when you corrected him?" Phoebe asked.

"I did not correct him."

Phoebe's brow puzzled even further. "Why ever not?"

She sipped her sherry before responding. "Because if I *had*, he would not have made an utter and complete fool of himself."

Phoebe laughed incredulously. "But he does not *know* that he made an utter fool of himself."

"He will when I choose for him to know it. I am more tempted, however, to let him dig the hole of his humiliation deeper still." She had been considering inviting Mr. Drake to join her on a small shooting expedition. That would be amusing indeed.

And dangerous, which was what had decided her against it.

She rested the glass against her lips, remembering some of the moments from Mr. Drake's visit with nostalgia. "There was something so very delicious about hearing him speak of a fowling piece as being *too long in the mouth*. Or having him warn me that no one might be willing to pay for one that I saw George pay thirty guineas for with my own eyes." She laughed softly.

It was maddening that Mr. Drake would have the gall to pretend expertise on a topic upon which he was mind-bogglingly ignorant—all in an effort to pursue her fortune. Yet, not just any man could fumble his way through such an ordeal with so much entirely unmerited confidence and leave her somehow amused rather than aggravated—and, if she was being entirely honest with herself, slightly charmed.

Phoebe finished her sherry, her eyes wandering somewhere across the room. There were a number of handsome young gentlemen present, and Selina had noticed her attention wandering from the music more than once. The object, she was nearly certain, was a man named Mr. Evenden, a good-looking man with a ready smile—and ready compliments. "And after all that, you sent him home with Pip?"

Selina's smile grew. "Oh, yes. He stepped all too willingly into that trap. But you may count me shocked beyond reason if we do not receive a visit from him soon, returning Pip to our care with some excuse or other about why he can no longer house the creature."

"And if he does not?"

"He will. You were not present for the havoc Pip wreaked before Mr. Drake's visit, Phoebe. I would not be surprised if that monkey was the devil incarnate."

"But he has such a charming face!"

Much like Mr. Drake, Selina thought. "Charm can be a dangerous weapon against female vanity, my dear. Better to be on your guard against it."

"Of course," Phoebe agreed.

Mr. Evenden found his way over to them shortly after, and while Selina was occupied speaking with Mrs. Winser, she kept an eye on Phoebe and him. Phoebe's cheeks were more than usually pink and her laugh never more than a few moments away. She doubted Mr. Evenden's conversation merited such ready and ripe amused responses. He was charming Phoebe. That was all there was to it.

"What can you tell me about the Evenden boy?" Selina asked Mrs. Winser.

Mrs. Winser took great pride in her abundant knowledge of anyone of consequence, and her gaze searched for Mr. Evenden until she found him. A knowing look entered her eyes. "Worried, are you? He flirts with everyone, but it is simply his way. Never a breath of scandal attached to the Evenden name. I believe he has a respectable fortune coming his way. You need not worry your head over his showing attention to Miss Grant, though."

Selina was not entirely reassured. Phoebe's tendency to think the very best of everyone was as dangerous as it was admirable. The fact that she had but a small dowry to offer prospective matches made it unlikely that Mr. Evenden meant anything serious. Whether Phoebe would realize that was less certain.

Selina excused herself from Mrs. Winser presently and gently but firmly interrupted Mr. Evenden and Phoebe.

The glow in Phoebe's cheeks lasted until they reached home some time later. Mr. Evenden's name came up more than once in their carriage conversation until Selina determined to say something as they reached Berkeley Square.

"Be careful, Phoebe, of the man who makes you feel like the only woman in the room. More often than not, he has made every woman in the room feel that way."

Phoebe's smile wavered. "You speak of Mr. Evenden."

"I speak of all men," Selina said. "But if Mr. Evenden has made you feel such a way, then, yes, I speak of him as well. I would not have you hurt."

Phoebe smiled gratefully as the carriage came to a stop. "I know. But I do believe he enjoys our conversation as much as I do."

"Of course he does," Selina replied kindly. "You are the easiest person in the world to speak with! I merely wish for you to listen not only to your heart but to your head also. The heart can so easily be deceived. I wish someone had said as much to me at your age. It might have saved me a great deal of heartache."

Despite that hard-won experience, it was heartache Selina had been on the cusp of courting yet again when she had met Mr. Drake.

Thank heaven Mr. Haskett had helped her avoid following the string of her curiosity any farther.

Now, Selina had Mr. Drake on *her* string.

⁘

Nearly a week had passed, however, when Selina sent yet another note to see how Mr. Drake and Pip were getting on. She thanked him profusely for the service he was providing.

It was dinnertime when one of the footmen brought Mr. Drake's response.

Selina forced herself to open it casually, setting it upon the table to read as she removed her gloves.

"What is it?" Phoebe asked as Selina's mouth spread into a grin.

Selina picked up the note and read from it:

> *If it is not too much trouble, I thought Pip and I might call upon you tomorrow.*

She set down the note again. "Ten to one, he will manage things so that he leaves empty-handed and we are saddled with the monkey again."

To give credit where credit was due, Mr. Drake had lasted far longer than she had expected. She had begun to wonder if Mr. Drake simply did not mind the chaos of the monkey—or perhaps her fortune was ample enough to compensate for the trouble.

But even if he did depart without Pip on his visit tomorrow, she had another plan in store for Mr. Drake—a way to force him into revealing his hand, she hoped.

Her anticipatory smile lasted all throughout dinner and even through the evening she and Phoebe spent at Almack's.

Mr. Evenden was present, and Phoebe was the first person he asked to dance. Phoebe accepted, but Selina was gratified to see her less quick to be delighted by him.

⁂

The most difficult task for Selina as she and Phoebe awaited Mr. Drake's visit the following day was to tame her self-satisfied smile.

If she had truly been facing the prospect of taking Pip back, perhaps she would have felt more dread than satisfaction, but she was only renting Pip and could return him at will. The small daily fee she was paying was nothing to the pleasure of torturing Mr. Drake.

"I feel for him," Phoebe said as they awaited his arrival in the drawing room.

"It was his suggestion to take Pip, Phoebe," Selina said with amusement. She had intended to ask it of him eventually, but he had beat her to it. "No one forced the monkey upon him. And do you know *why* he offered to take the monkey?"

"Because he wished to be of help to you."

Selina laughed indulgently. "May Mr. Drake endeavor to deserve the benefit of the doubt you bestow upon him so willingly, dear Phoebe. Why do you suppose he wishes to be of help to me?"

"Out of the goodness of his heart?" Phoebe offered, but there was little conviction behind the words.

Selina merely smiled at her as the door opened.

"Mr. Drake," the butler announced. "And...the monkey."

Selina and Phoebe rose simultaneously as Mr. Drake stepped into the room.

All the composure Selina had worked so valiantly to gather crumbled, the greeting on her lips dying a sudden death.

On Mr. Drake's left shoulder sat Pip, but it was not the Pip she had sent him home with.

The small monkey wore a miniature crimson waistcoat, complete with one small button. The bottom of the waistcoat was concealed by a wide strip of dark linen, which had been wrapped between and then around his legs, then finished off around the waist with a knot at his small belly. A hole in the back of the apparatus allowed his tail to trail behind him.

"Is Pip wearing...a clout?" Selina asked incredulously as the monkey jumped down from his shoulder and scampered over to Phoebe.

Mr. Drake walked over to Selina and bowed. "It is only until he is properly breeched." He leaned toward her and spoke in an undervoice, as though trying to keep the sound from Pip. "Though, to be quite frank, I am not entirely certain that time will ever come."

Selina had no response for this. She was still watching the monkey, astounded at the oddly dapper yet infantile image he presented. She had intended to use Pip to test Sebastian's limits, not provide him an ally.

Phoebe laughed as Pip fiddled with the button on his waistcoat. "How very handsome you are now, Pip."

"Pip," Mr. Drake said in a severe tone. "Propriety demands we not disrobe in polite company."

Pip scampered over to him, apparently forgetting about the waistcoat, and jumped onto his arm.

"Good man." Mr. Drake smiled and pulled a bonbon out of the pocket of his tailcoat.

The monkey reached for it, but Mr. Drake put it out of his grasp. "You have not yet made your bow." He cleared his throat significantly. "Make a leg, Pip."

Somewhat reluctantly, Pip hopped back onto the floor and, in an unmistakable attempt at a bow, he leaned forward.

Selina looked on with her mouth agape while Phoebe clapped enthusiastically, her face wreathed in smiles. "You have trained him!"

"I have worked on a few things with him that I hope will serve to make him a less overwhelming pet," Mr. Drake replied modestly.

Pip snatched the bonbon Mr. Drake offered, then went to enjoy it in the corner of the room in peace.

Selina, who had not yet managed to utter anything beyond her original, bemused question about Pip's clout, felt a sudden rush of victory. "You mean to leave him here, then?" Her gaze darted to Phoebe, seeking an acknowledgement that, despite the unexpected progress Mr. Drake had made with Pip, he had still come with the purpose of ridding himself of the monkey.

"Oh, no," Mr. Drake said. "I am happy to take him with me for as long as it is of help."

Selina was bereft of speech yet again.

"However did you manage to make such a gentleman out of him, Mr. Drake?" Phoebe asked with wonder. "It must have taken a great deal of work."

"It was nothing," Mr. Drake insisted as the monkey returned to his place on his shoulder. "We have amused ourselves greatly together, have we not, Pip?"

Pip's response to this was to turn to Mr. Drake and begin searching through the hair near his temple, grooming him.

Mr. Drake smiled but made no move to stop Pip, instead taking a seat. "He is training to become my valet now." He winked at Selina.

The door to the drawing room opened, and a footman appeared. His eyes darted to Mr. Drake, then back to Selina.

"What is it, James?" Selina asked, though she already knew why he had come. Indeed, she had insisted he do so.

"You have another visitor, ma'am. Mr. Tolliver is waiting in the entrance hall."

"Oh dear," Selina said in feigned discomfiture. "How foolish of me to have forgotten. Erm..."

Mr. Drake rose. "Pip and I shall leave you to your visitor, ladies."

"No, no," Selina hurried to say. "You have only just arrived. If you do not mind overmuch, Mr. Tolliver may join us." It would be too bad if she was obliged to endure the presence of Mr. Tolliver without the joy of watching him compete with Mr. Drake.

Mr. Tolliver could not stand to be near her in the presence of another gentleman without trying to prove himself superior.

Mr. Drake paused for a moment, then gave a nod and took his seat again. "As you wish." Meanwhile, Pip again escaped to the corner of the room, where he consumed the fruit he had stolen from Mr. Drake's pocket.

The footman bowed and soon returned with Mr. Tolliver, whose benevolent expression lasted through his bow to Selina and Phoebe, only to disintegrate the moment he noticed Mr. Drake.

"I pray you will excuse my thoughtlessness, Mr. Tolliver," Selina said. "I lost track of my engagements, which is why you find us with a friend. Allow me to introduce you to Mr. Sebastian Drake."

The Herculean effort Mr. Tolliver's forced smile required of him had Selina fighting her own amusement as he bowed stiffly to Mr. Drake.

Mr. Drake seemed to be similarly amused by Mr. Tolliver's attitude toward him, for the corner of his mouth twitched, and his gaze flicked to Selina.

She strived to control her expression but feared she had failed, for Mr. Drake's eyes danced as they held hers, eliciting a strange stutter in her heartbeat.

It was precisely what she had warned Phoebe against: the man who made one feel as if she was the only woman in the room. And yet, he still managed to evoke the feeling, all the same.

"A friend, you say?" Mr. Tolliver repeated as he stared at Mr. Drake. "I have not yet had the pleasure of hearing Mrs. Lawrence mention you."

Thoroughly diverted already, Selina watched the effect of this on Mr. Drake with interest.

Mr. Drake smiled knowingly. "Whereas she has spoken of *you* multiple times."

Her amusement dissolved. She had done no such thing.

"She...she has?" Mr. Tolliver asked, apparently taken off his guard, though not unpleasantly so.

"Oh, yes," Mr. Drake said as Pip galloped up and hopped onto his arm.

"Good heavens!" Mr. Tolliver stumbled backward in surprise.

"Come, now, Pip," Mr. Drake chided the monkey. "Is that any way to greet a visitor?" He pulled out what appeared to be a piece of dried fruit, which Pip's eyes fixed on hungrily. "Make a leg."

Pip reluctantly hopped down and executed his simple bow, though his eyes remained fixed on the treat at every possible moment. In exchange for his sacrifice, he was awarded the desired fruit.

Mr. Tolliver blinked at the strange performance, then looked at Mr. Drake. "Do you bring that...thing with you on all your house calls?"

Mr. Drake laughed. "No, though he is certainly helpful for pushing past polite conversation."

Mr. Tolliver frowned deeply. "I cannot see why anyone would wish to *push past polite conversation*, as you put it."

Mr. Drake's gaze met Selina's again, and she raised her brows to signify that she too was interested to hear Mr. Drake's response, though she privately agreed with him and was nearly certain he knew it.

"No, indeed," Mr. Drake replied, humbled. "Someone like you, who so clearly excels at conversation, need never resort to such barbarous methods."

Mr. Tolliver seemed not to know what to make of this comment, perhaps because he was watching Pip, who had come up to Selina and was interested in her reticule. "Is that creature bothering you, Mrs. Lawrence?"

"Oh, no," Selina said genially. "He is quite all right."

"She is accustomed to managing him," Mr. Drake reassured him. "Pip belonged to Mr. Lawrence."

Selina's muscles tightened. She had been so focused on putting Mr. Drake in an awkward situation that she had not thought carefully enough about this encounter and how Pip would be discussed.

"Belonged to George?" Mr. Tolliver repeated with incredulity. "I never knew George to have a pet."

Selina forced a laugh. "Nor would you. George could be surprisingly private, you know."

"It was Mr. Drake who trained Pip, though," Phoebe chimed in. "Is it not marvelous the way he is dressed and how he bows just so? Such skill it must have required."

"You overwhelm me, Miss Grant," Mr. Drake said. "It was simply an idea I took into my head, but I am happy to know it has found favor with you."

"How could it not?" Phoebe asked. "Is it not the most charming thing, Selina?"

Selina opened her mouth without any idea how to respond to this. It *was* charming, but she did not particularly care to compliment Mr. Drake.

The obligation to respond was removed by Mr. Tolliver. "I once trained a falcon so that, if I threw my glove into the air from horseback, it would retrieve it and return it straight to my hand."

Mr. Drake's brows shot up in tandem with Selina's.

She forced herself not to meet his gaze, for she felt certain that if she did, she would burst into laughter.

She happened to know that Mr. Tolliver was very mediocre indeed at both riding and falconry, which was when the next idea occurred to her. "Mr. Drake is an accomplished hunter, Mr. Tolliver."

"Are you now?" Mr. Tolliver took up the gauntlet without the slightest bit of hesitation.

Selina could hardly contain the eagerness she felt to hear just what fools both men would make of themselves on a topic neither of them knew well.

Mr. Drake gave a laugh and rose to his feet. "We shan't bore Mrs. Lawrence or Miss Grant with tales of the hunt today. Pip and I will allow you three to enjoy the conversation you intended to have. We still have some training to be getting on with, don't we, chap?" He strode over to Selina, who had settled in for another ten minutes at least of competition between the suitors but could not think of a way to force Mr. Drake to stay. He did not seem terribly inclined to compete with Mr. Tolliver.

She rose and faced him.

He met her gaze with that familiar glint of shared amusement in his eyes that made her feel short of breath. "I cannot pretend I have the skill to teach Pip to retrieve your glove as Mr. Tolliver might manage, but I will do my poor best to instill him with a bit of discipline." He put out his hand to welcome hers, and before she knew what she was about, she had granted it to him. "Thank you for allowing us to call upon you." He pressed a light kiss to the back of her glove, sending her heart racing and warmth into her cheeks.

Mr. Tolliver shot to his feet and cleared his throat. "You had better leave the monkey with me, Drake. I will teach him anything Mrs. Lawrence desires. Better he be with a friend of George's, you know."

Selina stared at Mr. Tolliver in chagrined amazement, then at Mr. Drake.

Had Mr. Drake foreseen this outcome? Had he somehow brought it into being?

"I am sure Mrs. Lawrence and I would not wish to put such a burden upon you, Mr. Tolliver." Mr. Drake turned to her. "Would we?"

She blinked, more confused than ever. "No, of course not."

"Nonsense," Mr. Tolliver replied, coming over to retrieve Pip from Mr. Drake. "It is no burden at all when Mrs. Lawrence needs something. She is accustomed to asking me."

Selina struggled to think of anything she would ask Mr. Tolliver for, but any reply was swallowed up in the way Pip resisted the man's efforts to take him from Mr. Drake.

Mr. Drake was obliged to oil the hinges with fruit in order to persuade Pip to accept the idea.

Before Selina could decide on a response to the entire situation, Mr. Drake had bid them farewell and was leaving without Pip on his shoulder.

She and Phoebe were obliged to sit through another half hour of Mr. Tolliver's company, a great deal of which was taken up by his frustrations with Pip, who insisted on searching and then re-searching every pocket or hiding place he could find in Mr. Tolliver's clothing, presumably for something to eat.

She made one other attempt to persuade Mr. Tolliver against his intention to train Pip, for she had little confidence that he would even know how to care for the monkey, but he would brook no disagreement, and she did not particularly wish to be saddled with Pip now that Mr. Drake had left. She could not help feeling that, for all her plans to torture Mr. Drake, he had come out on top with awe-inspiring dexterity.

When Mr. Tolliver finally left and the door closed behind Pip and him, Selina slumped into her chair, exhausted.

"Well," Phoebe said, "that went a different way than you had planned."

Selina looked over at her, unable to suppress a smile. "And you are thrilled, aren't you?"

"Well, when you pit someone as amiable as Mr. Drake against someone as boring and self-important as Mr. Tolliver, what do you expect? Do you still cling to your notion that he is merely hunting your fortune?"

"Of course I do! You heard Mr. Haskett. He *is* a fortune hunter. There is no doubt on that score."

"Well, for my part, I would not mind having a fortune if it meant Mr. Drake was the one hunting me."

"Phoebe!" Selina cried out, shocked and amused all at once.

Phoebe grinned. "Do you mean to play the same games with Mr. Tolliver that you have been playing with Mr. Drake? Tolliver is a fortune hunter too, after all."

"Good heavens, no," Selina said, disgusted at the mere thought.

"Why not?" She stared at Selina with a bit too much innocent curiosity.

Selina did not reply, for if she did, it would confirm something she had no wish to confirm: she was enjoying this game with Mr. Drake. It would be entirely miserable if Mr. Tolliver were to take his place, however.

How she hated that knowledge.

Chapter Nine
Sebastian

"You managed to persuade Tolliver to take Pip?" Yorke asked with patent admiration in his eyes as he and Sebastian sat in the morning room at the townhouse in St. James's. Fairchild had gone to visit his uncle in Kent for a few days.

"It was not something I had planned." Sebastian stretched his legs out and crossed his ankles. "I had no idea he would be there, you recall. But he could not bear to see Mrs. Lawrence rely upon me for anything when he felt so certain he could do it better."

Yorke's head fell back with laughter.

"I would pay good money to see Tolliver attempting to train Pip," Yorke said. "And even more to see him covered in marmoset droppings, for that is far more likely than him managing to train the little hellion."

"Not a hellion, surely," Sebastian said. "We managed to civilize him quite well, I thought."

Yorke looked around at the tranquil scene. "It *is* a bit boring here without the fiend, isn't it?"

Sebastian's lip lifted at the edge. Life was markedly less chaotic without the monkey, but a small part of him missed the creature. A very small part.

"What did Mrs. Lawrence make of Pip's transformation?" Yorke asked, letting his head fall back on the chair and closing his eyes.

Sebastian reflected on the visit for a moment before responding. "You know, I believe she and Miss Grant were quite impressed."

"You had better hope so, or else you let Tolliver make off with your ticket to her fortune."

Sebastian frowned slightly at this coarse way of putting things. The truth was, he had not been thinking of her fortune for the past few days. He enjoyed himself enough in her company that he was not obliged to keep her money at the forefront of his mind in order to wish to spend time with her. At times, she had a guarded feel about her. But without fail, there were moments when their eyes met in silent laughter. Sebastian found himself wanting more and more of such interactions, for they were intoxicating.

He glanced up and found Yorke watching him. "What?"

Yorke smiled. "You dislike that thought, don't you? Tolliver winning her fortune."

Sebastian considered his boots for a moment before answering. "I certainly have no wish to lose it. Tolliver's attempts to woo her do not keep me awake at night, however. He seems an old fool."

"Mrs. Lawrence may have an affinity for old fools," Yorke said. "She married one before, after all."

Sebastian's mind went to the diamond ring and the way she was always fiddling with it. Was she still in love with him? Perhaps the times when he had thought he had seen a guarded look about her were due to the lingering loyalty she felt to her late husband.

"Forgive me," Sebastian said with incredulity, "but are you implying that Mrs. Lawrence might prefer someone like Tolliver to me? I have a mind to call you out."

"As long as you intend to shoot me with a twin-barreled musketoon, I shan't attempt to stop you," Yorke said. "But, for what it is worth, I merely meant that if you are set upon Mrs. Lawrence, you may need to exert yourself a bit more."

"I *am* set upon her," Sebastian said, as much to himself as to anyone else. Barring the sudden discovery of Mrs. Lawrence possessing hitherto masked and unbearable qualities, he could not imagine finding anyone else who suited his needs and wishes as well. If he had not been obliged to make wealth his primary aim in marriage, she was precisely the type of woman he would have taken pleasure in courting.

Yorke continued to watch him, his eyes slightly narrowed. "Have you become enamored of your target?"

"Enamored," Sebastian repeated with amusement. "I admire her, certainly. Who would not?"

There was a knock on the door, which opened, revealing a servant holding a letter. "This arrived with the post for you, Mr. Drake." He brought it over, bowed, then left.

Sebastian's heart skittered at the sight of the handwriting on the front. It was uneven and unpracticed, the writing of a boy. It was not even sealed with a wafer but appeared to have been stuck shut with some sort of flour paste.

With a knot in his stomach, he unfolded the letter and consumed its short, barely legible contents.

Sibastian,

I hope this leter finds you well. I must be quik befor Hollis returns. He does not know I am righting this and would punish me if he discoverd it. I wishd to ask one thing: when will you pay us a call? Hollis leaves us each evning to go to the freehous. You could come then. I hate it here and miss you tarribly.

Pleas come soon.

Felix

Sebastian's heart twisted, his throat growing thick with emotion. He had been plying a mischievous marmoset with sweets while Felix was living under the thumb of Hollis.

Apart from the content of the letter, the writing itself made Sebastian sick. The penmanship and spelling should have been better for a boy of Felix's age, evidence that Hollis was neglecting their education.

"Unwelcome news?" Yorke asked.

Sebastian cleared his throat and folded the letter. "Nothing out of the ordinary."

Why he felt it necessary to keep the problems of his siblings private from even Yorke, he did not know. Perhaps he wanted to spare Margaret, Hugo, and Felix the embarrassment they might feel later on if people were aware of the struggles and deprivations they had experienced.

That was assuming, of course, that he could bring an end to such deprivations.

Pleas come soon.

The words repeated again and again in his mind.

It was not a convenient time to make the sixty-mile journey to see them, given the developing situation with Mrs. Lawrence.

Hollis would certainly not appreciate it if he found out.

But how could Sebastian say no? How could he deprive Felix of something that would bring joy to his otherwise bleak life?

The bell to the front door rang, pulling him from his thoughts.

"Are we expecting anyone?" Yorke asked with a frown.

Sebastian shook his head.

They listened as muffled voices sounded, followed by footsteps, a knock, and the door opening to reveal the same servant.

"You have a visitor, Mr. Drake," he said, resignation etched into the tired lines of his face. "Shall I show Mr. Tolliver in, sir?"

Sebastian blinked. "I suppose you had better."

He nodded and disappeared.

"Tolliver!" Yorke exclaimed softly. "If this is the company you are beginning to keep, you may need to find new lodgings, Drake." He pushed himself to his feet. "I will give you privacy."

But the little screeches that made their way through the open door made both of them freeze.

Those were sounds they knew all too well.

They were the sounds of Pip, who scampered through the door, Mr. Tolliver on his heels.

"Come back here," Tolliver grunted, reaching futilely for the monkey.

Pip took quick stock of the room and ran to Sebastian, leaping to his shoulder as though it was a church and he had come to claim sanctuary.

"Mr. Tolliver," Sebastian said. "To what do we owe this... unexpected pleasure?"

Tolliver straightened, his cheeks red from apparent exertion. "I apologize for calling upon you in this way, Drake, but I am afraid I must leave Pip with you for a time."

Sebastian's brows rose. Based on the way Pip's nails gripped him, no amount of effort on Tolliver's part could convince Pip to leave his shoulder. "Is that so?"

"Yes. Very unfortunate business, for I have made a great deal of progress with him already, but I have been called away on urgent business."

Sebastian's gaze flicked to Yorke, who was smiling with unabashed amusement.

"Nothing too serious, I hope?" Yorke asked, not even bothering to appear concerned.

"There is simply no telling," Tolliver said gravely. "It is a regrettable thing, for I was intent on having the monkey trained for Mrs. Lawrence within the week, but I fear you will have to do your best in my absence."

"Perhaps the training could wait?" Yorke offered.

Tolliver's eyes widened slightly. "That will not be possible, for...there is no certainty that I will return to Town in a timely manner."

"I quite understand," Sebastian said, masking his amusement as well as he could as Pip fiddled with his ear. "Mrs. Lawrence will have to settle for my unsatisfactory efforts—and company."

Tolliver showed the first sign of hesitation, but another glance at Pip seemed to steel him to the unsavory prospect of leaving both Pip and Mrs. Lawrence in Sebastian's care. "She may rest at ease that I will return as soon as possible and call upon her."

Mrs. Lawrence might have been dissatisfied with Sebastian's training of Pip, but Pip himself was more than happy to be back in his company. So happy, in fact, that he took to bringing Sebastian little trinkets and odds and ends, seemingly to show his appreciation for him. These gifts took various forms—a half-eaten apple stolen from the kitchen, a watch chain from Yorke's bedchamber, and a dead beetle, which he offered to Sebastian like it was the last bonbon on earth.

The respite from Pip had rejuvenated Sebastian so that he viewed such well-intended mischief with more amusement than exasperation—and a growing fondness, if he was being honest with himself. He was beginning to understand how Mr. Lawrence had kept Pip as a pet.

Tolliver had returned a Pip bursting with unexpended energy, and after an evening of chaos, Sebastian resigned himself to taking him to the Park twice the following day. Unlike in the mornings, the Park was busy in the afternoon, but as the alternative was a mess at the townhouse, Sebastian set out to the Park near three o'clock.

Pip climbed the trees in a less-frequented corner of the Park and searched for anything he could feasibly eat while Sebastian looked on thoughtfully. Pip's return complicated his planned journey to his siblings, and yet, he could imagine nothing that would delight Felix or Hugo—or Margaret, for that matter—more than meeting Pip.

He stared at the place where the monkey had disappeared through some dense branches, watching for the familiar rustling that would notify him of his progress. There was no movement, however.

"Pip?" he called.

He waited patiently, for though Pip sometimes ventured off, he always returned within a few minutes. The memory of bonbons was sufficient, no doubt. Perhaps Tolliver *had* managed to train him, and Pip had gone off in search of the infamous glove to return it to Tolliver's care.

"Mr. Drake?"

Sebastian spun around.

Mrs. Lawrence and Miss Grant approached on the nearest path, walking arm in arm.

Sebastian's mouth broke into a genuine smile, and he strode over to them. "Well, *this* is a welcome surprise."

He had been wishing he could see Mrs. Lawrence before leaving Town and had been trying to hit upon a way to do so.

"We walk this path every day," Mrs. Lawrence replied with a quizzical glint in her eye.

Did she think he had come for the express purpose of seeing her? He had not, though if he had known she made a habit of walking just here each afternoon, he would have done his best to happen upon her. Perhaps this would become Pip's and his regular daily outing.

"How are you faring?" Mrs. Lawrence asked. "Missing your four-legged companion?"

Sebastian glanced toward the trees, but still there was no sign of Pip. Better to wait to tell her Tolliver had returned the monkey to him until he was certain Pip had not abandoned him. "I have it on good authority that he has two arms and two legs rather than four legs. But no, I am not missing him."

"I wonder what tricks Mr. Tolliver has managed to teach him by now."

"Do you think he will manage to teach him *any*?" asked Phoebe doubtfully.

"Forsooth, Miss Grant," Sebastian said teasingly. "Before you know it, Pip shall be twirling atop Mr. Tolliver's left pinkie at the snap of a finger."

At that precise moment, Pip came sailing through the branches.

His sudden appearance took all of them off guard, but none more so than Mrs. Lawrence, who faltered toward Sebastian as Pip landed in front of them on the soft grass.

Her hands grasped Sebastian's arm, and he put a reassuring one atop them. There was something about having her hold onto him in such a way that sent a flood of warmth through him.

Her head whipped up to regard him, a questioning look in her eyes. She seemed to realize she was holding onto him, for she released him and took a step back.

Pip came to Sebastian's feet, then hopped up onto his arm.

"Mr. Tolliver did the honor of paying me a visit yesterday," Sebastian explained as Pip offered him the shell of an acorn. "He had...erm...urgent business that suddenly called him out of Town. He expressed the deepest regret that he would not be able to help Pip reach the dizzying heights he had in mind for him."

Mrs. Lawrence's mouth quivered at the edge before she managed to control it. "Indeed. So, he left him with you?"

Sebastian gave a little bow of the head.

Pip took this as an invitation to ascend to higher heights and scrambled atop it, then began picking through his hair.

Phoebe covered her laugh with a hand, and Mrs. Lawrence's eyes sparkled with unvoiced laughter.

"I bring Pip to the Park each day for a bit of unrestrained exercise time," Sebastian explained, trying to ignore the oddity he must present, "but normally I do so at an hour where I am less likely to be made a fool of in public." Pip reached lower and began grooming his right eyebrow.

"That is a shame," Mrs. Lawrence said. "Phoebe and I would happily make this spectacle part of our daily walk."

"Perhaps I could charge a fee," Sebastian said.

"We will be certain to bring our coins tomorrow," Phoebe said.

"Guineas, I trust. Bonbons for Pip." Sebastian patted his shoulder, and Pip returned to his place. "But I am afraid I will not be here tomorrow. Like Mr. Tolliver, I have been unexpectedly called out of Town."

Mrs. Lawrence's brows shot up. "You have? Does this mean you are leaving Pip with me?"

"I had rather hoped to take him with me, if you do not mind."

She blinked. "I...that is, of course you may take him. You are doing me a great service by caring for him. It has been much easier to sort through George's belongings without Pip trying to steal them."

Sebastian smiled. "Well, you may be happy to know that he has taken to bringing me the items he collects."

"Has he?" Phoebe asked with curiosity. "He must hold you in affection."

"Or he is hoping for a bonbon."

"I believe I have one in my reticule," she said, removing it from her wrist and loosening the drawstring.

Pip seemed inherently to know what this meant and left his place on Sebastian's shoulder in favor of what treats the reticule might hold in store for him.

Sebastian and Mrs. Lawrence looked on as Phoebe coaxed the monkey onto her arm. Pip's eyes locked on the reticule, keeping him more still than usual.

Sebastian looked at Mrs. Lawrence beside him. She wore a soft smile on lips that matched the color of her bonnet ribbon.

Was it strange that he would miss her, short as his trip to Oxfordshire would be? What had begun as an attempt to acquire a fortune had transformed significantly, and now he found himself impatient to see her, eager for excuses to call upon her.

"May I see you when I return?" he asked.

Her head turned slowly, and her eyes met his for a few seconds, searching for he knew not what.

For a moment, he feared she might deny him his wish.

She nodded, and his heart fluttered with relief and anticipation. He didn't know which he looked forward to more: seeing his siblings or returning to London with the prospect of seeing Mrs. Lawrence.

The home of Edward Hollis was located outside of the village of Bicester in Oxfordshire. Making the journey with Pip would certainly have been more convenient in a closed carriage, but Sebastian simply did not have the money to afford it.

He was obliged to take the monkey with him on horseback, setting out at an ungodly hour in order to arrive by evening with the hope that Yorke's horse was equal to the grueling journey. While Pip spent a good part of the day perched in his place on Sebastian's shoulder, Sebastian had decided to wear a leather satchel where Pip could retreat—or, in an emergency, be shut inside.

But the marmoset behaved himself quite well, only leaping from the horse twice over the course of the day, both times due to the sight of something he hoped to eat. He drew a fair bit of attention when they stopped at coaching inns for refreshment, and the satchel was soon lined with the odds and ends he had managed to acquire from fellow travelers eager to please him and observe his strange behaviors. Sebastian suspected some of the trinkets had been snatched rather than given willingly.

Dark had fallen some time ago when Sebastian slowed his horse to approach the Hollis home warily, muscles aching with weariness. It was unlikely Hollis would deviate from his habit of going out for a drink—or a half-dozen—each evening, but it was better to be careful. Sebastian could manage the man's temper well enough—indeed, he would be happy for an excuse to plant him a facer—but the last thing he wanted was to cause his siblings more trouble.

And then there was the matter of the Court of Chancery. If Hollis made a fuss about the unwelcome visit, it might prejudice them against Sebastian.

His body ached from the long journey as he looked over the small house. There was but one window with any light, and as Sebastian drew nearer, it was suddenly extinguished, causing him to pull back on the reins and wait.

"Steady, Pip," he said quietly as the monkey threatened to jump down.

Sebastian watched for any sign of movement, but it was too dark. He coaxed Pip into the satchel near his waist with a bonbon.

"Just for a moment," he assured the monkey as he fastened the clasp.

The door of the house opened suddenly, and Sebastian squinted.

Two small figures came running toward him, and his mouth broke into a smile. Margaret brought up the rear, closing the door behind her eager younger brothers.

Sebastian swung down from his horse just in time to receive Felix's and Hugo's embraces. He forced down the lump in his throat with a swallow, feeling the thin frames of both boys.

"You came!" Felix said with delight.

"Of course I did." Sebastian squeezed them so tightly that they both groaned, then he pulled back. "And what is more, I brought a surprise."

The spark in Felix's eyes might have lit the house and its surroundings. "What sort of surprise?"

Sebastian quirked a teasing brow. "You will have to wait until we are inside to see." He pulled Margaret into his arms, and she gave a little sigh of relief that spoke volumes of the weight she had been laboring under and how she viewed his arrival.

Felix took him by the hand and pulled him toward the house,

impatient for his surprise. Pip too was impatient, squirming in the satchel.

Sebastian allowed Felix to guide him toward the door while Margaret took the horse to graze and drink in the nearby stream.

"How long do we have?" Sebastian asked when she joined them at the door.

"Three hours, at the least," Margaret replied. "On some nights, he does not return until after two."

Sebastian's jaw tightened. This was the man charged with their care, and he abandoned them for nearly a quarter of every twenty-four hours? Not that they likely wanted him home. "I worried when I saw the light extinguished that he had seen me."

"Oh, no," Hugo said, speaking with all the confidence of youth as he led the way inside. "We heard the horse hooves, and I blew it out, fearing he had returned early."

Sebastian frowned, ducking under the door. "Are you meant to be sleeping?"

"We are not to use candles when he is not at home," Felix explained.

Sebastian glanced at Margaret, who offered something between a smile and a grimace. So, Hollis left them at night *and* refused them light, presumably because he did not wish to pay for the candles.

"I will fetch a candle," Margaret said. "This is a special occasion."

Felix turned toward Sebastian expectantly while his sister disappeared. "Well? What have you brought? Is it sweets?"

Sebastian chuckled. "Yes and no. Sweets *were* brought, but they are not, strictly speaking, for you. And if you take one, Pip might take violent exception to it."

"Pip?" Hugo repeated.

Sebastian winked at him, then undid the latch on the satchel as Margaret reappeared with a small candle.

Pip climbed out of the bag and onto Sebastian's shoulder. "This is Pip."

All three children stared with open mouths, Margaret stopping mid-stride.

"Would you like to hold him?" Sebastian asked Felix.

Felix's head bobbed up and down, his jaw slack.

The children laughed and played with Pip by the light of one small—and increasingly smaller—tallow candle. Their laughter did his heart good, but the dim candle, the fear of Hollis's footsteps, and the knowledge that he would have to leave them there were difficult to ignore.

"Take this." He handed Margaret a fistful of banknotes while Hugo and Felix hid from Pip with bonbons to lure him to their places. "Do not, for heaven's sake, allow Hollis to see it. You will have to be wise how you spend it so as not to raise suspicion."

She nodded, and it pained him to realize the level of responsibility she had been forced to take up as the eldest of the children. Sebastian had only been six months shy of his twenty-first birthday when Henry Hollis had died, which meant he had not been of an age to act as their guardian. Six months was all that had stood between him and custody of his siblings.

"I am hopeful that the Court of Chancery will allow the transfer of guardianship," he said in a low voice, "but it is simply too early to say anything for certain. I merely want to assure you that I am doing everything in my power."

She smiled. "I know."

He opened his mouth to tell her of Mrs. Lawrence, only to decide against it. He was certain Margaret would like her. The boys too. How could they not?

But it would be better to keep the details to himself. A little hope was vital, but some part of him—a superstitious part, he supposed—feared that telling them his precise plan might turn fate against him.

"You will tell me if your situation becomes more dire," Sebastian instructed, holding Margaret's gaze.

She nodded.

"You know my direction in London."

"What do you think you are doing?" The chill but slurred voice jarred them from their conversation, bringing their heads toward the door to the bedchamber the three children shared. Hollis stood in the doorway, his face ruddy from drink and anger.

Sebastian stepped toward him, putting himself between Hollis and the children. His nostrils burned at the smell of spirits. "I came to see my brothers and sister."

"You have no right to be here," Hollis said. "Get out."

Sebastian stood his ground for a moment, trying to decide what to do. Just the sight of Hollis made his blood sizzle with anger.

"Get out before I call for the constable," Hollis yelled.

"There is no need," Sebastian said through gritted teeth. Being taken by the constable would not be looked upon kindly by the Chancery. "Come, Pip."

The monkey scampered over to him and into his usual place, and both Hugo and Felix drooped with disappointment. Part of Sebastian wished to leave Pip and see what havoc he might wreak for Hollis. But it was the children who would suffer.

He went over to Felix and Hugo and embraced them.

"Out!" Hollis barked. "Now!"

Margaret gave Sebastian a nod and a little reassuring smile, and with his jaw set grimly, he strode toward the door.

He stopped just shy of Hollis. "If you lay as much as a finger on them," he said through gritted teeth, "I will see to it that you are made every bit as miserable as you have made them." He stalked past the drunkard, not bothering to keep his shoulder from jarring Hollis's on the way.

Chapter Ten
Selina

May I see you when I return?

They were such innocuous words, and yet, the way Mr. Drake had looked at Selina as he said them—and the way it had snatched her breath like a thief—had been anything *but* innocuous.

Her heartbeat quickened even now, remembering the moment—and the one after when she had barely managed to eke out an agreement. An agreement that should never have been given.

This game she was playing was beginning to feel more dangerous. Had she truly learned nothing? Was she so vulnerable to flattery and a charming smile that she could ignore that she was mere prey to a fortune hunter? That she was no better than a fox running to the hounds hunting it, submitting itself for ravaging?

Of course not. She would never allow herself to be used in such a way again. Never would she allow herself to believe a man cared for her, only to be forced to face that she was but a means to an end.

Before the game was up, Mr. Drake must face humiliation. He must be made to admit that his charm and his acts of service had not been motivated by love for her but by love of the money she possessed.

She must hit upon a way to test the limits of his conniving—something that would test his resolve in new ways. There must be some point at which he would admit the truth of his intentions—or simply leave her be and make someone else his target.

With more force than was merited, she set down the correspondence of George's that she had been sorting through. She was tired to death of trying to determine what merited keeping. She would happily throw it all away, and yet her conscience would not allow it. Much as she might resent George, she owed all of her current comforts to him. Comforts Mr. Drake intended to make his own.

A commotion in the entry hall brought her across the room and to the door of the study. She had just opened the door when her brows drew together at the sound of a familiar voice.

"Where is Aunt Selina?"

There was no doubting that sweet, high-pitched tone, and Selina hurried toward it with a mixture of concern and anticipation.

"Is that my little Kitty I hear?" Selina asked, coming round to a view that had her stopping short, her eyes wide.

In the entryway stood her brother, Richard, her sister-in-law, Jane, and all four of their small children. Phoebe held the youngest, Lou, in her arms, while various portmanteaux and valises had been and were continuing to be stacked around the group by the servants.

Selina blinked.

"Oh, dear," Jane said at the sight of her. "You do *not* look as though you were expecting us." She turned to her husband. "You promised you had sent the letter, my love."

"I did!" he insisted with all the defensiveness of someone who had not sent the letter.

Jane looked at Selina with a grimace full of shared understanding. Richard was absent-minded on the best of days.

"We had hoped to spend a bit of time with you and Phoebe," Jane said, "but if it is inconvenient, we will leave immediately."

The resounding chorus of all four children rejecting this offer outright brought a gurgle of laughter from Selina.

"Do not be ridiculous," she said. "You are always welcome here. But not, mind you"—she gave all four children a stern look—"if I have to wait even one more second for the proper greeting from my little troublemakers."

In one motion, the four of them—from seven-year-old Arthur down to two-year-old Lou, who squirmed down from Phoebe's arms—ran over to Selina. She crouched to receive them.

The warmth and vivacity of their embraces nearly made her lose her balance, but she managed to stay upright. The feel of their arms around her brought a strange lump to her throat.

Why couldn't everyone's affection be as trustworthy and reliable as those of children?

Arthur, who was the eldest, pulled back, his eyes intent. "Aunt Phoebe says you have a monkey."

"And that his name is Pip!" five-year-old Teddy added.

Selina laughed and stood. "Aunt Phoebe has told the truth, but unfortunately, Pip is not here."

The look of disappointment that met this information would have been comical had it not been so genuinely crushing.

"He is being taken care of by...a friend." The last word came out strangled, and the explanation did nothing to temper the blow she had dealt them. "But," she said, watching their ears perk up, "perhaps we can arrange for him to visit?" She had no desire to have Pip back from Mr. Drake. Was there a way that she could persuade him to leave the creature for an hour or two, then take the monkey home with him again?

The shift to elation was instantaneous, and again, Selina was swarmed with little arms eager to thank her. Had she not been accustomed to the clamor of her nieces and nephews, it would have been utterly overwhelming.

And that was when the idea occurred to her.

How would Mr. Drake fare under such an energetic entourage? How would his cool, collected charm endure such an assault, under the sometimes-brutal frankness of four opinionated children?

Selina smiled.

May I see you when I return?

Oh, he would certainly see her. Whether he would enjoy it was another matter, however.

※

Her pulse fluttered when the note arrived from Mr. Drake the following day, asking if it would be convenient for him to call upon her in the late morning hours.

Unable to suppress her smile, she responded quickly in the affirmative, then went off to encourage Jane, Richard, and Phoebe to leave the children with her for a few hours while they enjoyed a day on the Town.

Their resistance was short-lived and feeble, for that was precisely what they had come to Town hoping for: time with Phoebe without the constant tumult of children to interrupt conversation. They wished to hear of her time in Society, and Phoebe was undoubtedly anxious to recount it to them.

The children, for their part, were more than happy to wave farewell to their dear parents for a few hours with the prospect of spending time with Selina, who had happily taken on the role of indulgent aunt, for there was no prospect of having children of her own now that she had settled upon life as a widow.

As the indulgent aunt, it was only fitting that she offer them an entire platter of marzipan and sugar plums shortly before Mr. Drake's anticipated arrival.

The four of them munched on the sweets, Lou making a terrible mess of the marzipan, which ended up soiling both face and clothing. Kitty did not manage much better, but rather than cleaning them up, Selina allowed them to remain in all their glory.

The sudden influx of sugar into their small bodies produced the anticipated effect, and soon all four of them were speaking over one another and moving about in the most comically haphazard manner.

"You mustn't bounce on the chaise, Teddy," Selina said with ill-concealed delight, "and those pillows are not for throwing, Arthur."

The bell rang out, and the children went still and quiet, looking at her with a question in their eyes.

"That will be Mr. Drake, who asked to call upon me," she said, her body trembling with nearly as much energy as little Lou's. "Now, I must tell you one or two things about Mr. Drake. Firstly, he loves nothing more than to be climbed upon."

"Like a tree?" Teddy asked, his brows bunched together, no doubt because his father was always telling him not to hang upon him like a branch.

"*Just* like a tree," Selina confirmed. "He is very strong and claims he can lift anyone."

Kitty's eyes widened, her cheeks smeared generously with marzipan paste. "Could he lift us all?"

"Oh, most certainly. Another thing he loves is questions. All manner of questions! And being tickled."

The children had never known such a person existed and looked as though they were on the cusp of meeting true greatness.

A final thought occurred to Selina. "His favorite question of all is about whether he intends to marry me. Now, just a moment, and I will return with him. You must be sure to give him the warmest welcome you can manage when I give you the nod. Like this..." She demonstrated it. "Yes?"

They all agreed eagerly, impatient to meet the impossibly perfect specimen.

Normally, Selina would have waited for a servant to show Mr. Drake in, but she had realized that one element of her plan was missing—one which required her to provide him with a bit of context before he was subjected to the children.

When Mr. Drake came into Selina's view, he was in conversation with the butler in the entry hall.

Her heart somersaulted at the sight of his handsome face, and she clenched her teeth.

Mr. Drake's gaze swept to her, and he smiled.

Oh, that cursed smile of his and the things it did to her!

Well, he would not be smiling for long.

Pip was nowhere in sight, and Selina realized with a sinking of the stomach that he had never stated his intention to bring the creature. She had simply assumed he would because he always had. The children would be murderous.

The butler moved out of the way, and Mr. Drake came toward her. "You *are* at home to visitors. Your butler was not certain."

"Ah, yes. Well, I suppose *you* must be the one to decide whether you wish to remain. My brother and his family arrived in Town unexpectedly yesterday, and I suggested they take Phoebe out and leave the four children with me. I should have written you a note to inform you, but I have been so very needed by them."

He grinned. "I can imagine! I have no wish to intrude..."

"Not at all! They were very eager when they heard the bell ring, in fact, and demanded an introduction to Mr. Drake."

"Then I would not for the world dream of denying them such a thing."

She smiled, almost feeling pity for him. Almost. "I admit I am happy to hear you say that, for they are very dear to me and visit often. Come, I will take you to them."

He nodded and followed her to the drawing room, unable to see the satisfied smile she wore as she led the way, telling him the names and ages of the children, which he would never remember once he was being mobbed by them.

She stopped suddenly at the door, running a hand along the bodice of her dress. "Oh dear! The children wanted a little sweet, and I seem to have acquired some on my dress.

Perhaps I could pop away to see to it after introducing you?"

"Of course," he said quickly.

She offered him her most winsome smile. "Thank you, Mr. Drake." She turned the handle and opened the door.

Sitting around the table, the marzipan and sugar plums nearly gone from the platter before them, sat the four children. All eyes were on the door, however.

"Arthur, Teddy, Kitty, Lou," Selina said, moving aside to make room for Mr. Drake to enter, "allow me to introduce you to Mr. Drake."

Mr. Drake swept a bow. "A pleasure to meet you all."

"I shall return to you all momentarily."

"There is no rush," Mr. Drake assured her.

"Thank you very much," she said, then made her way to the door. When she reached it and was certain Mr. Drake's attention was on the children, she gave them the nod they were waiting for.

Their rise from the chaise was synchronized and yet chaotic, and they all came running toward Mr. Drake just as Selina slipped out the door, making her escape.

Rather than going to her bedchamber to see to the marzipan on her dress, she slipped into the morning room, which was situated beside the drawing room. The door which connected the rooms had been purposely left ajar.

On quiet feet, she made her way to it, though the sheer volume of noise coming from the drawing room made such a precaution unnecessary.

She peeked through the gap between the door and the frame and covered her smile with a hand.

Arthur was hanging off one of Sebastian's arms, while Teddy and Kitty hung off the other.

"Can you really hold us all?" Teddy asked.

Mr. Drake laughed as he tried to keep his balance with three children adjusting their grip on his arms and using his body like a tree trunk.

Selina suppressed her glee as he wobbled and corrected his stance to remain upright.

"Of course not," Arthur said. "He would have to be as strong as Pickles."

"I fancy I *am* a bit stronger than pickles," Mr. Drake grunted. "Unless they are the crunchy sort."

Kitty giggled. "Not *those* pickles!"

"What pickles, then?" Mr. Drake asked.

"Pickles is our horse," Teddy replied, as though this should have been obvious to anyone with half a brain. "And you are *not* as strong as him. You couldn't be."

"Well," Mr. Drake said. "Can Pickles do *this*?" He lifted both arms, his face screwing up with the effort of so much weight, and the children rose with them.

It was extremely impressive, Selina had to admit. Privately.

"Of course Pickles can't do that, silly," Kitty said, giggling with elation as her entire body hung from one of Mr. Drake's biceps.

With an enormous exhale, Mr. Drake lowered the three children to the floor again. "You see?" he said breathlessly. "I *am* as strong as Pickles. Stronger, even."

"We all rode on his back once," Kitty said. "Can we ride on yours?"

Selina tried to suppress a smile. Kitty could always be counted upon to call someone's bluff.

Mr. Drake's brow knit pensively. "I would hate for you to assume Pickles was stronger only because we didn't bother attempting it."

To Selina's surprise and the children's utter joy, he shrugged out of his coat, tossed it over the chaise, and began rolling up his sleeves, revealing a set of forearms ridged with muscle.

Selina had been married and had thus seen more than a man's bare forearms, and yet the sight affected her in a novel way, making her breathless. Feeling like a voyeur, she removed her gaze, but the image was etched upon the backs of her eyelids.

Mr. Drake lowered himself onto his hands and knees, the waistcoat stretched across his broad shoulders. Another very unneeded image for Selina's mind to store.

"Come on, then," Mr. Drake urged the children.

Grins wide enough to split their faces, Teddy, Kitty, and Arthur hurried over and clambered onto his back, laughing and arguing over who should be in front.

"I have no reins," Kitty said from her coveted place at the front. "Ah, here." She grasped two fistfuls of Mr. Drake's hair, and Selina was obliged to cover her mouth again to stop the horrified laugh that broke through her lips.

"Just so," Mr. Drake said with effort but plenty of energy. "But where is our fourth rider?"

Lou stood a dozen feet away, her thumb in her mouth and a watchfulness in her eyes.

"Come, Lou," Arthur prompted.

She shook her head.

Selina watched her niece with sympathy. Lou was the slowest to warm to new people, tending to be quieter and withdrawn until she felt comfortable.

"We need you," Mr. Drake said. "How can we ride to battle without our Princess Lou to protect?"

The barest hint of a smile tugged at Lou's lips, but she did not move.

Her siblings urged her to come, but she simply looked at the floor.

Mr. Drake turned his head toward the children on his back, no small effort given that Kitty still had his hair in her hands. "Will you give me a moment?"

They climbed down a bit grudgingly, and he went over to Lou, crouching in front of her, his elbows resting on his knees.

Selina leaned forward in order to hear.

"What is it?" Mr. Drake asked Lou softly. "We cannot ride without our princess."

She looked down at her dress. "I sticky."

Mr. Drake followed the direction of her gaze to the marzipan smushed generously into her clothing. He tilted his head to the side consideringly. "It is the perfect dress to wear into battle. Better not to waste your prettiest and cleanest clothing on battle day. Besides, you are not simply a pretty princess, though you are certainly that." He tweaked one of the curls that hung by her temple. "You are a strong princess about to lead us to war! Can we rely upon you to guide us to victory?"

Lou fought a smile, then nodded with ill-concealed delight.

Selina's throat was tight with unexpected—and unwanted— emotion.

It was not only the care with which he had set Lou at her ease. It was what he had said.

You are not simply a pretty princess...You are a strong princess about to lead us to war.

George had made Selina feel much like a pretty princess. He had been proud to parade her about and call her his, but he had never seen her strength or allowed her to explore it in the way Mr. Drake was allowing Lou to in a mere game.

Rather than allowing her to hunt, which she enjoyed immensely, George had insisted she remain at home where she was safe. When she had inquired about affairs giving him trouble, he had refused to take her into his confidences, insisting *such ugly matters would mar her pretty face.*

"Would you like to hold the reins, Lou?" Kitty asked.

Lou thought about this for a moment, then nodded.

"Our fearless Princess Lou shall guide us to victory," Mr. Drake called out, lowering onto his hands and knees again. The children helped Lou into place at the base of Mr. Drake's neck, then followed by climbing on his back behind her. They barely fit, requiring the greatest care on his part to keep them from tumbling onto the floor.

Lou grasped his hair with both hands, eliciting the merest wince from him.

"On to victory!" Mr. Drake grunted, and with a Herculean effort, he inched forward, the children laughing as they rocked.

Selina looked on with the strangest tangle of feelings. She loved to see her nieces and nephews enjoying themselves. What was she to make of Mr. Drake, though? He had taken four excitable children and made watching them look like the easiest and most natural thing in the world.

"Faster!" Lou said, yanking on his hair.

"This is more of a battle march than a race," Mr. Drake eked out. "Slow and steady wins."

"This battle is boring!" Arthur slipped off Mr. Drake's back. "I want to be king!" With an imaginary sword, he jabbed his steed in the ribs.

Mr. Drake crumpled dramatically, and the three remaining children giggled and shrieked as they fell to the floor along with him in a tangle of limbs and laughter.

Selina couldn't stop a smile, but her heart twinged, and her fingers toyed with the ring on her finger.

She hated Mr. Drake for this mirage of happiness.

The laughter subsided, and all five of them lay on the floor, staring at the ceiling.

"Are you going to marry Aunt Selina, Mr. Drake?" Teddy asked.

Selina's heart stuttered. It was a question she had prompted them to ask, and yet she held her breath all the same.

Mr. Drake turned his head toward Teddy, which concealed his face from view. Selina went up on her tiptoes, though it made no difference. She could not see him.

"If you are the knight guarding her," he said, "I am not certain I stand a chance."

Teddy smiled, then copied his older brother and stabbed a fantastical sword into Mr. Drake, who clutched at the spot and went limp.

"No, Teddy!" Kitty cried out. "I like him!"

"It is just a bit of fun," Teddy replied, and as if to make certain she understood this, he began to tickle Mr. Drake.

Still lying upon the ground, he doubled over and was soon covered in grubby children's hands, tickling him under the arms, the neck, the boots—Lou seemed not to realize this would not produce results—and, to Selina's laughing dismay, his backside.

He was incapacitated for a time but seemed to realize the only way to stop the madness was to go on the offense. Soon he was giving as good as he had got, and presently, all five of them seemed to lose steam and give up.

Kitty caught her breath first and looked at Mr. Drake, whose broad chest rose and fell in a way Selina found mesmerizing. "Are you in love with Aunt Selina?"

Every muscle in Selina's body tightened, the breath in her lungs suspended as she looked on in deep dismay.

Mr. Drake's eyes opened from his pretended and violent death, and he went up on his elbow, looking thoughtful for a moment.

Selina's heart knocked against her ribs, and she nearly pushed through the door to intervene, but something kept her feet planted in place.

"Your aunt," Mr. Drake said, "is one of the cleverest and kindest people I have met. I admire her very much. Don't you?"

Selina searched for the manipulation or guile in Mr. Drake's answer, but she could not find it. It angered her deeply. How could he be so convincing when she *knew* he wanted her money? How could she be so blinded by her desire to be loved and wanted for reasons outside of her appearance or wealth?

All four children nodded in response to his question.

"And today she gave us as many helpings of marzipan as we wanted," Teddy said as they all began to rise to their feet.

"I think you should marry her," Kitty said with the authority of someone whose opinion was of paramount importance.

"As soon as you can," agreed Teddy as he lunged toward a pretended enemy with his imaginary sword. "Mama says Aunt

Selina is very beautiful and is bound to lose her heart to someone while in Town."

Selina's eyes widened. This scene was supposed to be for her entertainment and Mr. Drake's undoing, but it was turning out quite the opposite. It was time to put a stop to it.

Fanning her cheeks to cool them for a moment, she pushed the door open.

"Are *you* the friend taking care of Pip?" Arthur asked Mr. Drake as she entered, changing the subject in an abrupt way that had Selina wishing to wring his neck and thank him all at once.

Mr. Drake turned at the sound of the door closing behind Selina. He smiled at her, and his gaze dropped to the bodice of her dress.

With a wrenching in her stomach, she realized she had forgotten to attend to it.

His gaze flicked back to hers.

"My maid was so occupied, I could not bear to bother her with such a minor issue," she explained. "I hope you will forgive the state of us all."

Mr. Drake looked around. "Forgive it? I feel quite overdressed being the only one without marzipan on my clothing."

Did he never lack a charming answer? This man would be the death of her.

"Ah"—Selina strode to the table, picked up the last piece of marzipan, and pressed it against Mr. Drake's clean, pressed shirt—"there you go."

The room froze with silence.

Heart beating erratically and hardly believing her own audacity, she met Mr. Drake's gaze, feeling a jolt when she realized how near his face was to hers.

He was unbearably handsome. Alluring. Skilled with children. And he smelled divine.

But he was a miserably manipulative fortune hunter.

His eyes explored hers, sparkling with amusement. "Thank you, Mrs. Lawrence. I feel quite at home now."

She took a step back and looked at her nieces and nephews, wide-eyed at what they had just witnessed. If she knew Kitty, a lecture was well on its way.

"*Are* you the friend with Pip?" Arthur asked, recovering from his surprise enough to refocus on that most important question.

"Guilty," Mr. Drake said.

"Why did you not bring him?" Teddy complained.

"It is for the best I did not. If I had, he would be crawling all over the lot of you, trying to eat the marzipan from your faces and fingers and clothes. And his teeth are quite sharp."

"Can we meet him?" Kitty asked, and beside her, Lou nodded her head fervently.

"We will take baths tonight if we must," Teddy said, a lamb prepared to surrender itself for slaughter.

"That is a great sacrifice indeed," Mr. Drake said. "But this is your aunt's home, and she must be the one to make that decision."

Five sets of eyes swept to Selina.

"Please, Aunt Selina," Arthur asked, and an echo of the same words followed from all of his siblings, including a *pwease* from Lou.

Selina could no more have refused them than she could have taught Pip to fetch Mr. Tolliver's glove on horseback. "Very well. Mr. Drake may bring Pip for a short visit tomorrow *if*"—she held up a hand to stem the tide of gratitude—"you take baths tonight, and *if* he has no other engagements."

All heads turned to Mr. Drake.

He covered the lower half of his face thoughtfully. "Hmm... have I any other engagements tomorrow?"

The children seemed to lean toward him with anticipation. Selina felt it too.

A grin formed beneath his hand, and he dropped it. "Tomorrow it is."

The four children swarmed Selina and Mr. Drake, as though they could not decide to whom they owed their thanks. The force of the gratitude pressed them together, and they shared laughing glances.

Despite the pleas of the children for him to remain, Mr. Drake made his excuses shortly after, something Selina supported whole-heartedly. She needed the time away from him to realign herself, remember her goal, and most importantly, to plan in what way she would next torture him.

For torture him she must.

She would be the princess, leading herself into battle on behalf of every woman who had been used for beauty or wealth. And tomorrow, Mr. Drake would leave with more than a smattering of marzipan on his clothing when it was over.

Chapter Eleven
Sebastian

Pip looked more dapper than ever as he perched on Sebastian's shoulder on their way to call upon Mrs. Lawrence and her nieces and nephews. Yorke and Fairchild had taken care of the monkey during Sebastian's call yesterday, and they had made him a monocle out of an old coin, which now dangled from his clout—the height of infantile sophistication.

Sebastian had asked them to look after the monkey with the intent that he and Mrs. Lawrence might find more time to converse and enjoy one another's company without the distraction of Pip.

The reality, however, was that Sebastian had barely spoken with Mrs. Lawrence. He had been too occupied with her nieces and nephews.

Little Lou had reminded him forcibly of a younger Margaret—adorably tentative—while the other three had the energy of Hugo and Felix.

A bloom of nerves spread through his stomach. He had received a letter from his solicitor, warning him that he could expect the Court of Chancery to request evidence of his fitness as a guardian at any time.

He had no such evidence, at least not if it referred to his financial fitness.

Today, he was determined to speak with Mrs. Lawrence and come to a better understanding of her view of him. If she would welcome a more purposeful courtship, he was more than ready to offer it. He was merely afraid of scaring her off. With the increasing affection in which he held her, there was more than a simple fortune at stake. He feared to lose her would mean losing his heart as well.

"For the love of everything good and beautiful, Pip," Sebastian said as they reached Number 14, "please behave yourself today."

When the footman welcomed him inside, the house was not quiet, as it had been upon his first visit. The muffled sound of children's voices could be heard from the entry. They quickly grew louder as the footman took Sebastian's hat and the four children came running into the hall.

Selina and the woman Sebastian could only assume was her sister-in-law came running up behind, urging the children to mind their manners.

Their comments and instructions fell on deaf ears as they huddled around Sebastian, staring up at Pip with grins of unfettered delight. Pip looked down on his audience curiously but stayed in his preferred perch.

With the focus on Pip, it was nearly a quarter of an hour before Sebastian was properly introduced to Mrs. Jane Randall, a woman very near his same age and with a great resemblance to her sister, Miss Grant.

Mr. Richard Randall came in presently, and Mrs. Lawrence introduced him to Sebastian as well while the children played with the monkey, who had lost any qualms about his eager entourage the moment he had discovered the crumbs on Kitty's shirt. There came a point, however, when the rowdiness of the play grew to be too much for Mr. Randall, who insisted they take the monkey out to the garden.

"Perhaps you could supervise, then, my dear," his wife said.

"I am happy to do so," Sebastian intervened, seeing how little Randall liked his wife's suggestion.

"That is very kind, Mr. Drake," Mrs. Randall said with a generous smile, "but it is a great deal to ask any one person to supervise a monkey *and* four unfamiliar children. Normally, I would ask Phoebe, but she has not yet returned from her walk in the Park with the Winsers."

"I will go along," Mrs. Lawrence said.

Sebastian smiled at her, eager to have the time by her side.

"I had hoped to ask you a small question, Selina," her sister-in-law said apologetically.

"Oh, then perhaps Richard can go with Mr. Drake, and I can come and spell him once we have spoken?"

Everyone agreed to this plan, and the children led the way, followed by their father, while Sebastian and Pip brought up the rear.

The garden attached to the townhouse was larger than any Sebastian had seen in Town. It was long and narrow and enclosed by brick walls, with gravel paths lined by plants and flowers winding through it. A small fountain and a number of trees and benches offered plenty of opportunity for Pip and the children to wiggle and laugh and talk without causing their father undue annoyance.

Arthur, who had cast himself in the role of liaison between Pip and the others, welcomed the marmoset onto his shoulder, then took him to the fountain, his siblings at his heels.

"It was kind of you to bring the monkey," Randall said.

Sebastian rather thought Randall would have preferred he *not* bring Pip, but it was a civil thing to say. "Pip is in his element," Sebastian said, watching with amusement as the children encouraged him to climb the tree. "He will sleep all the better tonight for this, so I can only thank your children for the service they are providing."

"He certainly looks to be a handful," Randall commented as

Pip hopped deftly from one branch to another, making the leaves rustle.

"Two handfuls at least—and more than that before I trained him a bit. I cannot imagine how your sister and Mr. Lawrence got along with him before."

"They must have managed fairly well, for Pip was never even mentioned until Phoebe's latest letter. I had always thought George disliked animals."

Sebastian frowned, for Tolliver had said something quite similar. "He enjoyed hunting them, at least, as I understand."

Randall smiled. "The only thing he and Selina had in common."

Sebastian's frown deepened. Despite the gap in their ages, it surprised him to know they had shared little in common. Though, he supposed, that was not necessarily a prerequisite for affection. But what, precisely, was the commonality Randall referred to? The timing of his comment was confusing. "They shared a dislike of animals?"

"No, they both liked hunting. Though, George never approved of Selina engaging in such pursuits, you know." He gave a soft chuckle, his eyes glazed over as he stared at some distant point in the garden. "She always managed to hunt despite that."

"Did she?" Were they speaking of the same person? Mrs. Lawrence had always managed to hunt? She knew nothing about firearms.

"Oh, yes. Selina might have been a docile wife in many ways, but she was never about to be told she could not ride to hounds or hunt. She can be quite stubborn when her will is crossed, and she developed a taste for the sport from a young age—something our father came to regret, I believe, for he was the one who introduced her to it. I can only think he did so in hopes of making her a more informed prospect on the Marriage Mart. Now she knows more than any woman I have ever met. A crack shot too. Puts me entirely to shame."

Sebastian did not respond, for he hadn't the slightest idea what to say.

Mrs. Lawrence, a crack shot? Knew more than any woman her brother had ever met about hunting?

The description bore no resemblance at all to the woman who had smiled sweetly while Sebastian had taught her about rifles.

Taught about rifles *he* knew nothing about.

Heat crept under his cravat and into his face as unwelcome memories presented themselves.

He clenched his eyes shut.

The things he had said! And the confidence with which he had uttered them!

Breeches and counterbalances and twin-barreled musketoons.

And she had not even bothered to correct him.

She had accepted help she did not require, and she had pretended ignorance when he had betrayed his. But why?

To spare his pride?

That, at least, was a comforting thought. Or half-comforting, at least.

"Mr. Drake! Mr. Drake!" Kitty came running up to him. "Pip will not come down from the tree!"

Sebastian cast his embarrassment aside. "He will not, will he? Let us see about that."

He followed Kitty on the gravel path through the garden, but she was right. Pip was quite content in the tree and would not respond, even to Sebastian's coaxing. The bonbons Sebastian had been certain he had left in his pocket were absent—no doubt Pip had found them without his knowledge.

"This may require more persuasive tactics," Sebastian said to the increasingly worried children. "Give me but a moment."

Randall agreed to supervise while Sebastian stole inside to ask the servants for some bonbons. He encountered one of the maids in the corridor and explained the situation to her.

"You understand the predicament, no doubt, for you know Pip better than I."

She gave him a funny look. "No, sir. I barely know the creature."

"Ah. I assumed you would have had plenty of opportunity to acquaint yourself with his mischief since your late master acquired him."

She laughed. "Oh, no, sir! Mr. Lawrence could not abide animals. He always said they were only good for shooting. The monkey was here but one night before you took him in, bless you."

The housekeeper came around the corner, her lips pressed together with displeasure as she looked at the maid, who dropped her gaze from Sebastian's immediately. "I will fetch the bonbons directly, sir." With a curtsy, she passed Sebastian, leaving him thoroughly and utterly befuddled.

Had he imagined Mrs. Lawrence saying Pip had belonged to her late husband?

No. Certainly not, for Tolliver had also expressed surprise to hear her say the monkey had been Mr. Lawrence's pet. As had Mr. Randall.

Mrs. Lawrence's response to Tolliver had been to say that her husband was surprisingly private. Was it possible he had owned such a chaotic animal without his friends or brother-in-law knowing of it?

Perhaps.

But his own servants?

Sebastian had cleaned up after Pip enough times to refute that possibility without hesitation.

Even if the maid was a recent addition to the household, she would be familiar with Pip. She would likely have been called upon to clean up after any number of messes he had made.

The monkey was here but one night before you took him in, bless you.

That was what she had said, but what in the blazes did it mean?

And why would Mrs. Lawrence say such things about Pip and her late husband if they were untrue?

It seemed that she herself must have acquired Pip, but then why claim him as her husband's? And why be so thankful to Sebastian for taking care of him if she was fond enough of the monkey to have chosen him as her own pet?

And then there was the bit about hunting.

Sebastian assumed she had spared his pride out of sympathy or due to a desire to spend time with him, regardless of what it required. But what if...

A growing unease began to creep into Sebastian's chest.

What if the reason behind all of it was *not* benign? What if it was the opposite?

He frowned.

No. If Mrs. Lawrence had heard tales of his reputation, she would not go to such trouble to tease him—allowing him to make a fool of himself over hunting equipment, acquiring a monkey and foisting it upon him. She would have simply rebuffed him instead.

Wouldn't she?

She can be quite stubborn when her will is crossed.

The maid approached, a little burlap sack in her hand, which she held out to him. "There you are, sir."

"Thank you," he said absently.

She curtsied and turned to go.

"Wait."

She stopped and faced him again, waiting for his orders, though her eyes darted down the corridor, no doubt to ensure the housekeeper was not near.

He hesitated, trying to decide how to form his question. "What made Mrs. Lawrence acquire Pip?"

"I couldn't say, sir. The monkey made quite a stir when he first arrived, as you can imagine, but Mrs. Lawrence promised us it would only be the one night."

Heartbeat pulsing in his neck, Sebastian smiled at her. "Thank you."

She gave another curtsy, then left him to his thoughts, which raced.

Perhaps he *was* going mad, but it sounded as though Mrs. Lawrence had acquired Pip with the sole intent of sending him home with Sebastian, knowing full well the chaos that would ensue. And she had done it by making him think Pip had been a cherished pet of her late husband's, who had been giving her trouble since her arrival in Town.

A muffled laugh from down the corridor yanked him from his thoughts, and he looked down at the sack in his hand.

The children were waiting outside. The children Mrs. Lawrence had left him with yesterday while she went to see to the stain on her clothing.

The stain that had still been there when she returned nearly half an hour later.

And today Aunt Selina gave us as many helpings of marzipan as we wanted!

It was almost as though she had done it on purpose, then left him with the children to fend for himself.

He tried to find other explanations for each of the circumstances, but the pieces fit together but one way.

There was no way around it: she knew. She knew his reputation and was trying to make a fool of him. She had purposely made him believe he had a chance of winning her hand, when all this time, she was wasting his time. His precious time.

His chest clenched painfully, and he swallowed the feeling of betrayal rising in his throat. A sense of loss was bubbling beneath it.

Had none of it been real, then? None of the moments he had come to look forward to, none of the camaraderie he had felt with her?

It had all been a lie, a cruel game at his expense.

Sebastian's jaw tightened. She could not be permitted to get away with such a thing.

With purposeful steps, he strode toward the drawing room, only to check mid-stride.

He could not barge in and read her a lecture in front of her sister-in-law. And what would he say even if he did?

No, he needed to allow his temper to cool. Only then could he think properly about what should be done next. All he knew was that he would no longer play the fool.

He strode back to the garden, his pulse thrumming as he considered his next move.

The children were still congregated at the trunk of the tree, Randall standing behind them.

"Ah, there you are." Randall looked behind Sebastian, as though he might see his sister or his wife. "What is taking the women so long, I wonder?"

Sebastian could not even bring himself to answer, but Randall did not require a reply. "I will go ensure nothing has befallen them."

What he imagined could befall two adult women in one of the finest townhouses in London, Sebastian did not know. It was a thin excuse to leave, but he did not prevent the man's departure. He was too grateful to be left alone with his thoughts, his mind too occupied to engage in meaningful conversation.

The children came over, and he absently ceded the sack of bonbons to them, hardly caring whether Pip went on a sugar-crazed rampage as a result. Mrs. Lawrence deserved that her garden be torn to shreds.

Minutes must have passed when the children ran up to Sebastian and pulled him from his abstraction.

"Mr. Drake," Teddy said urgently. "He found a pigeon."

"Hm?" Sebastian felt as though he had missed something important.

"Pip," Arthur clarified. "He found a pigeon. Come see."

The tide of their demand was simply too strong to be ignored, and Sebastian followed them to where Pip was, indeed, holding a pigeon.

A dead pigeon, it seemed, for it did not flutter or struggle against Pip's handling.

"Did he kill it?" Sebastian asked. The monkey was not generally violent, but Sebastian would not have bet against the possibility if someone laid him odds.

"I believe it was already dead," Arthur said.

A little, distinctive sniff drew Sebastian's attention from the spectacle.

A few feet away, Lou stood with her thumb in her mouth and her eyes full of tears.

"Oh, dear," Sebastian said, pulling a handkerchief from his pocket. "Kitty, will you see to Princess Lou? I will handle the pigeon. Arthur, keep Pip near, if you will." He draped the handkerchief over the pigeon. "Why don't you all find hiding spots in the garden, and I will come find you presently?" The corner of his mouth quirked. "The last one to be found wins a trip to Gunter's with Aunt Selina—and as many helpings of ice cream as desired."

The children scattered immediately, and Sebastian hurried toward the door that led inside.

Chapter Twelve
Selina

"Is something the matter?" Selina asked her sister-in-law as they sat on either side of the pale yellow chaise longue. She felt a degree of impatience with this little tête-à-tête, for Mr. Drake was in her home.

He had been there before, of course, but always with a plan on Selina's end—a way she intended to rattle him. She had no such plan today, and she was desperate to hit upon one.

"No, no," Jane said, arranging her hands in her lap in a way that might have been thought to belie her assurances. "I simply wished to speak with you before Phoebe returns."

"By all means," Selina said, turning her knees toward her. Whatever Jane's claims, Selina sensed that something important was about to be communicated. It made her just the slightest bit nervous.

There was a pause, and Selina had the distinct feeling that Jane was gathering her courage.

Jane's face spread into a smile. "Tell me about Mr. Drake."

Selina blinked. "About...Mr. Drake." That was why she had pulled Selina aside? To have a chit-chat about him?

"Yes. He is obviously head over heels for you, Selina, and I find him to be utterly and completely engaging. Given his presence here two days in a row—and Phoebe has mentioned other visits—I can only assume that you are agreeable to his suit."

An incredulous laugh burst through Selina's lips. She should have known Jane would fall under Mr. Drake's spell, just as Phoebe had done. It was precisely why Selina dismissed her impulse to tell Jane precisely how she felt toward Mr. Drake.

Jane's gaze grew bemused at the strange reaction.

"My dear Jane," Selina said, "let us leave discussion of Mr. Drake behind for the moment and rather speak of whatever it is you wished to speak about with me, for I sense something is troubling you, and not for the world would I have that be the case."

Jane gave a nervous laugh. "Oh, not troubles, precisely. It is only that...well, it is something Phoebe said yesterday while we were out."

Selina nodded, urging her to go on, while she racked her brains for what could have been said to require this private audience in the middle of Mr. Drake's visit. Leaving him with Richard was not her preferred scenario, for Richard was often thoughtless in what he said.

"Naturally, I asked her about the young gentlemen she has become acquainted with while in Town, and I was pleased that there were so many mentioned. You have obviously gone to great trouble to ensure this, for which your brother and I are sincerely grateful, of course."

"But..." Selina supplied when there was a pause.

Jane licked her lips nervously. "But there was one she mentioned—indeed, the one I inferred she was most interested in —called Mr. Evenden."

"Your inference was correct, I believe," Selina said, wondering if perhaps Phoebe and that young gentleman had somehow managed to do something untoward—not that she could believe such a thing of Phoebe, but infatuation could make one do strange things.

Jane's brow knit as she regarded Selina, as though considering her next words carefully. "Though naturally Phoebe is too modest to say so, it sounded to me as though Mr. Evenden has evinced a marked interest in her—and that she returns this interest."

Selina waited for her to go on.

"I inquired further and discovered that Phoebe essentially cut off the acquaintance."

Selina raised her brows. "Did she?"

Jane nodded.

"Well, no doubt she had good reason for it."

Jane frowned. "That is just it, though. Her explanation was a bit difficult to follow, but Richard and I agreed afterward that it sounded as though it was your idea—or at least done at your urging. That you had put it into Phoebe's head that Mr. Evenden's attentions were not to be trusted."

Selina's fingers tightened their hold on each other, and her heart clenched.

Jane's gaze grew sympathetic. "Now, I know, Selina, that you have Phoebe's best interests at heart, and it is the height of kindness for you to play chaperone to her, particularly given that you share no blood relation. But I admit that I was troubled to hear of this particular turn of events from Phoebe, and I wondered if perhaps we requested your chaperonage too soon after George's death, may he rest in peace."

"Too soon," Selina said incredulously. "It has been over four years since his death, Jane."

"I know that," she hurried to say, "but..." She hesitated.

"Speak plainly, Jane," Selina said calmly. "I can bear it, whatever it is."

Jane pressed her lips together. "It is only that I think Richard and I both underestimated just how unhappy you were and how your marriage to George affected you."

Selina swallowed forcefully and kept her expression curious. "You mean to say that you think that my unhappiness in marriage is poorly affecting Phoebe."

"I *think*," Jane said with deliberation, "that you are trying your very best to protect Phoebe from the pain of what you experienced. But I wonder if perhaps your fears are a bit...inflated."

Selina's lungs tightened and her pulse pounded. "Inflated."

Jane nodded, her brow wrinkled with sympathy and worry.

"Mr. Evenden is a flirt, Jane. He is a charmer, and Phoebe's lack of experience in Society makes her susceptible to reading too much into his behavior toward her. In warning her against him, I was simply attempting to spare her unnecessary heartbreak."

"But is there not the possibility that you have instead deprived her of the opportunity for courtship that might have turned into more?"

A sick feeling swam in Selina's stomach. But Jane did not know of what she spoke. She was older than Phoebe and married, but she had married for love, and she had done so in her first Season. Her understanding of the world had formed based on such experience. She knew little of heartache, and she had Phoebe's same inclination to assume the best of everyone.

"The risk of pain from Mr. Evenden's quarter seemed greater than the possibility of such a thing," she settled upon replying.

"There is no reward without risk, Selina," Jane said, "and while a just world would see Phoebe receiving the attentions of any number of gentlemen based upon her admirable character, we do not live in a just world. She does not have your wealth or your beauty, as pretty as she is. She does not have the luxury of turning away suitors based on ungrounded fears."

Ungrounded fears.

The two words rattled in Selina's head and heart.

Jane thought she was being irrational in guarding Phoebe against men like Mr. Evenden. She had no notion that Mr. Drake, who she seemed to regard very highly indeed, was the very grounds for her fears.

But even if Selina told Jane that Mr. Drake was nothing more than a black-hearted fortune hunter hiding behind a handsome face, and even if Jane somehow believed it, she would undoubtedly point out that Phoebe was not a target for such wiles.

Selina stood, her heart racing. "You must excuse me, Jane," she said as evenly as she could manage. "I have to see to my guest, but I will endeavor not to shield Phoebe from eligible gentlemen, whatever my concerns may be."

Jane let out a sigh and did not stop Selina from leaving the room.

Selina seethed and hurt all at once. Jane had all but accused her of denying Phoebe a match, of tainting Phoebe's happiness with her own *ungrounded fears*.

She was Mr. Drake's prey, and yet somehow *she* had been cast as the huntress, shooting down innocent suitors willy-nilly.

There was nothing innocent about Mr. Drake, however, and yet people refused to see it. They must be made to, which was why Selina was in such dire need of the next part of her plan.

She strode toward the garden, her mind racing in an attempt to strike upon her next step. She turned at the end of the corridor and ran headlong into something solid.

"Oh!" she cried out, placing her hands out to guard herself from further injury.

"Forgive me," Mr. Drake replied, taking a step backward. "Have I hurt you?"

Selina's surprise gave way to the irony of his asking such a thing.

"No," she said with extra force. He had not hurt her, and he *would* not.

Her gaze dropped to his hands, which seemed to be guarding something, though it was difficult to see in the dim corridor. "Is everything well?"

The pause before his response was longer than expected.

"Yes," he finally said. "Pip seems to have found a pigeon in the garden, and the sight upset Miss Lou, so I have come to dispose of it."

"A pigeon?" she repeated blankly.

He lifted the corner of the handkerchief to confirm.

Selina drew back at the sight of the dead bird. She had never liked the birds. They were dirty and ugly and forever getting in one's way.

The way Mr. Drake held the creature and the slight downturn of his lips made it evident that he was no lover of them, either.

Selina stilled, an idea forming in her desperate mind. A ridiculous, laughable idea.

It was not enough to repay Mr. Drake's crimes, but it would serve until she found a better plan.

Chapter Thirteen
Sebastian

Sebastian had not seen Mrs. Lawrence since realizing the game she had been playing, and he watched her with interest that both seethed and ached.

He had dismissed his impulse to barge in upon her and her sister-in-law to charge her with her offenses, but now she was quite alone.

And yet standing before her, he knew it would not be enough. Everything he had admired about her—her beauty, her wit, her kindness—*kindness!*—were now irreparably tainted. Where they had before invited him to draw nearer, now they mocked him.

His jaw clenched. Simple verbal assault would not be enough.

"Oh, dear." Mrs. Lawrence's hand stole to her mouth. "Sweet Montague!"

Sebastian was pulled violently from his vengeful ponderings. "I beg your pardon?"

"It is Montague, George's prized messenger pigeon."

Sebastian's gaze fixed intently on her—the brows knit so tightly, the forlorn, anguished look on her face. An hour ago, it might have convinced him. But not now. Now he wondered if she had practiced it in the mirror.

What was her game, though?

"A messenger pigeon," Sebastian repeated.

Mrs. Lawrence nodded, covering her mouth again with a hand, as though overcome with emotion. "George was so very fond of Montague."

Sebastian's jaw worked from side to side. He would play this game with her and see where it led. "I am unspeakably sorry, Mrs. Lawrence. I had no idea..."

Her gaze lifted to his. "No, indeed. How could you have?" Again, her hand stole to her mouth.

He began to suspect she was not concealing emotion so much as she was trying to hide a smile.

She sniffed. "Forgive me. It is just...the sight of something he loved so dearly...such an important part of him."

Was she truly expecting him to believe that her husband loved a common pigeon?

Was her opinion of his intelligence so little?

After the incident with the hunting equipment, perhaps so.

She ran a hand along the handkerchief covering the pigeon's wing, likely because she did not wish to touch the actual bird. "Another goodbye to say. Another part of George that will be buried and gone."

Sebastian could hardly keep from rolling his eyes. Mrs. Lawrence's sudden sentimentality did not fool him for a second. But he still failed to see what she intended with this.

He said nothing, determined that she be the one to reveal her hand.

She turned her face away in a fashion Sebastian found melodramatic. "It is difficult to even see Montague like this. I should hate for it to be the last memory I have of him."

Sebastian kept his silence, aware that she was waiting for him to say something.

Her eyes finally lifted to his. Those beautiful, hateful blue eyes. "I have troubled you so much already, but might I ask one last favor of you?"

Only with the greatest self-mastery did he suppress a scoff.

Every bit of trouble she had given him had been intentional. And here she was, plotting more.

"Anything," he said.

"I would be so grateful if someone were to preserve Montague's memory somehow. A portrait, perhaps, to keep his memory alive so that I may remember him the way he was in life. Whoever did it would need to see Montague, of course, for he is so very distinctive."

Sebastian glanced down at the lifeless pigeon in his hands. In a crowd of ten, he could not have picked it out. It was the same drab gray, with haphazard flecks of white in places. Indistinguishable from the majority of other pigeons, in fact.

Did she wish to inconvenience him, then? To force a disgusting, dead creature upon him in an effort to humiliate him?

"He truly is," Sebastian said, "and I would be honored to take on this task, Mrs. Lawrence."

She smiled up at him sweetly. Wickedly. "You are too good to me."

"Impossible," Sebastian responded. "You may safely leave the matter in my hands."

───※───

IT WAS IN THE DARK HOURS OF THE MIDDLE OF THE night when Sebastian hit upon the idea.

He must have looked like the devil himself, grinning in the dark like a villain who'd just escaped the gallows.

It was Mrs. Lawrence's own words that had given him the idea. *I would be so grateful if someone were to preserve Montague's memory somehow.*

She had suggested a portrait, but Sebastian knew no one capable of such a thing.

That word *preserve*, though...it had remained with him, and it inevitably brought someone particular to mind.

Sebastian did not take Pip with him to Blackstone's a second time. The doorman, Plockton, insisted upon announcing Sebastian's arrival to Lord Blackstone personally, however, and Sebastian suspected the man had been given specific instructions not to allow Pip to return.

Sebastian was left kicking his heels in the drawing room, trying to ignore the wild boar head hovering above him. The patch covering its left eye gave it a menacing air, as though it had just pillaged one of His Majesty's ships. The truth, as Sebastian understood it, was that the animal had lost an eye while being hunted, and there had been simply no way to salvage things.

There were a handful of other gentlemen in the drawing room. Most of them seemed to be congregating around a gentleman named Smart.

Leaving the wild boar, Sebastian made his way over, choosing a place beside John Aubin to bide his time while Plockton conferred with Blackstone. Aubin was too focused on what Smart was saying to take notice of him.

Smart was recounting some history with an earl who had engaged in dubious financial activity that had since come to light. Why anyone seemed surprised to discover such things was beyond Sebastian, who teased that the earl in question might just become the next member of Blackstone's.

Aubin seemed not to appreciate this bit of humor. Indeed, he seemed to be very much lost in intent thought.

Plockton returned, preventing any conversation with Aubin when he came up behind Sebastian. "His lordship is ready to receive you, Mr. Drake."

Sebastian bid farewell to Aubin, then followed the doorman to Blackstone's study. Apparently, he was not welcome to see himself there after the events of his last call. Perhaps Blackstone feared he would somehow manage to smuggle Pip into the club and force the monkey's presence upon him.

As if anyone could force Pip to do anything he didn't wish to.

Blackstone's face filled with relief at the sight of Sebastian entering alone.

"Drake!" he said jovially. "How do you do? Did you manage to train that marmoset of yours?"

"A bit, my lord. A bit. His manners will never be welcome at Almack's, I fear, but he has acquired a few more polite habits than when I first met him. I thank you for recommending the trainer."

"Do not even mention it," Blackstone said kindly. "What can I do for you, then?"

"I was hoping you might offer me a bit of counsel. I need to have a pigeon preserved."

Blackstone stared at him blankly. "A pigeon."

"A pigeon, my lord."

The corners of Blackstone's mouth turned down, and he surveyed Sebastian as though reconsidering his decision to welcome him into the hallows of his club.

"What was the name of the taxidermist you mentioned before?" Sebastian asked. "The one who had done poor work."

Blackstone's frown deepened, as though the mere mention upset him. "Fratch, you mean?"

Sebastian snapped. "Fratch! That was it. I could not for the life of me remember it. You do not happen to have his direction, do you?"

Blackstone took a moment before responding. "Drake, do you mean to have Fratch preserve this pigeon you speak of?"

"I do, sir." Sebastian could not suppress a smile, so gleeful did he feel.

Blackstone was becoming more certain by the second that Sebastian was mad.

"It is a strange request, I realize," Sebastian said. "I have my reasons, but I will not bore you with them. If you have Fratch's direction, I will take it and leave you in peace."

Blackstone looked at him another moment, then heaved a resigned sigh and pulled the quill from its stand while Sebastian tried and failed to suppress his exultation.

If Mrs. Lawrence believed she was the only one who could play a game, she was about to discover her error.

Chapter Fourteen
Selina

Selina had quickly come to the unwelcome conclusion that nothing she could do would try Mr. Drake's desire for her money to its limits. Thus far, everything she had thrown his way, he had caught deftly—and with that heart-stopping smile of his.

He seemed aggravatingly equal to anything.

He had civilized a monkey and entertained a group of sugar-mad children, but she was eager to see how his dignity would fare under the task of carrying around a dead pigeon and paying for a portrait to be painted of it—particularly when it had belonged to the deceased husband of the woman he was attempting to woo. Surely his pride would smart under such a task. Her one regret was that she would not be there to see the face of the artist when he made the request.

She went to sleep that night with a smile on her face, content at least that she was making Mr. Drake's life considerably less pleasant.

The children begged for her to invite him back the following day.

"I would, my dears," Selina said with a grimace, "but Pip must rest after yesterday's excitement."

There was a disappointed silence.

"Cannot Mr. Drake come on his own?" Teddy asked.

"Yes, let him come without Pip," Kitty agreed.

Selina required a moment to school her consternation into a proper response. "I think we should allow Mr. Drake a rest as well. But perhaps he can come another day this week."

She was obliged to resort to other tactics to appease the children and ended by taking them all to Gunter's, where she was obliged to buy no fewer than five ice creams for Arthur.

The children were not to be put off indefinitely, however—not even by ice cream—and Mr. Drake called upon them the following day, accompanied by Pip.

Richard, Jane, and Phoebe had taken advantage of the opportunity to go out in search of a new bonnet for Phoebe and gloves for Jane. Things between Selina and Jane were painfully civil after the difficult conversation, but Jane seemed determined to smooth things over. When Richard had voiced slight concern over leaving Selina with a bachelor, his wife had swept aside his concerns.

"What sort of indecency do you imagine Selina and Mr. Drake might manage when they have four mischief-makers to watch over?"

"Jane," Selina had cried out, her cheeks turning rosy in spite of herself.

Richard had seemed to take the point, however, and had made no more fuss over the matter.

Despite having been tasked with handling the preservation of an ugly dead pigeon, Mr. Drake arrived in high spirits, positively oozing charm and good humor.

Jane had dismissed Richard's concerns over the danger Mr. Drake posed to Selina, but Selina had to privately agree with her brother after an hour in Mr. Drake's company. He was more than usually vivacious, shooting her teasing looks and smiles that snatched the breath from her lungs.

He made no mention of the pigeon, but Selina's curiosity was strong enough that she broached the subject herself.

"I hope I have not put you out too much with the care of Montague, Mr. Drake," she said as they sat in the garden watching the children play.

"Not at all," he insisted. "I am more than happy to help."

More than happy to help yourself to my money. "I feel a wretch for taking such advantage of your kindness. Between Pip and Montague..."

There was a short silence before he responded. "I have great admiration for the deference you have given your late husband's wishes, Mrs. Lawrence. I am certain he would be pleased to know the lengths to which you have gone to ensure his belongings—whether they be rifles or prized pets—are seen to in a way befitting the esteem in which he held them."

Selina avoided his eye and ignored the warmth creeping up her neck. She had given little thought to how George would feel to know how she had been using his name in this game with Mr. Drake.

"You must miss him," Mr. Drake said gently.

She met his gaze, heart skipping at the suddenly sentimental turn.

How could he sit there, pretending to care how she felt about George when he had his eye on the fortune George had left her? In that moment, more than ever, she wanted to raise his hopes so that she could dash them into oblivion when the time was right.

"Terribly." She turned her head away again and dug her nails into the skin of her hand until her eyes began to water from the pain. "One becomes accustomed to having a strong, capable man at one's side." She let her gaze rise to his, and her heart thumped at the strength of the implication she was making.

He searched her face, his own inscrutable. "I assure you, one would never assume you wanted for strength or capability, Mrs. Lawrence. But I suppose appearances can be deceiving."

Her eyes locked on his, for she could hardly believe he dared utter such a phrase—and to look her in the eye as he did so.

Had he no shame in that entire well-formed body of his? Was

there no part of him that cared a jot for decency? No stray bit of conscience niggling him?

Lou's cry interrupted them, and they both hurried to her side, for she had fallen on the gravel path and scraped her knee while chasing after Pip.

"You are too quick for your own good, Princess Lou." Mr. Drake scooped her into his arms and took her to the nearest bench.

After ensuring the scrape was nothing serious, Selina stepped back and watched.

The gentle care with which Mr. Drake attended to Lou, making her smile amidst her tears, tending to her injury, then encouraging her not to be put off from playing more—it confused and angered Selina.

What if she had not come upon Mr. Haskett that day in the pet store? What if she had continued on, ignorant of the truth about him?

She would have been utterly and completely taken in. In Mr. Drake, she would have seen the incarnation of everything she had not allowed herself to want, everything she had never permitted herself to hope for. For, try as she might, she could find nothing but genuine care and concern in his eyes as he sent Lou off after Pip.

He must be the most convincing and persuasive fortune hunter to walk His Majesty's land. So convincing and persuasive that Selina lay awake that night, trying to fight the part of her that encouraged her to reconsider his intentions—to entertain the possibility that his attention to her did not only stem from greed and selfishness.

What if she was *not* so gullible as she feared? What if his admiration for her, his desire to see her and help her, was pure?

It might be nothing more than coincidence that had led him to propose marriage to another heiress after a mere week of knowing her, then pivot his focus to Selina quickly after.

That such humiliatingly implausible thoughts were the ones she fell asleep to made her hate Mr. Drake all the more.

It was but two days later when a note arrived from Mr. Drake, asking when it would be convenient for him to call upon her.

Selina had still not decided upon the next action she would take against him, and the thought of again welcoming him into her home without that made her feel uneasy. But Richard, Jane, and the children would be leaving the following day, and her nieces and nephews would never forgive her if they were not permitted to say farewell to Mr. Drake and Pip before their departure.

The fact that her entire family was so enraptured by Mr. Drake was equal parts reassuring and aggravating. After all, it demonstrated that it was not some deficiency unique to her that made her react to his charm. Yet, knowing that so many people she loved were so deceived by him made her all the more determined to teach him the lesson he needed.

So, she surrendered to the wishes of her nieces and nephews, aware of the irony of allowing them to see Mr. Drake once more despite the fact that he was not the man they thought him.

The joy on the children's faces when he arrived had her suppressing a sigh. In the years Selina had been married to George, her nieces and nephews had never connected with him, and yet Mr. Drake had wrapped them around his finger within half an hour of meeting them.

"Shall you marry Aunt Selina, Mr. Drake?" Kitty asked as they sat in the drawing room, playing spillikins.

Selina's eyes widened.

"Kitty!" Jane cried out, her tone half-censure, half-amusement.

"What?" Kitty said, not understanding what she had said amiss. "I did not like Uncle George half so much as I like him."

"Neither did I," Teddy said, his mouth turned down in disgust. "I am glad Uncle George is gone."

"Heavens above," Jane said, reaching a hand across Teddy's mouth to prevent him saying anything else shocking.

He pulled it away. "What? He was so boring. Always falling asleep and complaining of gout."

Mr. Drake seemed to be fighting off his own amusement, but as Lou was attempting to climb onto his lap, he had an excuse for not responding.

"You need not even ask Aunt Selina's father for her hand," Arthur said, "for he is dead too. But perhaps you could ask *my* father. He is bound to say yes, for he said last night that he thinks you a right good stick."

The color of Selina's face would have put any beet to shame in that moment, but she was obliged to cover her mouth to keep from laughing. She generally adored the naive frankness of children, but it was a different experience to be the one embarrassed by it.

The glance she stole at Mr. Drake only threatened her composure further, for his eyes danced in that particular way that made it so difficult to believe him the manipulative, selfish fortune hunter he was.

"That is very kind of your father," Mr. Drake said, bouncing Lou up and down on his knee so that she giggled adorably. "I think him a right good stick as well."

"Do you think Aunt Selina a right good stick too?" Teddy asked.

Mr. Drake's eyes flitted to Selina just as Jane grimaced apologetically at her.

"No," he said, his gaze thoughtful.

The baldness of the word sent a jolt through Selina.

"A stick is too plain," he said. "I would rather describe her as"

—his eyes searched her face so that her heart beat quickened—"a rose."

Their gazes locked, and for the hundredth time, Selina sought the crack in his façade, the evidence of his artifice. It was only a game, of course, but sometimes it felt far too real.

"A right good rose?" Teddy offered.

Mr. Drake's mouth spread into a grin, and he chuckled. "Precisely."

"Well, if you mean to marry Aunt Selina, you had better ask my father permission today, for we are leaving, you know."

"Teddy," Jane said sternly. "You may safely leave Mr. Drake's affairs to *him*, my dear. If he wishes to pay his addresses to Selina, he need ask no one but her. She is her own mistress."

Selina's eyes widened. Apparently, it was not only the children she needed to worry about saying embarrassing things.

Jane seemed to realize she had only made matters worse, for she colored up and shot an apologetic look at Selina.

When it was time for Mr. Drake to leave some ten minutes later, he said his farewells to the children and Jane before coming to face Selina. "Might I have a private word with you before I leave?" His voice was pitched lower, speaking to the private nature of the request.

Selina's heart skipped, and her eyes flitted to Jane, who had clearly heard and jumped to the same conclusion as Selina—a ridiculous one. Mr. Drake did not truly intend to pay his addresses to her right now, of all times.

Did he?

"Of course," Selina said with as much composure as she could muster.

"In the study, perhaps?" he suggested.

Surprised as she was that he had a particular room in mind for this tête-à-tête, Selina's heart was beating too fast and her mind too caught up trying to determine if she should be preparing for an offer of marriage to do anything but agree to it.

What if this *was* the moment? What if Mr. Drake did mean to propose marriage to her?

What would she say to him?

She would refuse, of course, but then, why in heaven's name was she so nervous? She should be exultant, but she was simply not prepared for the sort of lecture she had intended on reading him. She wanted him to leave Number 14 Berkeley Square with his tail between his legs and his character torn to shreds. When she was done with him, she wanted to be absolutely certain he never would dare seek out another heiress.

"Thank you for agreeing to speak with me privately," he said, closing the door behind them.

Selina felt suddenly breathless now that they were alone together. It was not the first time, but it *was* the first time he had asked for a private audience, and she was unsure what to expect.

What if he tried to kiss her?

She had hated when George would kiss her, but at times, she had wondered if it was because she found kissing repulsive or rather because George had done it poorly.

She was not yet aware of anything Mr. Drake did poorly. Except perhaps having a heart. Or a conscience.

So taken up was her mind with such questions that it was a moment before she noticed the box sitting upon the desk. It was large—too large to hold a ring without seeming ridiculous.

Mr. Drake picked it up and offered it to her. "I hope it pleases you."

Selina stared at the box, then at him. There was a strange light in his eyes as he watched her. The box was moderately heavy, and she was obliged to set it upon the desk again so that she could open it.

With fingers that trembled slightly, she undid the latch, then slowly lifted the lid. She sucked in a breath of shock and stepped backward.

Inside the box was a pigeon, entirely and utterly still. Its wings were splayed crookedly, as though one had broken and it was mid-fall. The feathers on its breast were not smooth and orderly but disheveled. It was the eyes that terrified her most, however. The glassy orbs bulged from its head as though they had been taken from a bird three times the pigeon's size. They leered at her threateningly.

The effect of it all was ghastly.

"It is not a portrait," Mr. Drake said, "but you mentioned preserving him, and I could think of no better way than this. I think he did a fine job, do you not? There is so much life and vivacity in him, even in death. He looks as though he has an extremely important message to deliver."

Selina glanced up at him.

Was this his idea of a joke?

He was watching her carefully, his expression intent but inscrutable.

He knows.

The words came into her mind unbidden. Without a doubt, they were true. He knew what game she had been playing, and this was his way of telling her.

His bright, fixed gaze challenged her, silently asking *what will you do now?*

"Oh, Mr. Drake," she said breathlessly, putting a hand to her chest, "it exceeds all expectation." She stepped forward to examine the bird more closely, though everything within her screamed at her to give the grotesque pigeon distance. She reached a hand toward its eyes, as though she might touch the macabre globes. Bile rose in her throat, but she forced it down. "The artistry is magnificent. Why, one can almost imagine Montfort might fly away at any moment." She smiled up at Mr. Drake.

"Montague, you mean," he said, his eyes never leaving her face.

"That is what I said," she replied evenly.

Their eyes locked, and a silent battle ensued, as though they were both determining whether to end the charade or continue it.

Selina would certainly not be the one to end it. Now, more

than ever, she was determined to win this war. Mr. Drake would leave it bloodied and bruised, humiliated. He would admit his crimes aloud.

"How can I ever thank you for this masterpiece?" she asked.

His smile had a sardonic tilt to it as he responded. "I have no doubt you will hit upon a way, my little rose."

She gritted her teeth, only managing to keep her pleasant expression intact by some small miracle.

"You are too kind," she replied.

He put out his hand for hers, and after a brief hesitation, she granted it to him. "Unthinkable." He brought her hand to his lips and pressed a long, soft kiss to the back of her glove.

Her heart fluttered even in its anger.

It was then she realized that his likening her to a rose earlier might not have been the compliment it had appeared to be. It was very likely he had been referencing not her beauty but her thorns.

He would soon learn just how sharp they could be.

Chapter Fifteen
Sebastian

"What are we to do now, Pip?" Stretched out on the chaise in the drawing room in St. James's, Sebastian cut a piece of the apple in his hand and offered it to the marmoset.

Pip munched on the fruit, providing no helpful suggestion.

Though it was past noon, Sebastian had yet to stir from this place. He simply hadn't the motivation to do so.

Now that the excitement of presenting the pigeon to Mrs. Lawrence had worn off and she had taken the wind out of his sails with her calm reaction, the reality of his situation had settled in.

"Back at square one." He let his head fall onto the arm of the chaise and stared at the ceiling.

The weight of his siblings' situation weighed heavily on him now that there was no prospect of Mrs. Lawrence's fortune. What was he to do now? And with the Court of Chancery expecting evidence of his suitability as a guardian soon?

The answer was not at all evident.

And yet, there was a sadness that permeated his entire body and mind, entirely separate from the burden of helping his siblings. His affection for Mrs. Lawrence had been genuine, his anticipation for a future by her side true.

He had been falling in love.

But she had never reciprocated. The entire time, she had been making calculated moves, letting him believe she was seriously considering his suit while doing her level best to humiliate him.

And humiliate him she had.

How had he missed the signs? How had he not seen through the façade?

He had been duped, fully and completely. But he would never let her know that.

He had been so certain she would end the ruse when she saw the pigeon. She had not, however. She had continued to play along.

And so had he, for his pride had demanded as much. He would not let her have the last laugh.

Sebastian sat up suddenly, not bothering to stop Pip when the monkey took the remainder of the apple from his hand and ran away with it.

"You are right, Pip," Sebastian said. "The game *must* go on. If Mrs. Lawrence wishes for a suitor, she will have a suitor—devil fly away with subtlety." The more aggressive he was in his attentions to her, the more she would be forced to admit that she never intended to accept an offer from him.

Pip's only response to this was to take another bite of the apple, which he was guarding in the corner.

What would a suitor do? Beyond forever darkening her doorstep, of course.

His gaze landed upon the escritoire, and a little smile curled the edge of his lip.

Sebastian went to the seat at the desk that faced the window and took out a sheet of paper. He dipped the quill in ink and set it to the paper.

There was a period of silence, interrupted only by Pip's chewing, before the quill began to scratch across the page.

> *Selina, thou art like a roast, so rich, so rare, so fine,*
> *Yet also like a well-aged cheese, pungent and divine.*
> *Thy hair doth flow like river's tide, so soft, so full, so free,*
> *A bird would gladly build its nest if left nigh unto thee.*
> *Like ivy creeping up the wall, my regard for thee shall grow,*
> *And wrap thee in its sweet embrace, till ne'er thou canst let go.*

It was by far the worst bit of poetry he had ever read, much less written, which was precisely why he could not stop smiling. Mrs. Lawrence hated poetry, even at its best, and this was poetry at its worst. He had also taken leave to use her given name, which he imagined she would despise.

He could ill spare the money, but he sent a bouquet of red roses to accompany the poem, wishing he could be a fly on the wall to watch Mrs. Lawrence's reaction.

The next morning, a servant sought him out to inform him of a delivery, and Sebastian shot up from his chair.

He hurried to the entry hall, where a bandbox sat on the table there, a note atop it.

He broke the seal in a hurry, eager for her response.

> *To Mr. Drake, Purveyor of Fine Verse and Peculiar Compliments,*
> *Thy words were rich, thy rhymes most rare, thy sentiments divine,*

And thus, I send a gift to thee, in form as bold as thine.

A fruit so fair, its crown held high, its gold a hue sublime,

Its sweetness, like a poet's verse, doth ripen over time.

And cheese, so strong, hath ripened well. Its scent doth linger true,

A potency much like that bestowed by sonnets writ by you.

A little smile curling the edge of his lip, Sebastian opened the bandbox as Pip galloped up beside him, then hopped onto the table.

He coughed and stepped back, the stench overpowering him.

Pip lingered for a moment, then ran off and took refuge through the nearest open door.

Covering his nose with a hand, Sebastian stepped toward the box and peered inside. Beside the wheel of cheese was something he had seen representations of but never beheld in person: a pineapple.

He stared at the exotic fruit for a moment—the vibrant gold color of the bottom half, the spiked green leaves at the top. The cheese he understood. He had likened her to it, after all, and she was having her revenge upon him with its pungent odor.

But the pineapple...

Pineapples were rare, exotic, expensive. Perhaps it was nothing to someone like Mrs. Lawrence to pay for such a thing, but given her feelings toward him, why share it with him?

When the footman cut into it at dinner that evening, the reason became apparent: the fruit was entirely rotten inside.

Yorke and Fairchild drew back in disgust, but Sebastian merely smiled.

"Well played, Mrs. Lawrence."

That night, he lay awake for some time, trying to decide upon his next move. They were playing at chess now, and he would settle for nothing less than checkmate.

Should he offer more grotesque verse? No. That was too predictable.

A gaudy and hideous set of jewelry obviously made from paste? Tempting, but money was in short supply, even for counterfeit pieces.

Something more than this child's play was required. Enough of their interactions had been happening in private; it was time to challenge Mrs. Lawrence's pretenses by seeing if she would agree to a more public courtship—and perhaps just how committed she was to acting as though she returned his affection in private.

Chapter Sixteen
Selina

Selina took especial care as she prepared for the card party at Lord Blackstone's. Her maid had coiffed her hair in an entirely new way, with every lock coiled and plaited, then looped into a tidy chignon at the nape of her neck. She added a touch of rouge to her lips and sprayed her favorite perfume onto her wrists and neck. Her gown was new—a creamy silver silk that clung to her form, shimmering like moonlight on the water, while the gauze overlay dusted the floor.

Mr. Drake must have thought she would shy away from accepting the invitation to the viscount's party, where they would be seen together for the first time. The gall he displayed inviting her to the home of the man who had befriended him in spite of his fortune hunting was not lost upon her. She had not even responded to his last missive, inquiring whether she intended to attend.

He would be thinking he had won, which would make her arrival all the more of a surprise. She wanted him to see her and to be frozen with shock and awe, to admire her and want her, while knowing he would never have her.

Phoebe was waiting in the entry hall when Selina descended,

and she glanced up to see her chaperone coming down the stairs. Her eyes widened.

"Selina," she said with near reverence. "You look..."

"Thank you," Selina said, hoping for such a reaction from Mr. Drake. "And you look..." She let the sentence trail off just as Phoebe had, winking at her.

Selina's heart was pattering a quick rhythm against her chest when they arrived at Lord Blackstone's. The viscount and viscountess greeted them warmly and urged them not to hesitate in joining any one of the various tables set up in the drawing room and saloon.

They heeded their hosts' advice and went immediately to the drawing room.

Selina's gaze wanted to stray and survey every corner of the room in search of Mr. Drake, but she bridled it.

Mr. Drake happened to be standing just opposite the doors, however, so her self-control was for naught. And she did not regret it, for his gaze landed upon her and fixed there intently, a hint of surprise driving his brows upward. But it was what followed the surprise that most pleased her.

His lips parted, and he took in a breath that made his chest rise. His eyes dropped to her gown before returning to her face.

Only then did he remember to smile, followed shortly by making his way toward them.

Mrs. Winser and her daughter were before him, however, and after a short exchange of greetings, Phoebe joined them to play at piquet, for they needed one more to complete their game. Selina felt a degree of consternation at the realization that Mr. Evenden was their fourth player.

"Mrs. Lawrence," Mr. Drake said, coming before her and taking up her gloved hand. He bent over it and looked up at her through his lashes. "You have stolen my attention *and* my breath, and I am come to retrieve them." He let his gaze hold hers for a moment before pressing a kiss to the back of her hand.

Selina felt eyes upon them, but she steeled herself and allowed Mr. Drake to finish his performance.

It was clear that he meant to play for high stakes this evening, and she was prepared to raise them every time.

"You quite undo me with such compliments, Mr. Drake," she said once he had come up for air from an unnecessarily long kiss.

"And yet they are but feeble attempts to do justice to your beauty and charm. Please tell me you will join me for a game of cards."

"With the greatest pleasure in the world," she replied through a cloying smile.

"Casino, perhaps?" he suggested, naming a game possible for two to play.

"Certainly."

He smiled at her and tucked her hand into his arm, then led her to an open table in the corner. He pulled out a chair for her, and she took her seat just as a man stopped.

"Drake! I thought I saw you arrive."

Mr. Drake blinked with surprise, his confident charm suffering a sudden check. It was evident he did not recognize the man.

"Phillips," the man said. "I met you when you were curate at Birchhurst—my home parish, you know."

Selina's brows shot up. A curate? Surely the man was mistaken.

Mr. Drake laughed, though there was an unease in the sound. "Ah, yes. Forgive my lapse in memory. It feels a lifetime ago."

"Where have you taken up a living?" Mr. Phillips asked.

Mr. Drake's eyes flitted to Selina for the briefest moment. "I have left the cloth, in fact."

"Oh," Mr. Phillips said blankly. "Well, I trust you have found success in your other endeavors. I shan't keep you from your partner any longer." He shot a smile at Selina, gave a quick bow, and left.

Mr. Drake took his seat and seemed to be avoiding Selina's staring gaze, but once he was seated, he had no excuse to avoid it.

The quick exchange with Mr. Phillips had accomplished what Selina had failed to do in sending him home with monkeys and dead pigeons: it had rattled him.

His mouth pulled into a smile as he reached for the cards and began to shuffle them. "Shall we play?"

Selina hesitated for a moment, for she was still trying to grasp this new information.

It would keep, so she nodded.

"What are our stakes?" Mr. Drake asked as he dealt each of them four cards.

"Whatever you wish," she said with a careless shrug of the shoulder.

Mr. Drake's hand slowed as he placed four cards in the center of the table, and he looked at her intently. A little glint sparked in his eyes. Mischief.

"Whatever I wish?" he asked.

She met his gaze firmly, wondering what devilry was in his mind. He had no money, so he would not wish to play for that. What, then, would he choose? Her hand in marriage? And what would she say if that *was* his suggestion?

Her curiosity and her pride brought out her response. "Whatever you wish," she repeated. "What do you have in mind?"

His eyes raked over her face. "Something…memorable." His gaze settled on her lips, and Selina's heart thumped violently as the image of his mouth on hers presented itself to her.

"A poem, perhaps?" she teased, playing as though she did not understand his meaning.

He chuckled softly. "Tempting, but no. That is not what I meant."

"What, then, did you mean?" She raised her brows. She would force him to say it—to put a name to his wishes. Whether he truly wished to kiss her or was simply testing her limits, she did not know.

He leaned his elbows on the table and dropped the volume of his voice. "A kiss. I would play for a kiss."

Such stakes were nonsensical. "I find such a stake perplexing, I confess, for does it not ensure the outcome remains the same, no matter who wins?"

"Not at all," he replied, sitting back in his chair and regarding her. "If you win, you may, of course, choose to forgo your prize—though I admit to hoping you would not wish to do such a thing."

She nearly scoffed. He thought it would be a prize to kiss him?

She forced a smile. "I suppose the only way to find out is to play."

A glance at Phoebe informed Selina that she was still playing piquet with the same group. All four of them were smiling, and Selina knew a flicker of doubt. Had she done wrong to warn Phoebe against Mr. Evenden?

Mr. Drake insisted Selina begin the game, and her focus became, of necessity, consumed by the challenge before her.

Casino was a simple enough game: match cards or build up combinations to capture them. With Mr. Drake as her opponent, however, each play felt laden with significance.

Mr. Drake could not be permitted to win, though what she would do if she won, she could not say.

To decline her prize would feel like a sort of surrender or admission. But to take it?

She forced her breath to come evenly.

They both meant to win—that much was clear by the focus they both evinced and the halting conversation that took place as a result of their minds being engaged in strategy.

"You were a curate once, then," Selina said after finishing a play.

Mr. Drake's eyes flicked to hers, then away again. "A lifetime ago."

"I had not imagined you to be of a pious turn of mind."

He chuckled as he selected a card. "You imagined correctly."

He looked at her for a moment, then returned the selected card to his hand and chose another.

Selina rose a brow in question.

His smile grew broader as he laid down his card. "I could sweep the table now, but that feels too easy."

Her nostrils flared as she smiled right back. "Do not hold back on my account, Mr. Drake. I assure you, I am capable of winning without any assistance."

He had been winning, but the game took a turn shortly thereafter, and Selina wondered whether it was intentional on his part. But no. He was every bit as determined to win as she was.

Her hands trembled treacherously as the final cards were played and the points counted aloud by Mr. Drake.

Selina let out a shaky breath as he laid down the deck and looked at her.

"Congratulations, Mrs. Lawrence. You have won."

She could not even force a smile so jumbled were her feelings and intentions. What would she do now?

His eyes asked that very same question.

Would she take those lips with hers? Would she do so quickly, barely allowing them to touch? Or would she linger, exploring what it felt like? To kiss George had been to kiss someone to whom she was not attracted even a whit. What would it feel like to share that intimacy with a man she had once felt the inklings of attraction toward—a man she now hated?

Would the violence of their feelings lead him to take her lips ruthlessly, his hands gripping her to him in a display of dominance, while she fought to gain control, her hands threaded forcefully through his hair?

Something told her that kissing Sebastian Drake would be nothing at all like kissing George.

Her body warmed.

Even if she *did* claim her prize, it would not be in a card room teeming with other people. Widowhood granted certain liberties to a woman, but that liberty was not among them.

Her eyes flitted to Phoebe, but she was not there. Neither was Mr. Evenden.

Her cheeks still hot, Selina searched the room for them with no success.

"Excuse me," she said, grasping at the excuse to escape. "I must attend to Phoebe." Without meeting Mr. Drake's eye, she rose and left the table.

A search of the saloon did not reveal Phoebe or Mr. Evenden, and Selina's feet moved quickly as she traversed the corridor, going from the study to the library and then the morning room. She had her hand on the knob to another room when she spotted Phoebe farther down the corridor, arm in arm with a young woman Selina recognized as Miss Templeton.

Selina let out a sigh of relief, for both girls were smiling as they conversed animatedly.

"Selina," Phoebe said when she noticed her.

"I came to find you," Selina explained. "But I can see you are well."

"Indeed," Phoebe replied, smiling at Miss Templeton. "Would you like to accompany us back to the drawing room?"

Selina hesitated. She had no desire to return to Mr. Drake. She needed a bit more time to decide upon a course of action. "Thank you, but I am stretching my legs a bit. I shall return presently."

Phoebe and Miss Templeton continued down the corridor, and Selina watched them, wondering how Phoebe had come to leave the company of Mr. Evenden and the Winsers.

The drawing room door opened, letting an abundance of light into the corridor, and the silhouette of Mr. Drake appeared.

Selina grasped the door of the nearest room in her hand and slipped inside, pulse racing.

It was a music room, small but furnished with a piano, a harp, and a tall case of music behind. A sole candle lit the space from its place on the windowsill. The room was decorated in the Oriental style, the celadon-papered walls accented with motifs depicting blossoming trees, cranes, and peacocks, all glimmering with gold leafing in the limited candlelight.

Selina pulled in a deep, protracted breath, trying to steady her nerves as she took slow, deliberate steps into the room.

She was overreacting. What need was there for such an emotional response to Mr. Drake and his scheming?

She had but one consideration to entertain: winning this round of their game, just as she had won at Casino. To lose was not an option.

The door opened, and she spun around.

Mr. Drake stood in the doorway.

Every nerve stood on end as she met his gaze.

"I saw Miss Grant return to the drawing room," he explained, "but you did not. And then I thought I saw you rush into this room."

The words were benign, but the tone was not. It said, *You are trying to escape. You are afraid.*

"I was waiting for *you*," she said.

His brows rose. "Were you?"

She let out a laugh. "Of course. I have a prize to claim." A shiver ran from her crown to her toes at her own words.

Mr. Drake's gaze intensified. "Indeed, you do." He closed the door behind him.

Every nail of propriety that had been so carefully hammered into Selina from her childhood rattled tremulously at the sound of the click.

Hang propriety. What good had it ever brought her? Of what benefit was being a wealthy widow if one did not take advantage of the liberties it afforded?

Every step Mr. Drake took toward her doubled the speed of her heart, but she was determined not to give him the satisfaction of seeing her balk or stumble.

She stood her ground, waiting for him to come so that she could claim her prize.

He stopped a few feet shy of her, his eyes watchful, gleaming with something she could not name.

Would he come closer? Or would he force her to take those final, impossible steps toward him?

He remained where he was. "You wish to claim it, then?"

She could not bring her voice to cooperate, so she took three steps toward him in response, until she was obliged to lift her chin to meet his eye.

He gazed down at her, his expression inscrutable, his eyes searching, his body still. "The prize is yours to take," he said, his voice gravel.

Selina could barely breathe, and whatever air she managed to bring in was saturated with the intoxicating scent of cedar. But she had to do something. The thought of pressing her mouth to his made her feel faint, so instead, she lifted a trembling hand and touched a finger to his lips.

His drew in an uneven breath as she trailed her finger lightly over his bottom lip, tracing its soft curve.

His eyelids fluttered, then shut as a soft, unintelligible noise came from him.

A sense of victory trickled through her, but the roar of warmth in her veins surged over it, drowning it in a sudden desire to replace her finger with her lips, to know whether the softness she was feeling would be even greater under their touch.

Mr. Drake's hand shot up, grasping her wrist as his eyes flew open and fixed upon hers.

She saw it there—the flame of desire she felt. Or perhaps it was the fire of anger. He had no right to that anger.

Whatever it was, it fanned the hot embers inside her until she could not separate the hatred from the want.

His head lowered an inch, his eyes dropping to her lips.

Kiss me, she said with her eyes. *Dare to kiss me and see what happens.*

Kiss me, his eyes responded as they met hers again. *Dare to kiss me and see what happens.*

Did she dare? And what would happen if she didn't?

A burst of laughter erupted just outside the room, and they both blinked, the thread broken.

Selina stepped back, her entire body wracked with trembling. "I ought to see if Phoebe needs me."

He searched her face for a moment but said nothing.

She swallowed, wondering if he saw this as surrender.

She forced a smile to her lips, hoping it looked more confident than she felt. "Good night, Mr. Drake." She turned on her heel and left the room, releasing a tremulous breath when she closed the door behind her.

She had no idea whether she or Mr. Drake had emerged victorious tonight.

Chapter Seventeen
Sebastian

Sebastian remained in the music room for some time, waiting for his composure to return. It did not do so readily.

He was stopped in the corridor by Tolliver, who found it necessary to recount his journey away from town in great detail and mention all the ways in which he had helped Mrs. Lawrence since returning.

As he ran into three gentlemen from Blackstone's just after, by the time he returned to the drawing room, Mrs. Lawrence and Miss Grant were gone.

Perhaps it was for the best. He could use a bit of time to master his emotions. He had arrived at Blackstone's with confidence and determination; he was leaving with neither.

When he had suggested a kiss as the stake of their game, he had been thinking only of forcing *her* into a situation she would hate. He had not accounted for how it would affect him.

Why should he have? His anger toward her burned bright, after all. There was no way to anticipate that the feelings he had felt for her before learning of her duplicity would return in full force the moment she touched him.

The mere memory of her finger tracing his lips sent a shock of desire through him.

He tamped it down, gritting his teeth. What a fool he was.

He needed a glass of water over the head.

⁂

He settled for a glass of water down the throat when he reached home. Sleep was revivifying, and by the time he had partaken of breakfast, his determination was stronger than ever. He sat at the escritoire, smiling at the memory of the poetry he had written there, and composed a new note, this time asking for the pleasure of her company—and the first two sets—at the ball the Duke of Rockwood was holding on Saturday evening.

"She will never agree to it," Sebastian told an inattentive Pip as he sealed the missive with pleasure.

She did agree to it, though, in an overly flowery response, thanking him for his kind invitation. He could have sworn there were moments when she, too, had been undone by their near-kiss, but perhaps that was simply because he had not wanted to be alone in his reaction.

Yorke and Fairchild accompanied Sebastian to the ball, for the duke was Yorke's eldest brother and the only reason Sebastian had been invited.

He barely heard the conversation between his friends when they arrived, for his focus was on the door to the ballroom.

Would she come?

She would. He knew Selina Lawrence well enough by now to know that.

She had still not arrived, however, when Henry Branok approached him. Branok was a fellow member of Blackstone's and an avid birdwatcher. In what way a birdwatcher had fallen afoul of Society in order to be relegated to Blackstone's club, Sebastian did not know, but he quite liked Branok. His love of birdwatching was less disruptive to conversation than Miss Fernside's had been, at least. Eccentric as Blackstone might be, Sebastian had to admit that he chose his members well. He had yet to meet one he disliked.

Sebastian listened with interest—and a bit of envy—about Branok's most recent exploits: a birding expedition around England. It sounded so tranquil compared to the difficulties Sebastian was facing. He would gladly have spent hours watching for one of Miss Fernside's purple-dusted wimper willows rather than tearing his hair out over Mrs. Lawrence and the Chancery case.

The conversation with Branok took on a distinctly awkward tone, however, when Miss Fernside herself appeared before them. She looked them over with haughty brows.

"So, it is true, then," she said to Branok. "You two are friends. You *have* been helping him."

Sebastian frowned and glanced at Branok, who looked just as bemused.

"This clears up matters perfectly," she said.

"What matters?" Mr. Branok asked. "Miss Fernside, please..."

She merely shook her head. "It doesn't matter any longer."

NEITHER OF THEM HAD MANAGED A RESPONSE WHEN she walked away.

Thoroughly confused but feeling the need to enlighten Branok to the extent that he could, Sebastian explained the nature of his acquaintance with Miss Fernside. Branok was far too even-keeled to hold his crimes against him, however, and soon left to go in search of Miss Fernside.

Sebastian's gaze flitted to the door again, and his heart stuttered. Mrs. Lawrence and Miss Grant stood just inside the entrance.

She had come.

The confirmation that she was too game to sit at home for

this part of their challenge pleased Sebastian greatly, even if a flicker of self-doubt lay beneath it.

He had prepared himself, steeled his heart, which was why it was all the more aggravating to feel it respond to her presence. It was not only anger he felt toward Selina, despite her crimes against him. There was still a stubborn bit of want and longing.

But he would not allow himself to be undone by such ill-judged feelings tonight.

Mrs. Lawrence's burgundy gown was regal, bringing to mind a heady, intoxicating wine, while the crystals scattered across the bodice glinted and glimmered in the candlelight. Around her neck hung a single diamond pendant, simple but elegant, matching the two diamond drops that hung from her ears. The cool light of the stones contrasted with the warmth of her blonde hair, giving the illusion of silver and gold.

His gaze dropped to her hand, noting the diamond ring she had worn upon their first meeting—the one she loved to tinker with.

He could not keep himself from staring at the vision she presented. She had once been everything he hadn't known existed —grace, wit, kindness, and beauty in one riveting woman.

But it had been an illusion.

Perhaps that version of Mrs. Lawrence existed, but not for him. She despised him. She wished him ill. And she continued to play with him like a cat with a mouse.

The ache in his chest turned to a pinch as anger filtered through him. She had not merely hurt *him* with her scheming; she had hurt Margaret and Hugo and Felix, and they had done nothing to deserve it.

Mr. Tolliver appeared before Mrs. Lawrence and bowed over her hand, sending all Sebastian's thoughts fleeing.

The time for observation had ended.

He strode purposefully toward Mrs. Lawrence and came to a stop in front of Miss Grant, Mr. Tolliver, and her.

"Forgive me, Tolliver," Sebastian said with an amiable smile, "but I had the distinct pleasure of extracting a promise from Mrs. Lawrence for the first two sets, and both of us know she is nothing if not a woman of her word."

"The first two sets?" Tolliver repeated incredulously.

Sebastian's gaze fixed on Mrs. Lawrence, and hers on him.

He held his hand out expectantly, maintaining his smile as her jaw tightened, her eyes lighting with fire.

She wanted nothing more than to deny him the two sets, and the knowledge sent a flush of pleasure through him.

Go ahead. Deny me. Admit defeat.

She set her hand in Sebastian's, then turned toward Mr. Tolliver and smiled. "Perhaps the third set?"

There was nothing for Mr. Tolliver to do but ask Miss Grant to dance with him, a distinctly lackluster offer which she accepted more gracefully than Tolliver deserved.

"Are you well, Mrs. Lawrence?" Sebastian asked as he led her to the set. "You look a bit...put out this evening."

She laughed. "You positively overwhelm me with your compliments once again, Mr. Drake. Do I look so ill?"

"On the contrary." He led her to her side of the set and released her hand. "I have never seen you look as radiant as you do this evening. The way your eyes flash and your cheeks flush—it only adds to your beauty."

"You cannot imagine how pleased I am to know that my aggravation brings you satisfaction."

Sebastian smiled as he walked across the set to take his place.

Her eyes were fixed on him, bright and intent, her mouth arranged in a mechanical smile as the music began.

He bowed, and she curtsied, then they came together.

"I trust I have had no part in this aggravation," he said, taking her hand to begin the figures of the dance.

"Oh, Mr. Drake," she said in a cloying tone. "You could never be a cause of aggravation. You have been so *very* attentive to me from the moment we met. And what happy chance that meeting was!" Her face was arranged in a sweet, joyful expression, but there was a martial light in her eyes there was no mistaking.

"I consider any moment spent with you happy chance. You cannot fathom how fortunate I feel to have been singled out for a full two sets with you."

"I might say the same," she replied with saccharine sweetness.

Their gazes held as Sebastian considered what to do and say next. He despised her and admired her all at once, wanted to rake her over the coals for toying with him, then kiss her senseless.

Coals would do nothing. Selina Lawrence seemed impossible to discompose.

There was a final maneuver left in Sebastian's arsenal, however —one that would leave him the winner and put an end to this entire charade.

Part of him was reluctant to end it. There was a level of enjoyment and exhilaration in it, after all. But he needed all of his mental faculties for the more pressing problem at hand: how to liberate his siblings from Hollis's guardianship now that Mrs. Lawrence's fortune was not an option.

It never *had* been.

His fingers pressed more firmly into her waist, and their gazes held in mutual defiance and determined pleasantness until the first dance began to draw to a close. Sebastian took the opportunity of their last moment together to draw near to her, bringing his mouth to her ear.

Did he detect a tremble in her body?

"Might I convince you to take the air with me, Selina?" he whispered.

She pulled back to look at him, indignation flashing in her eyes.

"May I call you your given name?" he asked, unable to fully suppress the pleasure of her reaction. "I have been wanting to for some time now."

"Of course...Sebastian," she replied. "I could use the fresh air." She accepted his arm, the press of her fingertips the only evidence of the tension in her body as he guided her from the ballroom floor toward the doors that led outside.

"I do love dancing," he said, choosing an area on the stone balcony that granted privacy, "but I have been eager for a bit of privacy with you."

Her brows went up, instant watchfulness entering her eyes. "Have you?"

He smiled, though his heart thumped against his ribs. "Yes, but that is not unusual, of course. Tonight, I simply have a particular reason for wishing it."

Her gaze intensified, and her body grew more still. "And what reason is that?"

He took her hands, and there was the slightest resistance before she granted them to him. "You cannot stand in any doubt of my regard for you, Selina."

Her eyes flashed, but her smile was steady. "No, indeed. I am fortunate enough to have been aware how you regard me for some time now."

He couldn't stop the corner of his mouth from hitching at her calculated answer. "I have reason to believe you return a measure of that regard."

"Oh, Mr. Drake—"

"Sebastian."

"Sebastian," she corrected with a smile. "You could not possibly fathom the strength of what I feel for you."

His lips turned up at both edges in further acknowledgement of the barbed response masked with sweetness. She was skilled, certainly, and he reluctantly admired her for it.

But this game had run its course.

Her fingers were stiff in his, her body tense as he brought her hands to his mouth and kissed one fervently, then the other. "You make me the happiest of men, Selina." He fixed his gaze on hers, arranging his expression into one of lovelorn pleading. "Please tell me you will do me the honor of becoming my wife."

All traces of a smile disappeared from her face. Her nostrils flared and her eyes glittered with barely restrained fire as the silence stretched.

Sebastian waited. He waited with all the patience in the world for victory.

He had backed her into a corner, and she had no choice now but to surrender.

How very sweet it would taste.

She released a sudden breath, and her expression shifted, her taut lips stretching into a smile. "Yes. I *will* marry you."

Chapter Eighteen
Selina

Rash the decision might have been, but the reward of seeing Mr. Drake's face was ample compensation for Selina.

He had truly believed he had her beat. He had been almost crooning the entire evening.

But not anymore.

Now he was speechless.

Selina beamed with triumph, the flush of victory coursing through her like nothing in her life had done. And it was not even complete yet.

She took advantage of Mr. Drake's shock, pulling her hands from his and setting her palm on his warm cheek. "You have made *me* the happiest of women."

The door opened, and their heads turned.

Mr. Yorke and Mr. Fairchild checked at the sight of Selina and their friend in such close quarters.

Mr. Yorke's eyes flicked between Selina and him while Mr. Fairchild's brows lifted.

Selina let her hands drop, a flush creeping up her cheeks. This was not the opportune time for an audience.

"Perhaps we should return later," Mr. Fairchild mumbled to Mr. Yorke.

"No, no," Mr. Drake said, apparently gathering himself. "You are the perfect two people to felicitate us."

Selina snatched his hand and squeezed it tightly, warningly.

Mr. Drake adjusted his grip so that they were holding hands. "Mrs. Lawrence—my beloved Selina—has just done me the honor of agreeing to marry me." Turning his gaze to her, he brought her hand to his lips and pressed yet another kiss to it.

"That is famous!" Mr. Yorke said with a grin. "I *do* felicitate you, then."

"My deepest well wishes," Mr. Fairchild said with his own surprised smile and a bow.

Selina's stomach swam.

This was not what she had intended when she had agreed to marry him—for it to become known. Twenty more seconds was all that she required to turn the tables back on Mr. Drake. His friends could not have had worse timing.

Their appearance complicated things in a way that made her cringe. But there was no helping it now. She could at least still deal Mr. Drake the blow she had intended.

"Thank you both," she said warmly, turning toward Mr. Drake. "I have long been searching for the happiness you have given me, Sebastian. How joyful a thing it is to know that I shall have you to care for me and see to my every need! It sets me at liberty to do the thing I have most wished to do but could not do as a husbandless widow."

There was a glint of confusion and wariness in his eyes as he responded. "Anything you want, my love."

She smiled as broadly as her lips would allow and gathered up his hands in hers. "I mean to donate my fortune to charity."

If Mr. Drake's surprise before had pleased her, the abject horror on his face now would sustain her for the rest of her life.

Mr. Yorke and Mr. Fairchild too were speechless, looking on and staring at their friend.

Mr. Drake's hands tightened uncomfortably around Selina's, as though he could undo her words with sheer force.

At such a moment, Mr. Tolliver and Phoebe came through the doorway.

Phoebe's eyes widened, and Mr. Tolliver's gaze shifted back and forth between Selina and Mr. Drake.

"What is the meaning of this?" Mr. Tolliver asked.

No one answered, but the question had been more rhetorical than anything. The fact that Selina and Mr. Drake were on the balcony together with their hands intertwined and their bodies so near drew a sufficiently clear picture for even someone as thick as Mr. Tolliver.

And if Mr. Tolliver knew...well, there was no stopping things.

Selina forced herself to dwell on the victory of robbing Mr. Drake of the thing he had most wanted rather than the complication of the engagement being known. If only she had been able to tell Mr. Drake of her intent to donate the fortune *before* anyone had found them...

Mr. Drake would have retracted his offer, and no one need ever know she had agreed to marry him.

But that time was past, and if the news was to spread, Selina fully intended to utilize it against him. He was trapped now, and she would make him feel the walls closing in upon him, even if she herself was to be crushed by those walls in the process.

"Mr. Drake and I are to be married," she announced.

Phoebe's hand stole to her mouth. She let out a muffled, incredulous laugh, then hurried over and threw her arms around Selina. "I knew it!" she breathed. "I knew it from the moment you met. You two were meant for one another."

Even amidst the embrace, Selina's eyes flicked to Mr. Drake, who watched her with a hundred emotions in his eyes. Or perhaps no emotion at all.

Guilt flickered through her, but it was quickly stamped out by pride. What right had he to be angry with her? He had courted and wooed her for her money. He deserved every bit of anguish he was feeling.

Mr. Tolliver was less effusive than Phoebe in his congratulations. He said not a word before spinning on his heel and returning inside.

Phoebe finally pulled back from Selina, her face wreathed in smiles as she turned to Mr. Drake. "I cannot express how much joy this news brings me, Mr. Drake. You could not have found a better woman than Selina, nor, I am sure, could she have found a better gentleman than you."

The muscle in his jaw feathered, but he smiled. "Thank you, Miss Grant."

She whirled toward Mr. Yorke and Mr. Fairchild. "Is this not the happiest occurrence?"

Selina took advantage of the moment to turn toward Mr. Drake, drawing near to him just as he had done during their dance. His grip was still tight around her fingers as she whispered against his cheek, "Shall we return to the ball, *my love*?"

The intoxicating scent of cedar enveloped her, and her lashes flickered.

She drew back, and Mr. Drake's eyes settled upon her.

"By all means." He smiled, but oh, how sharp the edges were.

***

WERE TEARS AN EXPECTED SIDE EFFECT OF VICTORY?

They must have been, for Selina found her eyes full of them as she lay in bed that evening. The sense of triumph she had been so certain would sustain her for the rest of her life was not, unfortunately, untainted. Deep beneath the surface, she found less desirable emotions clamoring for her attention.

Anger, of course, was foremost amongst them, but as she sat with that anger and questioned its strength, she found it writhing and changing until it became something else: hurt.

She might claim victory over Mr. Drake, but victory did not

change her situation—and it did little to lessen the pain of knowing she had been used and manipulated for her money.

She had not truly intended to donate her fortune to charity—it had been said as a way to punish Mr. Drake—but the desire was growing quickly within her. What had the money brought her aside from grief and suspicion?

Her parents' admiration for George's wealth had led Selina into an unhappy, loveless marriage. Since George's death, she had avoided Society precisely because of the fortune. How could she trust anyone's intentions toward her to be pure?

Now, she was engaged to a fortune hunter—a fortune hunter who had somehow managed to pierce the armor around her heart despite his selfish and sinister motivations.

He was charming and capable, her family loved him, he made her laugh, he made her heart skip and bound. He was the type of man who could inspire love—and the type of man she had refused to believe existed.

And he did *not* exist. But she had begun to believe he had, and that was the tragedy. Despite all her best efforts, she'd started to hope. Foolishly. Quietly. Desperately.

But Sebastian Drake was all artifice and ulterior motives.

One thing was certain: she could not remain engaged to him, whatever the consequences might be. And if ending an engagement and donating the majority of her fortune to charity was the only way she could relinquish the bitterness and hurt in her heart, so be it.

A WOMAN WITH A PRISTINE REPUTATION TO GUARD would not have made a visit to St. James's in broad daylight.

But Selina did not have a pristine reputation.

At least not for much longer. Soon, she would not be Selina Lawrence, respected widow and heiress; she would be Selina Lawrence, brazen jilt of modest means.

The thought was strangely freeing. And perhaps just the tiniest bit lowering.

She was certainly testing the limits of the protection widowhood provided as she rapped the knocker against the door of Mr. Drake's townhouse three times and waited patiently.

The servant who answered it stared at her with raised brows.

"I am here to see Mr. Drake," she said firmly.

"Allow me to see whether he is at home to—"

"That will not be necessary," she said, pushing past him and into the entry hall. "He is expecting me."

He was not. But he would see her despite that.

The servant hurried to keep pace with her. "Allow me to show you into the morning room, ma'am."

"That will not be necessary, either. Which apartments belong to Mr. Drake?"

The servant blinked, but perhaps he was too intimidated by the force and confidence with which she spoke, for he replied a bit blankly, "Upstairs. First door on the left, ma'am."

Selina picked up her skirts and made her way up the stairs.

She did not bother knocking when she reached Mr. Drake's door, swinging it open and striding in as Mr. Drake whirled around from his current task: tucking his shirt into his breeches.

"What the devil?" he exclaimed.

Selina closed the door behind her and took a seat in the only chair in the room. "Good morning to you too, my love." She kept her eyes on his face, studiously ignoring his open shirt and the strong chest beneath it.

"What madness is this?" He tried to do up the buttons of his shirt quickly.

"Calm yourself," she said, shocked and emboldened by her own daring. "It is nothing I have not seen before."

It was not strictly true. George had been a man of middle age, and his body had betrayed as much. Sebastian Drake was in his prime, and *his* body betrayed as much.

He let out an incredulous scoff, but his hands slowed as they worked at the buttons. That they struggled with the task gave Selina a morbid satisfaction.

It was no small feat to discomfit Sebastian Drake.

"I wish to speak with you," she said.

"You might've sent a note."

"I might have," she said. "But I did not. I am feeling impatient today."

"And how will you be feeling when the servant gossip from your call makes its way through London?" he asked grimly.

She shrugged, thoroughly unconcerned.

He grimaced, then pulled the blue waistcoat from his bed. "What is it you wish to speak of?"

"Let us be frank with one another for once, Sebastian," she said. "You have no intention of marrying me once my fortune is gone, and I certainly have no intention of marrying a fortune hunter."

"Something you might have considered before accepting my offer of marriage last night," he said with a tight dryness as he slipped his arms through his waistcoat.

A little scoffing laugh escaped her. "The offer you fully expected me to refuse, you mean?"

"And the offer you only accepted so that you could rip your fortune from me the moment you made me believe I would have it?"

It was his first admission that he had only sought her for her fortune, and it felt like an arrow through her heart.

She dug her nails into her palms in an effort to distract herself from the pain. "Forgive me if I seem unmoved by the disappointment you have suffered."

"No, indeed." He took a step toward her, his waistcoat hanging open, the buttons forgotten. "You have gone to great lengths to intensify that disappointment, have you not? Making me believe my suit was welcome to you—"

She shot to her feet. "While *you* tried to make *me* believe your affection for me genuine."

"It is!" he nearly shouted.

There was a shattering silence, the only sound that of Selina's strong heartbeat, pulsing against her ribs.

They stared at each other from a half-dozen feet away, their nostrils flared, their eyes alight.

"Was," he corrected, his voice less intense. "Until I discovered I was nothing but a game to you."

She scoffed. "Oh, that is rich indeed! Poor Sebastian Drake seeks women for their fortunes and has his heart broken when they do not grovel and worship him in the process."

"And poor Selina Lawrence, acquires a fortune through marriage, then takes offense when a man seeks her with the same intent."

Her teeth ground against each other, and she stepped toward him so that their faces were mere inches apart. "I did not *seek* a fortune—I was pushed into marriage. And I suffered dearly as a result. You, on the other hand, schemed and strategized, trying to charm your way into my heart when my money was your true aim."

His focus on her flickered, but their gazes held. The responsive fire in his had dimmed, however, and it stoked her anger more.

How dare he back down at this moment when she wanted a battle? For weeks, she had been bridling her anger, channeling it into narrow paths, and now that she was able to give it full rein, he was uninclined to fight.

"Do you deny it?" she challenged, advancing toward him.

His brown eyes searched hers, then without warning, they dipped to her mouth.

Her breath stuttered—not from fear or even fury, but from something deep and traitorous.

Would he dare kiss her?

Her spine held firm at the thought but in her knees were the whisperings of surrender.

If a kiss was the only way he would engage with her, she would give him battle.

He stepped back and broke his gaze away. "This arguing is futile. All that remains to be discussed is what is to be done now."

Selina blinked at the abrupt shift in the air and let out the breath she had been holding, ignoring the flash of disappointment in her chest. Only a woman desperate for love and affection would settle for a kiss from a man who had just admitted to hunting her like a fox in the fields.

"It is safe to assume that word has made its way round the *ton*," he said, buttoning up his waistcoat, "which makes the situation precarious."

"And why is that?"

He looked at her for the first time since that electrifying moment. "Your opinion of me is obviously low, Selina, but I have no wish to mark your reputation with scandal."

"As you well know, Sebastian," she said with a falsely sweet smile, "there are plenty of gentlemen more than willing to overlook the scandal of a brief engagement for the sake of my fortune."

His mouth tightened into a thin line. "Perhaps you could store up all the barbed comments about my character until we have settled the matter of how to proceed."

"Oh, I *have* been storing them up. For weeks. I am simply unable to contain them any longer. But your conscience may rest, assuming you possess such a thing. I have no intention of entering into matrimony a second time, which means the subject of my reputation need not concern you. Nor need it concern anyone. It certainly does not concern *me*."

He stared at her for a long moment, making her feel as though *she* was the one in a state of undress when it was his collar that was twisted ridiculously. "Very well." He took his tailcoat from the bed. "Spread it about that our engagement has come to an end whenever you wish. Today, even."

"Why must I be the one to do so?" How very like him it was to put the difficult task on her.

He shot her a confused look as he shrugged into his coat. "I assumed you would prefer it. You may not regard your reputation as it concerns prospects of marriage, but I would think it far preferable for you to be the one who ended an engagement rather than the one jilted."

Dash him for being honorable about it! And dash that ridiculous collar on his coat, which was still twisted.

She pressed her lips together and stepped toward him. "You look absurd with your collar like that."

He watched her warily as she reached to adjust it.

His eyes rested on her as she did so, setting her heart beating faster than she liked.

He claimed that his affection for her had at one time been genuine. Not for a second did she believe such a thing, but it seemed a strange thing for him to say when his ruse was already spoiled.

She hated how much she wanted to believe it.

She finished with the collar and stepped back.

"Thank you," he said stiffly.

The door burst open, and Selina whirled toward it in time to see three children hurry through. For the briefest of moments, Selina thought them her own nieces and nephews, but a quick glance at the eldest of the three—a girl—put such a thought to rest.

The servant who had admitted Selina stood outside of the doorway, looking helpless and resigned.

"Sebastian!" said one of two young boys as all three children charged toward him.

Selina stepped aside, realizing she was an obstacle.

The children thrust their arms around Sebastian, whose eyes were wide with shock as he submitted to the tangle of limbs.

"What in heaven's name is this?" His arms wrapped around the children, the eldest of whose head came up to his chin.

The three of them were in a sad state, their clothing dusty at the hems, their faces, which were turned to rest against Sebastian now, dirty as well.

Who in the world were they?

"How did you...?" Sebastian did not finish but held them more tightly to him still.

The eldest pulled back, and the younger two boys followed suit.

"How do you come to be here, Margaret?" Sebastian asked.

Margaret clasped her hands in front of her chest. "I am sorry, but we could not remain with him a moment longer. I remembered your direction, and you said if the situation became more dire..."

"Of course." Sebastian's brow pinched. "I am not angry, simply worried and taken by surprise. Did you come on the stagecoach?"

All three shook their heads.

"On the Mail," the youngest boy said, and his dirty cheeks turned up in a little mischievous smile. "I got to ride with the coachman for a stage."

"And handle the reins," the older boy said sulkily.

Margaret exchanged a speaking look with Sebastian, whose mouth pulled up at one corner in incredulous amusement.

"Then it is an even greater miracle that you have all arrived intact."

"The coachman said I was a bang up whip, Sebastian," the boy said as someone defending his honor.

"Felix," Margaret said censoriously.

"Did he now?" Sebastian asked, his eyes alight with amusement. "I am sure he was right."

"Who is *she*?" The older boy stared at Selina.

"Hugo," Margaret rebuked him.

Sebastian's gaze flitted to Selina, and his smile faded, as though he had forgotten her presence and did not find the reminder welcome.

"What?" Hugo asked of Margaret. "She is in his bedchamber, after all."

Selina pulled her lips between her teeth to stop a smile while her cheeks filled with heat. The bravado with which she had entered Sebastian's bedchamber had long since fled, and while nothing Sebastian himself could have said would have embarrassed her, this young Hugo had successfully managed to awaken her sense of propriety.

"This is Mrs. Lawrence," Sebastian said with a hint of tightness in his voice and his own color heightened. "She is..."

"You may call me Selina," Selina said. "And to whom do I have the pleasure of speaking?"

Margaret glanced at Sebastian, who was staring at Selina, then stepped forward. "I am Margaret Hollis."

Selina smiled kindly at her. "I am very happy to make your acquaintance, Miss Hollis."

Margaret must have been no more than thirteen or fourteen, but she carried herself with a maturity beyond that. It was evident she was accustomed to taking charge, despite her youth.

She made a curtsy—unpolished but not awkward—then turned to the boys. "These are my brothers, Hugo and Felix—and Sebastian, of course, whom you obviously know."

Selina's smile flickered, and her gaze swept back to Sebastian.

He watched her, his expression sober.

Had she understood correctly?

These three children were Sebastian's *siblings*?

Chapter Nineteen
Sebastian

Sebastian had not expected Selina, he had not expected his siblings, and he had not expected the way in which Selina now regarded him. It was an arrested expression, as though she was looking at him but not truly seeing him.

But now was not the time to concern himself with what she thought of him. She had left little doubt of that, after all. According to her, she had been storing up all her unfavorable opinions of him for weeks. He had no wish to hear them all.

The urgent matter was Margaret, Hugo, and Felix.

"He has become more volatile since your visit," Margaret said, as though tracking his thought path.

Sebastian's jaw clenched. As usual, Margaret put things diplomatically.

Hollis had never been stable to begin with. If she was describing him as *volatile*, there was no saying what he had been subjecting them to.

The thought made Sebastian sick. "I should not have gone to see you."

"But then we would not have met Pip!" Felix said. "Is he here?"

Sebastian considered before replying. He needed to speak frankly with Margaret without the boys present—or Selina. There was no need for her to be involved in this conversation. Indeed, he would far rather she not be.

"Yes," Sebastian said. "He is in his room, no doubt tearing it apart, as I have been neglecting him this morning. He would be glad for some company if you and Hugo wish to join him."

He may as well have asked them if they would like a piece of chocolate cake.

They were gone almost before he had finished speaking, evidently confident they could find Pip's room without being told where it was. As it was just beside Sebastian's, he made no move to go after them.

He turned his gaze to Selina.

She was sharp enough to know with a simple look that he wished her to leave. Given her opinion of him, she was undoubtedly eager for an excuse to leave.

He gazed at her steadily, but her eyes were on Margaret.

"Are you hungry, Miss Hollis?" Selina asked.

Margaret let out a smiling sigh, as though relieved to be asked. "Famished."

Wishing he had thought to ask such a basic question himself, Sebastian tugged the bell chord, and a servant appeared with a rapidity that made him suspect he had not been at all far from the room. Ear to the keyhole, possibly.

He instructed that a platter of food and drink be prepared for Margaret and the boys, and the three of them were left to themselves again.

Still, Selina did not meet his speaking glance. Why? What mischief did she mean?

"You must be exhausted," she said to Margaret. "Why not have a seat?"

Margaret shot her a grateful look and sat down on the edge of Sebastian's bed. She looked at Sebastian, a hint of fear entering her eyes. "Do you think he will come after us?"

Sebastian grimaced. "I suspect so. And this is the first place he will come."

Margaret's brows pinched together. "I had not thought of that."

"If he discovers you here, he may tell the Court of Chancery that I took you from him."

Margaret's chin dropped to her chest, her eyes squeezing shut. "I should not have come. I simply did not know what to do."

Sebastian hurried over and lowered to his knees, taking her hands and waiting for her to look at him. "You did exactly right, Margaret. I should have taken you with me the night of my visit, not left you to endure his wrath."

Margaret met his gaze, her eyes brimming with tears.

He looked at her intently. "You do not belong with Hollis, no matter what the Chancery says. We will find a way forward."

That way forward simply could not mean their remaining there in the home of three bachelors in St. James's.

If only Yorke and Fairchild were not at Parliament, Sebastian might ask for their help. Yorke's brother, the Duke of Rockwood, lived in London, and though Yorke hated asking favors of him, perhaps he would make an exception in this case, even if temporarily.

"I will send a note to Yorke," Sebastian said. "He is attending Parliament today, but perhaps you could stay with his brother until..."

Until what? There was no saying when the Chancery would agree to see them in court or when they would make a decision.

"Let them stay with me."

Sebastian's and Margaret's heads turned toward Selina.

She met their gazes evenly. "I confess I am not acquainted with the particulars of the situation, but it seems that a primary concern is that this man you speak of not know where to find Miss Hollis and her brothers. If that is correct"—she lifted her shoulders—"he would not suspect *my* house, would he?"

Sebastian did not respond immediately. He was searching her

face, trying to understand why she would make such a generous offer.

But he knew why.

"No," he said blankly, rising to his feet.

Margaret looked at him, confusion etched in her young brow.

"Why not?" asked Selina.

Sebastian fixed his gaze upon her grimly. "You know why." He scrubbed a hand over his jaw and began to pace the room.

Selina walked over to him and spoke in a low voice. "This is not a game, Sebastian."

He stopped and looked at her. "A game is all it has ever been to you."

A glint of hurt flashed in her eyes. "I would never use children in such an abominable way."

"Would you not? What of your own nieces and nephews? Did you not use them in your attempts to teach me a lesson?"

Her jaw tightened, but he could see that she had taken his point. "That was different. They were never in any danger." Her gaze became more intent upon him. "My offer is genuine. I swear it."

Sebastian searched her eyes, finding no evidence of duplicity but still not wanting to believe her. Would he not be the world's greatest fool to do so? To put his vulnerable siblings into the care of the woman who had made it her mission to mortify him?

And yet, what other options did he have?

Even if Yorke agreed to ask his brother and the duke agreed to take the children in, the duchess was with child—and frequently unwell as a result, from what Yorke had said. The last thing they needed was three unfamiliar children to manage. Sebastian knew firsthand how wild Felix and Hugo could be.

He had seen Selina with her nieces and nephews; with them, at least, she was capable, kind, and equal to their mischief. She would have Miss Grant to assist her—and a number of servants besides.

"Why do you offer such a thing?" Sebastian asked.

There was a moment of hesitation, and a flicker of something in her eyes—nervousness, he almost thought.

Then her mouth pulled up at one edge in a wry half-smile. "We are engaged, are we not?"

Sebastian's mouth pulled into a thin line.

"You are...engaged?" Margaret asked.

Selina sucked in a breath, her expression stricken. She must have forgotten Margaret's presence.

Sebastian certainly had.

He cleared his throat, but what was he to say? He had just told Selina that she could spread news of the end of the engagement.

"Yes," Selina said, bringing Sebastian's head around swiftly. "We are."

Margaret's mouth stretched wide. "But that is wonderful! The most happy news imaginable. I would welcome the opportunity to come to know you better, Mrs. Lawrence. We are to be family, after all."

Sebastian's every muscle was tight.

"And I you," Selina said. "But please call me Selina. Tell me, Margaret. Do you think you and your brothers could be happy for a time under my roof? You would have your own bedchamber, and the two of them as well."

Margaret let out a laugh. "They will be beside themselves at the prospect."

Selina smiled. "We could even bring Pip with us. Perhaps you could ask them their thoughts?"

Margaret nodded, but Sebastian knew Felix and Hugo well enough to see the pointless nature of such a question. They *would* be beside themselves. And yet, a bit of privacy to speak with Selina was warranted.

Once it was an option, however, he found himself at a loss for words, caught in an awkward space between gratitude, frustration, worry, and wariness.

The two of them stared at one another in full silence, their eyes locked as they tried to understand one another and the fast-evolving—or perhaps devolving—situation.

The door burst open.

"You are getting married?" Hugo asked with the energy of someone who had forgotten the trials and adversities of an arduous journey to London.

Felix came on his heels, holding Pip like a baby.

"Yes," Sebastian said, unable to keep the stiffness from his voice. "And Selina has graciously offered to take you in until I can find a more permanent solution."

"With Pip too?" Felix asked.

Selina smiled. "With Pip too. I trust you will help me to watch over him."

Both boys nodded fervently.

"Shall we go once you have all had a bit to eat, then?" Selina asked. "You can wash up and have a proper meal. My cook makes the most delicious kidney pie."

Sebastian was borne inexorably on the tide of his siblings' eagerness, but their departure was delayed by the appearance of the food Sebastian had requested. It was far from ideal, but the children consumed it with ravenous energy.

Once they had finished, Selina's carriage conveyed them all—snugly indeed—to her lodgings in Berkeley Square.

The eyes of all three grew wide at the sight of the fine house and remained so as she showed them inside.

The level of energy that came with being shown to the bedchambers they would each call home brought a sad smile to Sebastian's face.

"We could fit seven of me in this bed!" Felix declared.

"Just so long as there are none of you in mine," Hugo said from the doorway as he compared Felix's room to his.

Sebastian chuckled, and his gaze met Selina's dancing one for a moment before they both looked away, smiles dampened.

So infatuated were the children that Hugo and Felix made no

complaint when Selina ordered Pip to be taken by the servants for a time.

Felix discovered the set of wooden soldiers in the trunk of his room with alarming rapidity, but when Sebastian went over to gently remind him that the toys did not belong to him, Selina intervened.

"You have found the troops," she said, coming over and kneeling down beside the trunk. "They belong to my nephews, Teddy and Arthur, but they are shamefully neglected when they are not here. May I trust you and Hugo to play with them?"

Felix was holding three soldiers in his hand, but he turned to Selina and regarded her with the somberness of a knight given a quest by his queen. "I give my word."

Sebastian couldn't help a smile.

Much as he disliked being beholden to Selina, there was no doubt his siblings would be happier here than perhaps anywhere else. He could swallow his pride—an increasingly large mouthful, it seemed—for their sakes.

While part of him wanted to stay to ensure everything went smoothly and the children minded their manners, he needed to leave. Their sudden arrival and the developments with Selina had thrown everything into upheaval, and he desperately needed to find a new path forward.

The futures and the happiness of his siblings relied upon it.

If the Court of Chancery made their decision in favor of Edward Hollis, there would be no recourse for Sebastian. Perhaps if he had been wealthy, he could have afforded the appeal to the House of Lords, but his lack of money was precisely why he was in this situation to begin with.

The children, who had already partaken of food at Sebastian's, were happily munching upon an inordinately large platter of sandwiches when Selina walked Sebastian to the door.

The two of them stopped in the entry hall and faced one another, Sebastian's heart thumping uncomfortably, for he knew what he needed to do now.

The words stuck in his throat.

"Do not worry," Selina said. "I will ensure they are happily engaged."

"I am not worried. You could lock them in any one of the rooms in this house together, and they would be more happily engaged than they have been in some time."

Her brow pursed. "Has life been so cruel to them?"

He nodded.

She searched his eyes. "Why did you not tell me?"

His brow bunched together. "Tell you what, precisely? That I needed your fortune to care for my siblings?"

She was quiet, and when she spoke, her voice was soft. "I merely thought the subject of them might have come up—particularly when my nieces and nephews arrived."

He shook his head firmly. "Almost no one is aware of Margaret, Hugo, and Felix, and I prefer to keep it that way. They have been through enough; they do not need a haze of *ton* gossip following them so early in life. Their connection with me is already likely to do them more harm than good."

Selina's lips pressed together in something between sympathy and a grimace.

Sebastian straightened. "Thank you." The words came out stiff and rigid. He forced out a breath and relaxed his shoulders. "Thank you for the kindness you are doing them. They will not soon forget it."

What he meant, of course, was that *he* would not soon forget it.

He had a sneaking suspicion that he would not soon forget anything about Selina Lawrence, for good or ill.

"I am only glad to be able to assist," she replied.

Sebastian found that difficult to believe. The two of them had been fighting like dogs just before the children had arrived, after all. And yet, she seemed sincere.

Perhaps this was her way of softening the blow she would deal him when she informed Society their engagement had ended. Would she tell everyone the real reason: that he was a fortune hunter?

"None of this changes what we discussed before," he said. "You may spread word of the end of the engagement immediately."

She was shaking her head before he had even finished. "We can discuss all of that later."

"What discussion is required? We have settled things well enough. There is no sense in waiting. I will inform the children myself, but as I said before, you may tell whatever story suits you, and you are at liberty to do so as soon as you wish."

She met his gaze but said nothing.

He took the door handle and opened it. "I am but a note away if any need arises," he said, stepping outside. "I will plan to call tomorrow at eleven if you have no objection."

"You may call whenever and as often as you wish." Her cheeks turned pink. "They will be more at ease if they see your face here frequently," she added.

He nodded, but his greater concern was the effect upon himself if he saw *her* face too frequently. The arrival of his siblings had thrown the two of them into an intimacy with which Sebastian was supremely uncomfortable. It had shifted the dynamic between them in a way that left him scrambling for a firm hold.

Since learning she had been leading him a merry dance, the last thing he wanted was to let her into the difficult parts of his life that he chose not to show even his nearest friends.

Worst of all, Selina had not used her newfound knowledge against him. On the contrary, she had thrown herself into his difficulties, ready and willing to take on tasks that were not hers to fulfill. She had been understanding and kind to the children, going so far as to welcome Pip into her home when Sebastian was certain she had no desire to reclaim the monkey.

She had gone from adding burdens to his back for the mere

pleasure of seeing him struggle to taking on his most taxing and important one with willingness and a smile. She was providing a soft place for him to land in a world of unrelenting hardness, and he wanted nothing more than to rest in that softness.

    This was a Selina that Sebastian did not know how to resist.

    But resist he must, for she was not his—and never would be.

Chapter Twenty
Selina

The house was full of chaos—three new children and endless noise—but even amidst it, ten words had haunted Selina since Sebastian's departure.

A game is all it has ever been to you.

Within them was the implication she desperately wanted to believe but which terrified her: that it *hadn't* always been a game to *him*.

She had marched into his bedchamber like a trollop, then proceeded to berate him like a naughty child. And she had felt justified in it.

But the fresh memory brought a rush of heat to her cheeks.

The arrival of his siblings had cast everything she had thought she knew about Sebastian Drake into an entirely new light.

More and more, it appeared that he was not a heartless fortune hunter seeking money for his own gain; he needed it to care for his siblings, who, from what Selina could gather, had been mistreated by this man Hollis, whoever he was. A relation, she inferred.

Her decision to offer her home to them had been impulsive, perhaps, but her heart couldn't help but respond to the sight of those children—travelworn, weary, and running into Sebastian's arms as though he was their only refuge.

If Arthur, Teddy, Kitty, and Lou had ever been in need of a home, she hoped someone would do the same for them.

There was a soft knock on the door to her bedchamber, and Phoebe appeared, her expression kind but hesitant. "May I come in?"

Selina nodded and stopped twisting her diamond ring. The skin beneath it had become red and almost raw.

She and Phoebe had not spoken of the engagement more than briefly since it had occurred two nights ago.

Selina suspected that was because Phoebe knew the subject was one of supreme confusion to her. She was providing Selina the time and space to come to terms with it.

Phoebe took a seat beside her on the bed. "The children are eating breakfast."

"I should hurry, then, or I will be left with nothing but crumbs."

Phoebe smiled. "It is quite probable. You should have seen their eyes when they saw the sideboard."

Selina grimaced sympathetically. "Poor things. I suspect they have not had a square meal in some time."

"It was kind of you to take them in."

Selina stood and went over to her dressing table, suddenly uncomfortable. "Anyone would do as much."

Phoebe was quiet, her silence an obvious but placid disagreement with the claim. The two of them seemed to be always at odds on subjects relating to Sebastian. It was part of why Selina had been avoiding anything more than superficial conversation with her. Phoebe's opinion of Sebastian was the one Selina wanted to believe. That did not mean it was the correct one or that she *should* believe it, so the last thing she needed was Phoebe adding her arguments on Sebastian's behalf to the ones already in Selina's mind and heart.

She opened her jewelry box and began fiddling with the contents. "He admitted everything."

"*Who* admitted everything?"

"Sebasti—" Selina's lips pressed together. "Mr. Drake. He admitted to courting me for my fortune." She stole a glance at Phoebe through the mirror.

Her brows knit tightly. "I do not understand. You are betrothed, are you not?"

Selina hesitated, fingering the diamond ring she had worn the night she had met Sebastian. "Only in a manner of speaking...and not for long."

There was a hint of a smile in Phoebe's voice when she responded. "I was not aware there were multiple manners of being betrothed. If he admitted to courting you for your fortune, why did you agree to marry him?"

"He did not admit it until *after* we were betrothed."

"But you suspected it all along, did you not? So, why say yes in the first place?"

Selina whirled around. "Because he expected me to say no. And because I wanted him to think he had won so that I might tell him of my intention to donate my fortune to charity."

Phoebe's brows nearly disappeared into her hair. "Do you mean to do so?"

"Yes! That is...no." Selina clenched her eyes shut. "I do not know what I intend anymore."

That, at least, was the pure and honest truth.

There was a short silence before Phoebe spoke. "You do not mean to...use the children against him, do you?"

Selina's eyes flew open, her face aflame. "Of course not!"

"No," Phoebe hurried to say. "I only thought..." She did not finish.

"I know what you thought," Selina said softly, regaining mastery of herself, "and I know why you thought it. Mr. Drake feared the same thing. But when I saw them, Phoebe, I saw Teddy and Arthur and Kitty and Lou—tired, dirty, and starving after somehow managing to find their way to London on their own. Can you fathom?"

Phoebe shook her head, her face twisted with sympathy.

Selina gripped the chair behind her with her fingers and stared at her slippers. "We have agreed to end the engagement."

There was a long silence before Phoebe spoke, tracing the pattern of Selina's bedcovers with a finger. "And you are happy with that decision...?"

"Oh, Phoebe, what does it matter how I feel? He only ever asked me to marry him because he was certain I would say no. And I should have! I should not have let my pride push me to do what I did. But what's done is done. The simple fact is that I cannot marry a man who chose me for my fortune, no matter how noble his reasons and no matter how many times he implies that his affection for me was genuine."

Phoebe's head came up. "Has he implied that?"

Selina sighed. Naturally, Phoebe would focus on that portion. "Twice. But what difference does it make?"

"All the difference, I would think." Phoebe rose and came over to her, standing before Selina until she met her gaze. "I have watched the two of you together, Selina, and it has been plain to me how well you would suit if only you could see past your prejudice against him. Would you truly prefer to marry a man who has no need of your money but does not appreciate your best qualities—and love you despite your worst ones? Surely, no man knows your stubbornness or your need for independence better than Mr. Drake. You have used him and tested him in ways most men would never endure."

"He endured because of my money."

"Did he?" She let that question linger for a moment before continuing. "Are there no other heiresses to be had? Ones who would gladly let themselves be charmed and wooed by the likes of Mr. Drake without requiring of him half so much as you have?"

Selina swallowed but said nothing, her throat sticky and full.

"I do not fault you," Phoebe said, her voice and eyes soft as down, "for being afraid of marriage. After all you have been through, anyone would be, and heaven knows I am no expert on love or matrimony. But I love you too much to stand by in silence while you push away the very man who could love you the way you deserve to be loved."

To her chagrin, Selina found her eyes watering. She blinked rapidly.

"Please promise me you will think on it."

Selina nodded, but the truth was, she could think of little else already. "What of Mr. Evenden?"

Phoebe's expression shifted, and she turned away, tugging distractedly at the bedclothes to straighten them. "What of him?"

"You played cards with him the other night."

"It was nothing—he already formed part of the group when I joined. I would not have done so if I had known."

Selina watched her for a moment. "Why not?"

Phoebe's gaze flitted to her, as though the question took her by surprise. "You were right, Selina. He is a flirt. He and Miss Winser were laughing together the entire game." She let out a sigh and smiled. "But it makes no odds. I must go write a letter to Jane. I promised her I would do so." She smiled, then turned and left the room.

Selina stared at the closed door, her brow heavy with a frown.

It was some time before she went down to breakfast. Despite her fears, the children had left an entire plate of food for her.

She ate what she could but found her appetite reduced and her nerves frayed. Rather than sitting and picking at the food, she offered what remained to the children, who pounced upon it eagerly.

Selina smiled and took her teacup with her as she paced the room. She watched the pedestrians and equipages on the street, sipping slowly in front of the window as the children debated the merits of different types of preserves.

What she wouldn't give to have that be the debate occupying her mind.

What debate *was* doing so was a perplexing matter, however. It was not as though she had to decide whether to end the engagement. She and Sebastian had come to an agreement upon that already. He might have harbored some affection for her at some point, but he had only ever referred to it in the past tense.

She had since given him a distaste for her.

The question, then, was when to end the engagement and what story she would tell.

She went still at the sight of Sebastian himself as he came around the corner. His brow was pulled together in a deep *v*, his mouth and jaw set tightly, his gaze unfocused as he walked distractedly toward Berkeley Square.

How much of that frown was her doing?

When he drew nearer, she stepped back. She needn't have, however, for he was too lost in his thoughts to take notice of her.

A knock sounded shortly thereafter, and soon he appeared in the doorway to the breakfast parlor.

Selina, whose heart had interpreted his arrival like a gunshot at the races, blinked at the sight of him grinning broadly at the threshold, his dark and somber expression entirely transformed.

"Good morning!" he said in a booming and cheery voice.

The mouths of all three children stretched into wide grins, and they went over to him, abandoning the last of the food on Selina's plate.

He embraced each of them heartily, then stepped back and cocked his head to the side as he regarded Felix. The corner of his mouth quirked up, and he brushed at Felix's collar, then straightened it. "I must have missed a delicious breakfast, based on the state of you and Hugo."

"It was the best breakfast I have eaten in my life," Felix said in a fervent voice.

"Mrs. Lawrence has the best cook in all of England," Hugo affirmed.

Sebastian's gaze flicked to Selina, whose heart shot into her throat.

His smile did not fade, precisely, but his expression grew a bit more watchful as he met her eye.

"Good morning," he said.

"Good morning," she replied with the best smile she could muster in her trembling state. "Cook has certainly never had a more appreciative audience. In fact, if I am not mistaken, she spent the better part of last night preparing a little surprise for all of you. Though"—she waited until their excitement had dissipated enough for her to be heard—"she gave strict orders that Pip not be given any."

"He shan't have so much as a crumb," Hugo promised, his devotion to the monkey disintegrating on the spot.

Sebastian's eyes gleamed with amusement, which was snuffed out the moment they met Selina's.

Suppressing a sigh, she walked over to the bell cord and gave it a tug. "Perhaps we could partake in the garden?"

Everyone was agreeable, so once the maid who responded to the summons had been given instruction, the five of them made their way there.

The children split ways to explore the space, but they beckoned to one another whenever they found something of interest.

"They have never seen such a well-manicured garden," Sebastian explained, his arms crossed over his chest. "And certainly not one where they can roam free."

Selina stole a glance at him from the corner of her eye. Phoebe had to be right. There must be any number of young women with enough money to solve Sebastian's difficulties—heiresses ready and willing to faint into those strong, capable arms and stare into those warm, intelligent eyes.

Did he decline to pursue them now because he feared she would put a stop to it? *Would* she?

"Where did they journey from?" Her skin tingled with nerves at the prospect of Sebastian refusing to answer. He had said he preferred people not know of his siblings.

He glanced at her for a moment, his eyes searching hers

briefly, then away again. "From Oxfordshire. They have been living under the guardianship of their uncle for some time."

"*Their* uncle," she repeated.

"My father died when I was young, and my mother remarried a man named Henry Hollis a few years later—an acquaintance of my father's, in fact. Margaret, Hugo, and Felix are their children."

"So, they are only your half-siblings." It was a statement rather than a question, spoken without thinking.

Sebastian turned his head to look at her. "Half-siblings or no, I love them just as dearly as you love your brother."

"I did not mean to imply anything by it," she clarified. "I am simply trying to understand the situation. I find it admirable that you take such an interest in them."

He frowned. "If not I, who? I can assure you, their guardian does not care a fig for them. He has frittered away the money meant for their care on spirits and foolish wagers, just as his brother frittered away my fortune before him." He turned his focus back to the children.

All this time, Selina had assumed whatever money he might have had had been mismanaged—used for gambling and tailors and heaven only knew what else. But that was not the case, it seemed. He had no money because his stepfather had spent it.

His next words came out softer, as though he was speaking them to himself. "And yet, somehow *I* am the one who must prove my fitness as a guardian."

Selina's focus became more intent. "It is their guardianship you seek?" So, it was not just money he needed.

"Yes."

Selina did not reply, her mind whirring at the information.

After a moment, Sebastian continued. "The Court of Chancery would rather keep the status quo, be it ever so harmful to the children, than to consider a new situation with a relative who has no wealth but would do anything to make the children happy."

Anything.

Fortune hunting included.

"I meant no offense with my comments," Selina said. "They were my poor attempt at expressing admiration. Consider that I had no notion of any of this before."

"You thought me selfish and money-hungry."

"And how *was* I to know any different?"

He met her gaze with his frowning one, and she held it.

"The extent of my knowledge," she said, "was that you were a fortune hunter who had asked a woman to marry him after but a week. And then you set your sights on me."

His jaw tensed, but after a moment, he let out a sigh, his shoulders relaxing. "You are right, of course. Forgive me. I fear I am poor company today. I am sincerely grateful to you for taking in my siblings, particularly given...our situation. And I do owe you an explanation."

She shook her head and opened her mouth to reply, but he put up a hand.

"I want to give it." He stared her in the eyes, his gaze clear and direct. "I want you to know."

She tried to breathe in evenly just as the door opened and the maid emerged with the platter of food.

Selina didn't know whether to be glad or sorry for the interruption. "Shall we call them over?"

"No need," Sebastian said with a half-smile she felt deep in her chest. "They can sense food from a mile."

Sure enough, within seconds, the children came to claim their surprise—sandwiches and berry tarts.

"May we eat it in the garden?" Hugo asked, gathering up as many sandwiches as he could hold.

"Yes, may we?" Felix echoed. "Margaret says we should not bother you, for you and Mrs. Lawrence are to be married, and married people wish to be alone."

Margaret's eyes clenched in consternation. "Thank you, *Felix.*"

"You may consume your treats wherever you like," Sebastian said with amusement and a slightly heightened color.

Hugo graciously granted two of the sandwiches to Selina and Sebastian after being chided by his elder sister, and the three of them soon left to enjoy their plunder in the garden.

"The delights of receiving something given by force," Sebastian said, inspecting the small triangular sandwich in his hand.

"It is no wonder they struggle with sharing food given the circumstances they have endured. They *did* leave me some breakfast, however."

"Margaret's doing, no doubt."

"Perhaps so, for when I hadn't the appetite to consume it, their charity also led them to volunteer their services in the eating of it." She took a small bite through her smile.

Sebastian let out a chuckle. "Their selflessness knows no bounds. They will be sorely disappointed when they leave here." He bit into the sandwich and shut his eyes in enjoyment.

Selina watched him, admiring the way the muscles in his jaw worked and how his lashes fluttered slightly.

Had he forgotten what they were speaking of before the children had interrupted? She was tempted to remind him, curious to hear what he had to say and what he wished for her to know.

He finished chewing, and his eyes opened slowly. "My mother died when Felix was a baby, so I was raised helping to care for the three of them. But when their father died, I was only twenty—not yet of an age to be considered for guardianship. Even if I had been, it became clear that Henry had taken great liberties as my trustee, leaving me with a heavily indebted property that I was obliged to rent out at the soonest opportunity. The guardianship was granted to the children's nearest relative of age: Henry's brother, Edward. He and Henry had never been on the best of terms, so while Edward resented and cordially disliked the children, he was pleased to have charge of the funds that came with the guardianship."

The muscles in his jaw feathered. "He was never particularly kind to them, but the mistreatment has grown worse over the years. I have always wanted to take over the guardianship, but my financial circumstances..." He broke off. "Their situation grew more dire some weeks ago, which is when I became determined to do whatever was necessary to pursue it. That required proving my fitness, including an income to support taking in three children. Edward does not have that, of course, but because he was appointed by the Court and I am the one petitioning, I must show it for my petition to find success." He lifted his shoulders. "After so many years of trying to build something out of what was taken from me unjustly, failing to make a living in the church due to my lack of connections, and watching fortunes trade hands at the gaming table or the altar, I came to the conclusion that the only way to protect my siblings was to play the game everyone else was playing. The only way I could see forward was to marry money."

Selina could not keep her eyes from him as she listened. How had she misjudged him so fully?

"Miss Fernside was the first heiress I came upon after making my decision. I was foolish and barely took care to hide my true motives. You know what came of that. I went to Markston's garden ball with the intent of finding a suitable woman to pursue. But this time, I would take care. Yorke and Fairchild pointed out several options, but"—he shook his head—"something in me revolted at the idea. I had no desire to prey upon a naive young heiress, fresh to the *ton*. I suppose it soothed my writhing conscience to avoid such options. But neither could I bring myself to marry *solely* for money. That was when they mentioned you."

His gaze rose to hers, and though he looked at her, she was certain he was seeing not her but the memory of that night. "You were a widow and had come by your fortune through marriage—the ideal situation for my conscience. How could you fault me for doing the exact thing you had done, after all?" His eyes glazed over as he continued. "And then I saw you, and your beauty stole my breath. But you were so much more than beautiful."

Selina's heart thudded painfully.

"You were intelligent and amusing and capable..." His eyes searched hers. "You intrigued me for reasons I could not understand. I began to wonder if perhaps I might have more with you than a match driven solely by my need for money."

She could hardly breathe, hanging on the edge of each word.

"But I was mistaken." He turned his gaze away.

Selina's chest twisted, throbbing until she feared her ribs would snap.

"If nothing else," Sebastian said, "I hope knowing this will help you understand that I never meant to hurt you."

"I know that now," she said quietly. And yet she *was* hurting.

She was hurting because of her own choices and folly, left to wonder what might have been if she had not been so determined to think the worst of Sebastian.

She had let her assumptions and her mistrust lead her into betraying the worst parts of herself. She had created more pain for a man and three innocent children already suffering.

"Is there anything I can do?" she asked.

"You are already doing more than you should be."

"I could do more," she said, "even if it is waiting to spread news of the end of our eng—"

"No." The word was blank, firm.

She swallowed. He wanted to be done with her as soon as possible. "Will the scandal not harm your petition with the Chancery?"

His jaw tightened. "I will manage. You need not worry your head over it. I did not tell you any of this to elicit sympathy. You are at liberty to make known the end of the betrothal as you see fit. I intend to tell the children today. They are becoming attached to you, and after all they have endured, it seems cruel to let them continue believing a lie."

She wanted to stop him, to say his name or reach for his hand. But the wall between them had been built brick by careful brick —and she had laid too many of them herself.

All she could manage was a nod.

Chapter Twenty-One
Sebastian

Sebastian had not told the children. He had fully intended to, for he had been sincere in what he had said to Selina: the last thing he wanted was to saddle the children with more disappointment after all they had been through.

But when the time had come for such a disclosure, his courage had failed him. They were so happy, so carefree for the first time in recent memory, and he had not been able to persuade himself to bring down their spirits.

He could only protect them from unwelcome truths for so long, however.

> Sir,
>
> You are hereby summoned to appear before the Court of Chancery for the purpose of presenting evidence and testimony in the matter concerning the guardianship of the minor children, to wit: Margaret Hollis, Hugo Hollis, and Felix Hollis.
>
> The matter shall be heard on the 25th of May, at nine o'clock in the forenoon, at Lincoln's Inn Hall, wherein it shall be determined whether you are a fit and proper person to assume said guardianship.
>
> You are required to furnish all supporting documents and

witness statements pertaining to your petition, including, but not limited to, proof of financial solvency, moral character, and capacity to provide for the well-being and education of the aforesaid minors.

Should you fail to attend or be found lacking in requisite proof, the Court shall proceed accordingly, and the matter may be resolved in favour of the present guardian, Mr. Edward Hollis.

By Order of the Court,
I remain, Sir,
Your obedient servant,
James Townsend
Clerk of the Rolls,
Court of Chancery

Sebastian folded the letter, trying to ignore the suffocating feeling descending upon him.

One week. That was all that was left him to find the means with which to provide for his siblings.

A meeting with his solicitor, Helliwell, led him to quickly discard the one option that felt within reach: a loan. There were a few people who might have granted him one, but Helliwell had made it clear in no uncertain terms that the court would not find mere money sufficient. They wanted evidence of both income and responsible financial management, not dependency upon others—and certainly not debts beyond the ones Sebastian already carried.

The irony, of course, was that Edward Hollis could prove none of those things. He was dependent upon the money the court had set aside for the children's maintenance. And upon the strong drink he used that money to afford.

Sebastian found himself delaying his visit to the children after his meeting with Helliwell, and though he hated to admit, it was more than his reluctance to reveal the truth to them. Time spent in the company of Selina had come to feel like torture. He was

Tantalus, forever tempted by the food and drink at his fingertips but never able to partake.

Adding insult to injury were the comments the children made about his impending marriage to Selina. They looked upon it with an eagerness that made his heart heavy.

The longer he waited, the more difficult it would become.

Thanks to his delays, it was well after three in the afternoon when he arrived at Number 14 Berkeley Square.

"I believe the children are in the drawing room, sir," said the footman as he took Sebastian's hat and gloves.

Sebastian thanked him and made his way there. Margaret was betraying her lack of proper musical education by plunking spontaneous notes on the pianoforte, while Hugo folded a piece of paper into something unrecognizable.

"Sebastian!" Hugo said with excitement. "We thought you had forgotten us."

Sebastian's conscience pricked. "Forgotten you? What nonsense is this?" He looked around. "Where is Felix?"

"He began feeling unwell during the night," Margaret said. "I did my best to make him comfortable, but Mrs. Lawrence insisted I rest awhile."

"Is she with him?"

Margaret nodded. "In his bedchamber."

"I will relieve her," he said, and he hurried from the room.

He took the stairs two at a time, but when he reached the door to Felix's bedchamber, he slowed. Taking the doorknob in hand, he turned it gently so that it made no sound as he pushed the door open slightly.

He peered into the bedchamber, and the sight within sent a jolting ache through his heart.

Felix lay on the bed, his head turned to the side, his cheeks rosy and skin moist. Beside him, pressing a damp cloth to his forehead, sat Selina, her brow knit with sympathy.

Felix let out a little groan, and she shifted closer to him.

"You are terribly uncomfortable, aren't you?" Her voice was so gentle, Sebastian barely heard it.

"My head feels like it will burst," Felix whimpered.

She wet the cloth in the nearby basin, squeezed the excess from it, then pressed it to his head again. "I know, my dear. Can I persuade you to take some of this tea?" She set down the cloth and picked up a teacup from the bedside table.

His face crumpled. "I hate medicine. It tastes like poison."

"Medicine *is* the most vile thing," she said sympathetically. "Shall I have some first? To ensure it is not, in fact, poison?"

He nodded.

Selina took a sip from the cup. "Mm." Her eyes shut with satisfaction. "If that is poison, it is the most delicious I have ever tasted. Cook made it herself—specially for you—and she has yet to poison anyone in this household." She took one more sip. "It tastes of honey and good health."

Sebastian's heart panged as he watched her caring for Felix. She was so gentle, so kind. He ached to know that part of her.

And perhaps he might have if only they had met in different circumstances. What if he had not so desperately needed money and she had not been set against him from the start?

But circumstances were *not* different. They had lied to and deceived one another until there was no fixing what they had broken.

Felix debated for a moment, but the memory of the other things Cook had made must have been recent enough that he was willing to give the tea a chance, for he finally nodded.

"Here." Selina set the tea down and began working to adjust the pillows behind him.

Sebastian stepped into the room, and Selina's head came around. He kept his eyes on Felix as he went to the opposite side of the bed from her. "What is this? A soldier down? This won't do at all." He scooped Felix up gently with one arm, then worked at arranging the pillows with the other while Selina assisted.

"I am terribly ill, Sebastian," Felix said in a weak voice.

"Not for long," Sebastian said gently.

"I meant to send word to you," Selina said, "but his fever has only worsened in the past hour, and he did not want me to leave his side."

Sebastian could certainly sympathize with that sentiment.

"Shall I call for the doctor?" she asked.

Sebastian met her gaze for the first time. "Is he discreet? I do not wish for word to spread of their presence here."

"I trust him."

He searched her face for a moment, then gave a nod, and she went over to the bell pull.

"Do not leave," Felix begged.

She gave it a tug, then came back to the bedside, sitting upon the edge and taking his hand. "I am not going anywhere."

Sebastian frowned, for he had come to spell her, but Felix kept hold of her hand as she put the tea to his lips. The act seemed to tire him, and he hovered on the edge of wake and sleep until the doctor arrived some thirty minutes later.

"A nervous fever," the doctor said after evaluating his condition, "likely brought on by the excitement of travel. His pulse is rapid, but his lungs are clear. Best to keep him quiet and avoid heavy meals. I see no need for a blister or leeching unless his condition is worse tomorrow."

He left them with instructions to send him word in the morning.

Margaret came to the bedchamber not long after, offering to take over, but Felix was adamant. He wanted Sebastian and Selina at his side, each holding a hand.

"Felix," Margaret chided softly.

"It is fine," Selina reassured her.

When Miss Grant entered with the same intent shortly after, she too was rebuffed by Felix. She left the room, promising to take care of Margaret and Hugo.

The arrangement that suited Felix left Sebastian and Selina directly across from one another as he both sought and fought sleep, tossing and turning. Selina managed to slip her hand out of his in order to apply cool compresses to his brow.

Sebastian tried not to admire her as she did so, but it was impossible. She was kind, competent, intelligent, and so intoxicatingly beautiful that it was a chore to take his eyes from her.

She glanced up, catching him in his stare.

"Perhaps he would consent to Pip taking over for a time," Sebastian said quietly.

A flash of amusement entered her eyes. "Before you arrived, he asked if I would allow Pip to lie with him."

Sebastian chuckled softly. "Lie with him? When has that monkey *ever* lain down quietly?" He bethought himself of something. "I do him an injustice. He *did* lie quietly in my arms one day. For nearly three hours."

Selina's brow grew quizzical. "Surely not."

"I swear it. But those three hours were preceded by his wreaking havoc on the house for just as long. He found his way to the kitchens and ate an entire sugarloaf."

Selina's eyes widened. "Good heavens."

"He was in rare form, I assure you, tearing all over the house and baring his teeth at anyone who dared keep him from whatever mischief came to him in the moment." Sebastian shook his head, smiling at the memory. "And then, suddenly, he grew listless. Lifeless, almost. I thought I would have to inform you I had killed your precious pet." He fixed his gaze upon her and cocked a brow.

Her face crumpled with apology, but there was the merest hint of a smile at the corners of her mouth. "I *am* sorry. It so happened that I learned of your history with Miss Fernside when Phoebe and I were at the pet shop. I was so upset that I used the first thing at hand to take my revenge."

"I suppose I should be grateful it was Pip at hand and not one of the rifles we inspected."

"Ah, yes. The twin-barrelled"—she narrowed her eyes in attempt to remember—"what was it?"

"Musketoon," Sebastian offered.

Her lip twitched, and their smiling gazes held for a few seconds as they remembered that day. In those seconds, the distance between them did not feel quite so vast.

"I have grown fond of Pip," Sebastian finally said. "Once you resign yourself to the chaos, it is not so very bad."

"A ringing endorsement," Selina replied with eyes dancing.

He narrowed his eyes thoughtfully as he regarded her. "It seems a brave choice to purchase Pip on the off-chance I would agree to take him in. What would you have done if I had not? Or when I inevitably insisted it was time to return him to your care?"

Her mouth twisted to the side guiltily.

"What?" he asked, intrigued by her reaction.

"I only rented him, and believe me, the owner was more than happy for a respite."

Sebastian let his head fall back as he laughed softly. "I can imagine he was! You mean to say you could have returned him to the shop at any point these past weeks?"

"He has been in such demand between my nieces and nephews and your siblings," she said defensively.

He shook his head at her, unable to suppress a smile. "Selina Lawrence, you are a veritable tormentor."

"Whereas *you* are a beacon of goodwill."

"Of course I am," Sebastian replied.

"Then, pray, how do you explain Montague?"

His lip quirked. "Ah, yes. Montague, your *other* beloved pet!"

"George's," she corrected.

"I imagine George would be astounded by the number of pets he has acquired since his death."

A little suffocated snort of laughter escaped Selina, who swiftly covered her mouth.

"Shh," Sebastian teased, though Felix did not stir. He was snoring lightly.

Their eyes met across the bed, full of silenced laughter.

This. This was what Sebastian wanted—not wealth or a title or the best connections Society had to offer. He wanted *this* connection, these moments. He wanted to care for his siblings by Selina's side, finding joyful moments together even amidst illness and adversity.

But what did *she* want?

She had told him she had no intention of marrying again—and certainly not of marrying a fortune hunter.

Sebastian *was* a fortune hunter, however unwillingly so.

Selina's gaze dropped away, her smile slowly receding.

"Have you told anyone?" he asked.

Her eyes flitted briefly to his, then away again. "Not yet. But I shall."

He nodded, ignoring the tightness in his throat.

"You have not told the children yet," she said. It was not a question but a statement.

"I intended to today, but..."

Felix began to toss and turn, and the opportunity for conversation passed.

His fever grew worse, and he seemed not to understand where he was, though when Selina left the room for a few minutes, he began to cry. He shifted and winced and tossed and turned, unable to find comfort.

And then, suddenly, he was shaking and cold.

Sebastian and Selina worked to appease his conflicting demands, sitting on either side of him on the bed.

Sebastian pulled Felix's clammy legs onto his lap, chafing them beneath the blanket.

Face crumpled with discomfort, Felix sat up, then wobbled.

Selina wrapped her arm around his back to support him. "There, there, my dear." She began to hum quietly, pulling up the blanket over his arms, and Felix's thrashing settled. He leaned in to her, exhausted from his struggle, and soon, his full weight rested upon her.

Sebastian helped her gently shift so that her back rested against the headboard and her arm against him. All the while, she continued humming. Beyond Felix's head turning from one side to the other, his eyes remained closed, a little furrow of pain on his brow.

"May I spell you?" Sebastian whispered after her humming had ended.

"We had better not make the attempt," she replied. "I am comfortable enough, and the sleep will do him good."

Sebastian frowned. "This was not what I had in mind when I agreed for the children to stay with you."

She smiled ruefully. "When it comes to children, having something in mind is the surest way to upset plans, in my experience."

That was certainly true. "At least let me put this pillow behind your head." As things stood, her neck was against the top of the headboard.

She agreed, and with clenched teeth and muscles on alert for any sign of rousing from Felix, Sebastian slipped the decorative pillow into place.

She rested her head against it, shutting her eyes and releasing a sigh.

It was a sigh Sebastian felt his whole body through. More than he had wished for anything in his entire life, he wished Selina Lawrence were his.

Chapter Twenty-Two
Selina

They sat in silence for a time, enjoying the reprieve from Felix's anguish.

Selina tried not to be aware of the press of Sebastian's body against hers or the way he smelled of cedar, but it was like fighting a rising tide.

"You are a skilled nursemaid," Sebastian said. "He would not have fallen asleep in my arms so readily."

"I have helped care for my nieces and nephews a time or two," she replied. "Richard has no patience for such things, and Jane is always managing the needs of the four children."

It was quiet for a moment.

"Did you nurse George when he took ill?"

Selina's head came around, and she met Sebastian's gaze for a moment before turning her focus to Felix. His lips were parted slightly, his chest rising and falling rhythmically. "He was a far more difficult patient than the children ever are."

Sebastian's gaze grew curious. "How so?"

"He was terribly stubborn and refused to follow the doctor's orders."

There was another silence, and she thought on those moments at George's bedside, caring for him, trying to persuade him to obey the doctor's orders when she knew in her heart that she would be happier with him gone. She was ashamed that she had felt such things.

"You loved him dearly, didn't you?"

Selina's breath stuttered at the gentle question. She did not respond immediately. What she truly wanted was to know why he was asking. "No." It was a terrible answer, but it was the truth.

He watched her intently. "But your ring...you are always touching it, fiddling with it. I assumed it was a gift from him."

She looked down at it. "It was." She thought for a moment, then reached her hand toward him. "Here. Take it. Look inside."

Sebastian hesitated, waiting for her to meet his eyes.

She did so and gave a nod.

His fingers grasped the ring, brushing her skin with his as he gently wiggled it from her hand. After taking a moment to admire it, he brought it closer and looked at the inscription as she watched.

"For my most beautiful diamond," Sebastian read softly. His eyes flicked to hers, questioning.

"That is all I ever was to him—something to adorn himself with. A pretty thing to look at. A possession to boast of. It took me too long to realize that." Her mind returned to those early days. They felt like a different lifetime—and she a different person. "George was five-and-forty and I but seventeen when we met. He showered me with gifts and compliments, almost from that moment. I do not come from wealth, so my parents were in transports over the prospect of my marriage to such an established, moneyed gentleman, and I was eager to please them—and to be deserving of such attention. I was too young and inexperienced to understand that what I felt was flattery, not love."

Her brow knit with memory. "He commissioned a portrait of me not long after our marriage. It was enormous, and of course, I was pleased that he would wish for such a thing. Whenever the artist came, George was present, offering his opinions and telling the artist to soften this feature or change that one. He insisted on unveiling it at a party."

Her eyes grew unfocused as she remembered it. "He had me on his arm all night. He was laughing and talking with the guests, complimenting me to them, but never speaking directly to me. When the portrait was unveiled, there was applause, and George was radiant. I remember staring at the portrait long after the party had concluded and coming to the realization that that was precisely how George saw me: something pretty to display to his friends and add to his consequence." She blinked away the stinging in her eyes. "He gave me the diamond shortly after that, and I began to hate him, I think." She met Sebastian's gaze.

He was looking at her intently, a sadness in his eyes.

She smiled wryly. "I must shock you with such confessions."

"No." His brows pulled together. "I am sorry, Selina."

She forced a soft laugh. "Sorry for what?"

"That you were ever made to feel such a way. You deserved better."

She swallowed, her eyes prickling again so that she turned her head away. "It is all in the past now."

Sebastian's gaze remained on her, but he said nothing.

She closed her eyes, and the stinging began to dissipate, leaving her tired.

Soon, she was asleep.

꩜

THE ROOM WAS DARK WHEN SELINA WOKE. THE CANDLE had guttered.

Felix was still asleep, but he had slumped over. There was a pillow beneath his head that had not been there before. Sebastian must have placed it there without her knowing.

She glanced to her right and went still.

Sebastian's head rested on her shoulder, his chest rising and falling with deep, steady breaths. A shock of hair had fallen over his forehead.

Her hand itched to move it. She could not have done so even if she had wanted to, though, for both arms were holding Felix. It was for the best. Her eyes explored Sebastian, admiring the way his dark lashes pressed against the top of his cheeks, how the line of his jaw sloped from his ear toward his strong chin. And his lips...

Felix shifted, and she winced, her body stiff from remaining in the same position for she knew not how long.

Sebastian stirred, and his face settled into the hollow of her neck.

Selina's every muscle went taut as his breath warmed her collar.

He breathed in deeply, then went still.

By the time Selina had considered feigning sleep herself, it was too late.

Sebastian pulled away, his eyes wide as they settled upon her in the dark.

"Forgive me," he said hastily.

"I think we all fell asleep," she replied, grateful there was no light to betray the heat in her cheeks.

Sebastian reached over and felt Felix's head. He let out a sigh of relief. "It has abated." He pulled his hand away and watched. "He seems to be sleeping deeply. If we can extricate ourselves, I think we can safely leave him."

Selina nodded, and for the next two minutes, they did their best to remove themselves from all the ways they were entangled with Felix...and one another.

She let out a sigh of relief when Felix remained still.

Sebastian led the way to the door, opening it slowly, then shutting it carefully behind them. "What time is it?"

"I have no notion." She glanced around, but the corridor was dark and deserted, the entire house silent with slumber. "Nigh on two or three, I imagine."

"I would think so," he said, but the way his eyes raked over her face made her think he was not thinking about the time anymore.

Her hand rose involuntarily to her hair, where it found mayhem and disorder. "I must look a catastrophe."

His hand went to the hair at her temple, gently brushing it toward her ear. "You have never looked more beautiful." There was none of the charm or flirtation she had come to expect from him in the words. His sincerity made her heart race.

This was not the man she had done everything in her power to mortify. He was gentle and caring, loyal to his family and self-sacrificing.

This was a man she could love—a man she feared she already *did* love.

She needed to stop it, to put an end to this feeling of falling.

It was too dangerous.

"I have hated you."

Sebastian stilled, his gaze fixing on hers. He stared at her intently, quiet, waiting for her to go on.

"From the night we met, I suspected you wanted me for my fortune. I was on my guard, determined to show Phoebe how to protect herself from the gentlemen she would come upon in Town. But then I met you, and against my will, I liked you. I let myself be persuaded that perhaps your interest in me was genuine. And then I spoke with Mr. Haskett..."

Sebastian's brows drew together, his lips pressing into a tight line.

"I was furious with myself for being taken in, just as I had been with George. To be flattered and charmed by someone who did not care for me but for only what they wanted *from* me. And my hope turned to hate in an instant."

Sebastian was quiet for a long moment, the furrow in his brow deep. When he spoke, his voice was quiet. "I deserve your hatred. Heaven knows I have hated myself."

She shut her eyes, trying to remember that moment with Mr. Haskett and the pulse of mortification and anger. She would do anything to recapture the hatred because at least then, she had felt in control. "Then why can I not feel it now?"

"Selina..." He brushed the back of his fingers along her cheek, and she trembled at the touch. His finger traced the line of her jaw, leaving her skin tingling in its wake until he reached her chin. He held it softly between his thumb and forefinger, then tilted her face up.

She opened her eyes, and the tenderness with which he looked at her made her knees shake.

"I want to hate you," she said, her voice a bare whisper, "but I do not."

"Nor I you." His thumb grazed her bottom lip, and her eyes fluttered closed.

The touch of his thumb disappeared, and the next sensation she felt was his lips brushing hers.

Sebastian's hands cupped her face, anchoring her to him as though the tide was not already sweeping her ruthlessly his way.

But his kiss was not ruthless.

It was intent yet gentle, full of something so sweet that Selina's entire chest ached. It was the type of kiss she had not known existed—had not dared imagine.

But it *was* real. The press of his mouth to hers, the touch of his fingertips on her neck and cheek, the mix of his breath with hers. All of it was real.

And the feelings within her...those were perhaps most real of all, overwhelming her with their intensity until she thought she might lose herself within them.

Nothing else mattered. Not the past, not the future. She wanted this. She wanted *him*, and she would give anything to have him.

She pulled away and stepped back.

His wide eyes watched her, grasping for understanding as his hands hovered in the air where they had just held her, as though she might come back at any moment to where she belonged.

"This was a mistake," she said, her voice breathless.

"Selina..."

She put a hand up and took another step backward. "No." The word was more of a plea than anything.

The corridor was still dark and silent, her thoughts clouded by the pounding of her heart and the tingling of her lips. It almost felt as though she was still kissing him.

She could not tell what was real anymore, which of her thoughts and feelings to trust.

She had thought George's love real, and it had cost her dearly. She had thought Sebastian's love false, and now...now, she did not know what to believe.

She had promised never to surrender herself again, never to belong to anyone but herself. But at the first touch of Sebastian's lips, she had been ready to give anything and everything, willing to forget the pain of the past and cede control of the future for... what?

"I am sorry," she said, her voice strangled. "I cannot do this. I will not." With a final look at Sebastian's concerned face, she turned on her heel and fled to her bedchamber.

Chapter Twenty-Three
Sebastian

Sebastian stood rooted to the spot long after Selina had disappeared down the corridor.

He had never known such bliss as kissing her—nor such defeat as her flight.

He shut his eyes, wanting to go after her but afraid he would only make things worse if he did.

This was a mistake.

That was what she had said.

It had certainly not felt like a mistake. At least, not to him. And she had certainly *seemed* willing.

For one moment, he had believed they might have a future together—not born of necessity or revenge but of something real. But in such a moment, she had only seen a mistake, and that hurt more than her hate ever had.

He stared at the place where she had disappeared, then sighed and slipped back into Felix's room.

Felix was sound asleep, and while Sebastian tried to let his head fall back and follow suit, his thoughts were too insistent. He finally gave up when the edges of the curtains at the window began to glow with the light of dawn.

A quick touch to Felix's forehead assured him that the fever had not returned. Rubbing at his eyes, he left the room quietly. His gaze flicked down the corridor to Selina's bedchamber.

Was she awake, as he was? Or had she managed to find refuge in sleep? Perhaps her allowance of the kiss had been nothing but a fit of fatigue, a lapse in judgment.

A door opened behind him, and Sebastian turned.

Margaret, still in her dressing gown, peered from her room. When she saw Sebastian, she shut the door behind her and hurried to him. "How is he?"

"Better," Sebastian replied. "The fever seems to have run its course."

She let out a breath of relief. "Thank heaven."

"May I leave him with you? I must return home for a time, but I shall come back."

"Of course," Margaret said. "I will sit with him."

Sebastian thanked her and made his way quietly to the front door, for the servants were only just beginning to stir.

He barely paid any heed to the path home, his mind on the problems at hand. Heaven knew there were plenty of them. The most pressing was the approaching Chancery hearing, but his heart insisted it was Selina.

To hear her admit she did not hate him, and then to have her melt into his arms and return his kisses with such fervor...

How was he to think of anything else? Or to settle for anything less?

And yet, it was not his choice.

I want to hate you, she had said. Whatever she felt for him apart from hate, was felt unwillingly. It was not what she wanted, much as her kiss had convinced him otherwise.

Once at home, he went straight to his bed and dropped onto it, not even bothering to remove his boots.

He woke some time later to a violent pounding sound. At first, he thought it was his own head, which throbbed as though he had drunk too much the night before. It became apparent, however, that someone was trying to batter down the front door.

Sebastian swung his legs over the bed, then winced as his head protested.

"I demand to see Drake!" a voice roared.

Sebastian shot to his feet, ignoring the throbbing, and hurried downstairs.

Edward Hollis seemed to have pushed his way inside, for he was in the entry hall.

"Hollis!" Sebastian called.

The man's head came up, and his gaze fixed on Sebastian, narrowing. "Where are they?"

Sebastian nodded at the footman to dismiss him. "Who?"

"Do not play the idiot, Drake. You know who I mean."

"It is the only part I am able to play, for I have no notion to whom you are referring."

Hollis's ruddy cheeks grew brighter. "The children!" he barked with unrestrained annoyance.

Sebastian's brows went up. "The children? How would I know where they are? Is that not your responsibility? They are under your guardianship."

"You took them! I know you did."

"I did not," Sebastian answered coolly. "But the fact that you have misplaced them says a great deal about your abilities as a guardian. I imagine the Court of Chancery would be interested to know it."

Hollis sneered angrily and took a step toward Sebastian. He reeked of spirits. "Not as interested as they will be to know of your role in the affair! I know you know where they are, Drake, and I *will* find a way to prove your involvement. The Chancery will never agree to your petition."

Sebastian's smile was brittle. "Then, for your sake, I hope your ability to find them is better than your ability to keep them."

"Then you won't mind me taking a look around," Hollis said.

Sebastian stopped him with a hand on his chest. "I most certainly do mind. You are not welcome here."

"What is this?" Yorke came hurrying down the stairs, his brow knit and his eyes shifting back and forth between Sebastian and Hollis.

"Hollis has done us the honor of calling," Sebastian said. "He seems to be under the impression that I am hiding my siblings from him here."

"Shall I help you throw him out?" Yorke asked.

"Shall he?" Sebastian asked Hollis.

Hollis's tight jaw shifted, his nostrils flaring as he stared at them. "I will be watching, Drake." He took a small step back.

"It *smells* like you will be drinking," Yorke muttered, his nose wrinkling. He walked over to the door and opened it. "Go on, then."

Hollis did not move.

"Allow me to explain how things are done in polite households," Yorke said. "You are a guest, so I have kindly opened the door for you. You reciprocate this thoughtful gesture by leaving through it—and by waiting to be welcomed in the next time you pay us a call, which I would cordially discourage you from ever attempting. If you feel incapable of passing back over the threshold, my offer to throw you out stands."

Hollis stared at Sebastian another moment, then turned and stalked out.

Yorke shut the door soundly behind him, then dusted off his hands and turned to Sebastian. "Charming fellow. Who is he?"

Sebastian drew in a large breath, then launched into a long-overdue explanation about Hollis, his siblings, and his situation.

Yorke stared at him for a moment once he had finished. "If you are refused guardianship in favor of that drunken fool, I will make it my mission to be elected to Parliament with the sole purpose of reforming the Court of Chancery."

"Be careful what you promise, Yorke," Sebastian said grimly. "I am unlikely to be granted the petition as things stand."

"Surely, you are joking."

"I wish I was."

"You are engaged to one of the wealthiest untitled widows in England. What further evidence could the Chancery want?"

Sebastian shook his head. "I am not."

Yorke studied him. "Word of the engagement is all over the *ton*. I offered you congratulations myself. What do you mean by saying you are not engaged? What happened?"

Sebastian rubbed his eyes, his fatigue returning now that Hollis had been dispatched. "I hardly know. She was told from the beginning that I sought her for her fortune—by Haskett. The entire courtship was her way of humiliating me. I finally discovered what she was about and determined to have my revenge. All of it culminated in our engagement."

Yorke could not have looked more confused if he had been handed Montague the pigeon. "That makes no sense, Drake."

"And yet, it is the truth. I have tried to apologize and assure her that my affection for her is genuine, and I had some hope that..." He grimaced. "Only time will tell, but our last interaction did not end well. I have been waiting upon her to spread word that the engagement is at an end."

Yorke let out a low whistle. "What do you mean to do about the children?"

Sebastian lifted his shoulders. "What *can* I do? They are at Selina's, but I cannot trespass upon her kindness indefinitely, particularly given our situation. I am due to appear at the Chancery in six days, and I have nothing that will satisfy the court that my finances are in order or that I can support three children. I am not in a position to take on their upkeep or education. Neither is Hollis, of course, but my solicitor insists they will be reluctant to change the arrangement without convincing evidence to the contrary."

Yorke's mouth turned down at the edges as he thought for a moment. "I am not particularly plump in the pocket, but—"

Sebastian shook his head, cutting him off. "It is kind of you, but I have been assured the court will not view gifts of money as sufficient. They want proof that the children will not be left to the mercy of others."

"And yet, they are happy to leave them to the mercy of *that* oaf?" He pointed at the door to indicate Hollis.

Sebastian pulled a wry face.

"It makes even less sense than the story of your engagement."

"There is little sense or justice in life."

"Not yet, perhaps," Yorke said. "But I mean to change that."

Sebastian gripped him by the shoulder. "You have my full support. Now, I must change my clothes and return to Felix. He took ill yesterday, and I was up with him all night."

"While Hollis was getting brandy-faced."

Sebastian chuckled and began to take the stairs with slow, listless steps. "You might safely append that same phrase onto the end of any sentence and be sure of its accuracy."

Chapter Twenty-Four
Selina

Selina slept even more fitfully than Felix. Her mind insisted on sending her headlong back into the kiss with Sebastian whether she was awake or asleep, and her heart was all too eager to take the journey.

Half of her regretted putting a stop to the most pleasurable moments of her entire life, while the other half berated her for allowing herself such an indulgence in the first place.

She needed all her wits about her to sort through the tangled situation with Sebastian, and those wits had been scattered to the four corners of the earth by those moments in the dark corridor.

Could she trust his assertions about his feelings for her? Or was all of it part of his attempt to acquire fortune, whatever his reasons for needing it?

When she considered her nieces and nephews, there were no lengths to which she would not go to protect them, so she could hardly fault him if that was the case.

But that did not mean she wished to be married for her fortune. She had sworn she would never marry again, never let herself be deceived into thinking she was loved when she was a means to an end.

If Sebastian truly loved her, though, did it matter that he also needed her money?

Was she willing to take the risk of marrying him to find out whether that supposed affection lasted?

Pushed to the edge of sanity by such impossible questions and the memories of his kiss, she forced herself out of bed and pulled the bell to summon her lady's maid. As she waited, she stared at the diamond ring she wore. The skin around it was red and angry, as though chastising her for veering away from her goal.

She felt more mistress of herself once she was dressed and her hair coiffed, but she knew she was holding onto her composure with a mere thread, and the moment she saw Sebastian again, it would unravel.

The maid assured her Sebastian had gone, and Selina was left to feel both grateful and disappointed.

Margaret sat by Felix's bed, her head lolled to the side and her eyes closed, but she woke when Selina opened the door.

"How is he?" Selina asked quietly, for Felix was asleep.

"The fever has not returned," Margaret said, adjusting her dressing gown and hair.

"You should have something to eat," Selina said. "I will send the maid to check on him in half an hour."

As though summoned by the mere mention, the door opened slightly.

"You have a visitor, ma'am," the maid said.

"A visitor?" she repeated.

She nodded. "One Mrs. Winser. Miss Grant is with her in the sitting room."

Selina shut her eyes in consternation. She would have preferred to have the servants inform Mrs. Winser she was not at home to visitors, but she could not leave Phoebe to entertain her.

Perhaps the call would provide a needed distraction, however unpleasant it might be.

"Very well," she said. "I shall go to her directly."

Selina took a moment to gather herself before opening the door to the sitting room.

Mrs. Winser rose immediately and walked over to her, hands out. "My dear Mrs. Lawrence! I have been wishing to call upon you, but we have been so occupied with the Redgrave party that I could not do so until now. Allow me to offer you my warmest felicitations! And"—her eyes twinkled—"to offer my assistance with a ball befitting the occasion."

Selina colored up. She should have realized the purpose of Mrs. Winser's visit. The woman was a gossiping busybody.

How was she to respond? Accept the congratulations when she had promised Sebastian she would be informing Society the engagement was at an end?

He had kissed her after that, of course, but there had been no discussion to give her reason to believe his wishes had changed. Even if there had been, her own were as clear as the Thames after a storm.

The last thing they needed was for Mrs. Winser to begin planning a ball in honor of them.

This was the precise moment to do what she had said she would: tell people she was not engaged to Sebastian Drake. She needed to do it before she lost the will to.

"That is very kind of you, Mrs. Winser," she said with as much calm as she could muster, "but the understanding between Mr. Drake and myself has come to an end."

Phoebe's eyes widened, and Mrs. Winser gasped and clutched at her fichu.

"Good gracious!" she said. "What ever happened, my dear?"

"We have agreed we do not suit," Selina replied, wondering if she had ever told a greater lie. Who on earth would suit her *better* than Sebastian Drake?

Mrs. Winser regarded her with so much pity, Selina could hardly bear it.

"It is better this way," Selina reassured her with a smile, expanding upon her lie without hesitation. She had no desire to delve into things with Mrs. Winser more fully, however. "I am terribly sorry, but we have illness in the household, and I must excuse myself to see to our patient."

Mrs. Winser took the polite dismissal with good grace, and soon Selina and Phoebe were left in the sitting room together.

Selina met Phoebe's gaze.

"It is at an end, then?" Phoebe asked.

"Yes."

Phoebe's chest rose with a long breath, and she nodded, but she watched Selina as though trying to ascertain the feelings behind the short answer.

"Oh, Phoebe," Selina said, "do not look at me that way. We have talked about this. Neither Sebastian nor I entered into the engagement with any intention of marrying."

"I know," she said. "But I had wondered if..."

Selina too had wondered. "I meant it when I told you I have no wish to marry again. Once was more than enough for me. I am quite satisfied with my life as a widow."

At least, she *had* been.

Phoebe nodded her understanding, but there was no missing the sadness in her eyes. "Mrs. Winser will have the news around London by dinnertime."

"I know."

"Do you not worry what the effect of it will be upon you? Or Mr. Drake?"

"In truth, I am tired of caring about such things. As for Sebastian, he is the one who has been encouraging me to make it known, Phoebe." Of course, he had also kissed her until she could hardly remember her own name...

A distinctive squeak brought their heads around.

Margaret stood in the doorway, her eyes wide.

Selina clenched her hands in stricken consternation. There was no saying how much Margaret had heard, but the expression she wore made it seem as though she had been standing there long enough to know more than she should.

"Forgive me," Margaret rushed to say. "I did not mean to eavesdrop. I thought I heard your guest leave, and I wished to ask whether Felix might have a bit to eat. He says he is hungry."

Selina nodded and went to pull the bell cord. "I shall have something taken to him."

"Thank you, Mrs. Lawrence." Margaret hesitated in the doorway. "Is it true? You and my brother are no longer engaged?"

Selina's gaze flicked to Phoebe, who grimaced apologetically. Sebastian had meant to tell the children himself, but Selina could not lie to Margaret.

"No," she said gently. "We are not."

Margaret stood very still, and Selina could have sworn there was a sheen in her eyes before she blinked, and it was gone. "I am very sorry to hear it, and Hugo and Felix will be too. We are all very fond of you, Mrs. Lawrence. And you, Miss Grant. Thank you for taking us in."

Margaret did not mean *taking us in* in the sense of fooling them, but that was how Selina heard it. Her heart panged. What would become of Margaret and her brothers now? "It has been our pleasure, Margaret."

She smiled weakly. "I shall inform Felix that food is coming."

Selina nodded, her throat thick as the door closed behind Margaret. She shut her eyes tightly. In ending the engagement, she couldn't help feeling she had consigned the children to an unknown fate. What good was taking them in for a few days if the end result of her presence in their life was so negative?

Phoebe had promised the children she would play at spillikins with them, and once Selina had ordered food to be sent to Felix, she took the opportunity for reflection away from the hustle and bustle of the house. She went to the room where George's sorted belongings had been stored. Several rifles and fowling pieces stood in the corner. She smiled sadly as she remembered Sebastian saying that one of them "jumps like a sack of flour."

He had been so certain of himself, yet grasping for ways to prove his knowledge. She would never forget how, when she had aimed one of the guns right at him, he had jumped and taken cover.

It had all been for his siblings, but what good had it done? Selina was all but ensuring they would return to Edward Hollis by ending the engagement. And yet, the thought of marrying Sebastian with no certainty his affection for her was real or would last?

No, she could not do that. She was too much of a coward.

But was the security and happiness of Margaret, Hugo, and Felix worth sacrificing just so that Selina could keep her heart safe and her fortune out of Sebastian's hands? It was a fortune she had come to hate, much like the ring she wore.

Her gaze grew more fixed. Perhaps there was another option.

Her heart began to patter, quick and soft.

She left the guns behind, picking up her skirts to hurry to the nearest escritoire. In the corridor, she passed Phoebe, who was carrying a chess board in her arms. "Is everything well?" she asked with concern.

Selina slowed. "No, but I hope to make it better, at least."

Minutes later, her heart pattered as she read over what she had written. As nervous as she was, however, there was a calm beneath it—a sense that this was what she wanted, as unreasonable or mad as it might seem to others.

She folded, sealed, and addressed the letter, then went to see it posted.

"Please see that this is posted without delay, Thomas," she instructed the footman she stopped in the corridor.

"I shall see to it immediately, ma'am."

Selina let out a long, slow breath as he strode away with the letter in hand just as the doorbell rang.

The footman paused and looked at her.

She nodded to indicate that he could answer the door. "I am not at home to callers today, Thomas."

"Yes, ma'am," he said.

She made her way to the stairs, only to stop at the sound of the footman's response to the low voice of the caller.

"I am sorry, Mr. Drake, but Mrs. Lawrence is not at home to visitors."

Selina gathered up her skirts and hurried to the entry hall. "It is fine, Thomas. Mr. Drake may come in."

The footman blinked, obviously confused by her conflicting commands, then quickly opened the door wider for Sebastian.

Selina met his gaze, instantly forgetting how to breathe.

His eyes were watchful but calm as he removed his hat and gloves.

What she wouldn't give to feel the calm he exuded.

"Felix is awake," she said, trying not to think how her lips had been on Sebastian's just hours ago.

"Good," Sebastian said as the footman left with Selina's letter. "Forgive me for the delay in my arrival—I slept longer than intended and was then...detained."

"There is no need to apologize," she said. At least one of them had slept.

"I will see Felix now," he said.

"Of course."

His eyes lingered on her for a moment, as though he might say something, but he merely nodded and swept past her.

"Sebastian," she said suddenly.

He stopped and faced her.

The words stuck in her throat, however. Why was it so difficult to say what needed to be said?

"I have some unpleasant news," she said.

His gaze intensified, and he stepped closer. "What is it?"

She swallowed. "I received a call from Mrs. Winser earlier." The heat filtered up her neck and into her cheeks. "She came to congratulate me on our engagement and offer her assistance in planning a celebration ball. I informed her that the understanding between us has come to an end."

His gaze flickered.

She made a pained expression. "Margaret happened to hear

the conversation Phoebe and I were having afterward. She knows."

Chapter Twenty-Five
Sebastian

Sebastian did his best to mask the intense sense of defeat permeating his entire body.

It was over.

Even after Selina's abrupt departure last night, he had harbored hope that perhaps she simply needed time. He had been wrong. That much was clear.

"Then it is done," he said.

She had only done what she had promised, after all—what they had decided together. Why, then, did it hurt so profoundly?

"I am truly sorry you were not able to tell her yourself," she said, and the way her brows pinched together made it clear she was.

"It is not your fault," he said. "I should have told them sooner."

She merely grimaced.

"I shall go to Felix." He offered a bracing smile, then continued on his way.

Sebastian's spirits might be in the gutter, but Felix's were not. He complained that he wanted mutton, eggs, and toast rather than thin gruel, but he had energy and a healthy color to his cheeks.

At least something was going right. Sebastian had been obliged to take a very circuitous route to Berkeley Square, for Hollis had been following him, true to his threats that he would be watching.

Selina peeked her head into the room half an hour later to inform Sebastian the doctor had arrived.

Sebastian stepped into the corridor to speak with him.

"I was passing by and thought I would see how my patient was getting on," the doctor said. "How did he fare during the night?"

"Not particularly well for the first half," Sebastian answered, suppressing the urge to look at Selina. "We spent the better part of the night trying to make him comfortable."

And kissing.

The doctor smiled at Sebastian, then at Selina. "This bit of practice will stand you in good stead as you welcome children of your own. I was remiss and failed to offer the two of you my congratulations yesterday."

Sebastian's muscles tightened, but he kept his eyes from Selina. "That is kind of you, sir, but Mrs. Lawrence and I are no longer engaged to be married."

"Oh," the doctor said, all awkwardness. "Forgive me, I..."

"Shall we go in and see Felix?" Sebastian suggested. If they stayed in the corridor a moment longer, they would suffocate on the thick air.

"Yes, yes," the doctor said, as eager to escape as Sebastian.

Sebastian pushed the door open to let the doctor in, while Selina went to speak with the housekeeper.

The doctor smiled at Felix. "You have your appetite back, I see."

"I could eat an entire horse," Felix stated.

"I think you might come to regret that choice."

"Not more than I regret being fed this." He let some of the gruel drip from his spoon.

The doctor chuckled. "Let me take a look at you, and perhaps we can see about something more substantial. You had better give up the idea of eating a horse, though. That is not a food I am in the habit of prescribing."

It was but a few minutes before the doctor was gathering up his things, satisfied the danger for Felix had passed. "Better not to let him do anything too strenuous, but he could take a short walk down the corridor—"

"And play with Pip?" Felix suggested.

The doctor's brows went up. "Who, pray, is Pip?"

"A marmoset."

The doctor's mouth hung open as he tried to decide how to respond to this unusual situation. "So long as you are not exerting yourself too much, I suppose it is well enough."

Felix grinned broadly, the trial of his gruel forgotten.

Margaret and Hugo were more than willing to facilitate and supervise the interaction between Pip and Felix, and Sebastian allowed them to do so as he accompanied the doctor to the door.

It would perhaps be for the best if he did not meet Pip. There was nothing calm about the creature, after all.

Selina emerged from the sitting room once the doctor had gone. "What did he say?"

"He is confident Felix is on the mend," Sebastian replied. "He believes he should take another day or two to recover before engaging in anything too exciting or demanding. He agreed to a visit from Pip, however, so I doubt we shall be able to keep that particular advice."

Selina's mouth stretched into a smile. "Pip is the very definition of exciting and demanding."

"On a good day."

Their smiling gazes held for a moment, then began to waver simultaneously.

"I am sorry for saddling you with illness," he said.

"There has been no saddling."

"We will not agree on that score, but either way, given the...

circumstances, it seems for the best that they stay elsewhere. I will find a place to house them as soon as—"

"I am more than happy to have them here, whether well or unwell, Sebastian. You must be the judge of what is best, of course, but they have been happy here, I think, and I would hate to disturb them after all they have been through."

Sebastian grimaced. He imagined he could find an alternative solution to housing them if he tried hard enough, but the truth was, he had other things on his plate that were already overwhelming him. He was being forced to reconsider the church as a way to make his way in the world, though little had changed from before. To make a living as a vicar or rector, he required someone to grant him a living, and he had no such option available.

"Thank you," he said with genuine feeling. "They will certainly prefer to remain where they are. It should not be much longer." He considered telling her the precise date of the hearing but stopped himself. Their lives had already become hopelessly entangled, and he needed to keep whatever distance he could. For his own sanity. She had already done enough. "I would like to stay, but I must see to a few matters—"

"Of course. You need not worry about them."

He gave a grimacing smile, then a quick bow, and made his way to the front door.

Miss Grant stopped him just shy of it, however. "You are leaving?"

"Yes. I have a number of matters to attend to."

She nodded. "I shall not keep you, then. I merely wished to tell you that I am sorry."

He raised his brows, but his heart sped. "For what?"

"That things have turned out this way between you and Selina."

He forced himself to swallow the lump in his throat and attempted a smile, aware it fell short of what he would like. "It is kind of you, Miss Grant."

She struggled for a moment before speaking again. "Selina's past holds a great deal of suffering."

Sebastian's brows pulled together at the thought of anyone making her suffer. Had he not played his own part in precisely that, though? She had been married off at a tender age, naive to the ways of the world, only to discover she was worth nothing more than her beauty to the man meant to protect and cherish her.

Then Sebastian had come into her life, choosing to court her for her money. He was no better than George Lawrence.

"I know," he said softly. "The last thing I want is to cause her pain."

"I think she knows that," Miss Grant said, "but fear is often stronger than reason." She offered one last sad smile. "Good day, Mr. Drake."

He was far from convinced that it *was* a good day, but whatever it was, he needed to make the most of it.

He went directly to his banker. His estate was entailed, but he had to see if there was any possible route for him to take that would help his case with the Chancery.

The response from the banker was not positive, however. Even if there had been no entail, the value of the estate was nearly equal to the debts against it.

Mrs. Winser seemed to have done a fine job of informing the *ton* of the dissolution of the engagement between Sebastian and Selina. Sebastian was offered grim condolences from two different gentleman in the street, then one at Blackstone's, each one twisting the knife in his heart a bit deeper.

With the distinct sense that the walls were closing in upon him, Sebastian spent the next four days trying and failing to find solutions that would satisfy the Chancery. His solicitor had obtained a statement from Margaret to help their case, and they had others attesting to Sebastian's character from Yorke, Fairchild, and Blackstone, but there was still a gaping hole in the evidence they demanded.

Sebastian kept his visits to Berkeley Square short, but the guilt ate at him, for it meant leaving the children to the care of Selina and her household. The alternative, however, was to force his presence upon her when their situation was awkward enough already. Every moment in her company was a special form of sweet torture.

His final act of desperation was a visit to the Duke of Rockwood to ask whether he possessed a living Sebastian might be granted. He had promised himself he would never return to that sphere, for it was at the mercy of money and influence just as everything else seemed to be. The income was far from robust, too, and would hardly be sufficient for sustaining three children the way they deserved. But it was something.

The duke regarded him with a frown, his hands clasped on his desk. "I am sorry to say, Drake, that every living in my gift is already occupied—and has been for some years. I would offer one gladly if it were in my power."

Sebastian nodded, swallowing painfully. "I quite understand. Do you know of any others, perhaps?"

The duke grimaced and shook his head. "I will certainly inform you if I become aware of anything."

Sebastian forced a smile and rose. "Thank you, Your Grace. It is more than I deserve."

He saw Margaret's brave face, Hugo's fierce protectiveness, and Felix's smiles over Pip. And then he saw them fading into the shadow of Hollis's care.

The thought hollowed him.

The day before the hearing arrived all too quickly, and Sebastian resigned himself to his one and final option: throwing himself upon the mercy of the court and hoping they would see the value in granting him guardianship despite his financial situation.

Chapter Twenty-Six
Sebastian

Sebastian had always been a confident man, but that confidence deserted him as he arrived at Lincoln's Inn Hall. Despite the early hour of the morning, the hall was already bustling with solicitors, petitioners, and barristers in full wigs. Clerks stepped out of large wooden chamber doors to call out names and case references.

Sebastian spotted his own solicitor, Helliwell, standing in conversation with the man Sebastian could only assume was his barrister, Mr. Sewell. He looked Sewell over, evaluating his rigid bearing and hoping it boded well for his case. He was paying a pretty penny for the man to appear before the court on his behalf today, and that was in addition to what he owed his solicitor, which was itself in addition to the filing fees and clerk fees he owed. He would be obliged to acquire a loan to meet such obligations.

Sebastian had only ever met with Helliwell in person once, and he wondered if he should have been more diligent in choosing the men who would represent him in front of the court.

He strode over to them to make his presence known. They seemed capable enough, however, and Sebastian satisfied himself that at least Hollis did not have the money to pay for the best solicitors and barristers money could buy. If the man ever regretted his affinity for strong drink, today would be the day.

There was no sign of Hollis as they talked over the case in the hall, and Sebastian began to harbor a hope that he might not appear at all. It was entirely possible that he had drunk well into the night and overslept.

But Hollis and a wigged gentleman appeared just as Sebastian, Helliwell, and Sewell decided to enter the chamber where the hearing would take place. Hollis looked less disheveled than usual, his hair groomed and his clothing pressed. He might even fool the court that he was capable of taking care of himself.

His gaze met Sebastian's, and his lip curled slightly.

The hearing chamber had high windows, dark wood paneling, and rows of benches and desks facing the elevated seat of Master of the Rolls, who would preside at the hearing. At the benches sat two dozen wigged barristers.

Sebastian was shown to the gallery meant for petitioners, his heart hammering.

The first case was a land dispute, found in favor of the heir, while the next argued for a new trustee to be appointed due to the misuse of guardianship funds.

Sebastian sat straighter as he listened to the arguments provided, but the Master of Rolls deferred judgment, requesting further evidence of financial misconduct.

Sebastian's barrister, Sewell, grimaced at this, sending Sebastian's heart to beating at a clipping pace.

Their own case was called next, and Sebastian could hardly contain his nerves as Hollis's barrister stood to make his arguments.

"My Lord," the man said, "I appear on behalf of Mr. Edward Hollis, the children's appointed guardian by prior order of this honourable court. I am instructed that Mr. Hollis has, since his appointment, exercised every reasonable care in the maintenance

To Hunt an Heiress

and supervision of his late brother's children, to whom he stands as both protector and legal steward."

Exercised every reasonable care? Sebastian could not help scoffing.

Helliwell shot him a dampening look.

Hollis's barrister continued, his voice full of energy that couldn't but draw the attention of everyone in the chamber. "It is with no small concern that we submit to the Court that the children were removed from Mr. Hollis's guardianship without his consent—indeed, without so much as a formal petition before this court to alter the current arrangement. The petitioner, Mr. Sebastian Drake, had neither legal right nor standing to take the minors into his household. Such an act amounts, we respectfully submit, to an extrajudicial removal bordering upon abduction, and must not be countenanced, lest it set a dangerous precedent in matters of guardianship and wardship."

Sebastian sat straighter, looking to his solicitor, who gave a slight shake of the head to discourage any further reaction.

So, Sebastian was to sit here calmly while Hollis's barrister told outright lies to the court?

The barrister was not finished, however. "The respondent, though of respectable birth, is not possessed of adequate means to provide for the children. His estate, I am informed, is encumbered by considerable debt, and his personal affairs are not such as would inspire confidence in a man seeking guardianship over three young lives. Mr. Drake has recently—very recently—engaged himself and, according to several reports, has since terminated the engagement under circumstances that suggest instability, both financial and emotional."

Sebastian clenched his eyes shut in consternation. Hollis's barrister was more capable than he had expected, even if he *was* spouting misinterpretations and lies.

"Mr. Hollis, on the other hand, has maintained the children within a proper household and provided for their care. No formal charge of cruelty or neglect has been substantiated, and I would respectfully submit that any discontent expressed by the children themselves must be viewed through the lens of youthful caprice. This is not a question of affection, my Lord, but of legal standing and capacity. The current arrangement is both lawful and sufficient. No cause has been shown to disturb it, while there is sufficient evidence to make the court wary in the extreme of granting Mr. Drake's petition."

Sebastian's nostrils flared, and he watched Hollis, who was calm and sober for perhaps the first time in his life, staring forward at the Master of Rolls with a somber expression that was meant, no doubt, to inspire confidence in his abilities as a guardian.

The time was granted to Mr. Sewell, and Sebastian hovered on the edge of his seat as the counterarguments began.

"My Lord, if I may—this is a petition concerning the guardianship of three minor children, who have, for the last several years, been under the guardianship of Mr. Edward Hollis. While this arrangement was initially sanctioned owing to Mr. Drake's minority, it is my submission that circumstances have altered sufficiently to warrant reconsideration."

Sebastian's hand fiddled in his lap as he looked around the room. The attention of those who had listened to Hollis's barrister was flagging at the sound of Sewell's rigid, monotonous voice.

"Mr. Drake is of age, is possessed of an estate—albeit, somewhat encumbered—and he has demonstrated a sincere commitment to the welfare of his siblings. They voluntarily left Mr. Hollis's care and sought out Mr. Drake, which, I think, speaks to their feelings on the matter.

"Mr. Drake has shown himself to be both willing and, I daresay, morally fit to assume responsibility for his family. If Your Lordship pleases, we would ask that serious consideration be given to placing the children with their elder brother in what we believe to be a more natural and affectionate arrangement."

Sebastian itched to stand and defend himself, to tell the court the truth of Hollis's supposed guardianship. If he and Hollis had been the ones making their cases to the court rather than having barristers speak in their stead, there could be no doubt of the result.

But Sebastian was obliged to sit in silence while Sewell provided a lackluster defense. He had to accept the distinct possibility that the court would find in favor of Hollis; Sebastian could hardly blame it given what they were hearing.

"In support of my client's position," Sewell said, "we have a sworn statement from the eldest of the children, Miss Margaret Hollis, who is thirteen years of age. She describes conditions in Mr. Hollis's household as...less than ideal. Troubling, even."

He fumbled with his papers, then drew one out. "If it please the Court, I can...read an excerpt?"

The Master of Rolls nodded.

Mr. Sewell put on his spectacles and cleared his throat. "'We are afraid in Mr. Hollis's house. He yells when he drinks and breaks things sometimes. When I had a fever, he left us alone for two days. We do not feel safe with him.'"

Sebastian's throat tightened painfully as Mr. Sewell looked up over his spectacles. "We believe this illustrates that the children's preference would be to remain with their brother, Mr. Drake."

The delivery of the evidence left Sebastian wanting, but at least there *was* evidence.

The Master of Rolls offered Hollis's barrister the chance to respond, which he was obviously eager to do. "My Lord, while I acknowledge the statement from Miss Hollis, I must submit that she is a child of merely thirteen years and hardly in a position to make judgments regarding her welfare that would override the authority granted by this court, which named Mr. Hollis as guardian.

"Children, my Lord, are easily influenced—especially by elder siblings with financial interests at stake. Mr. Drake, let us remember, is a man in debt, whose motives are not beyond question.

"We cannot allow a child's impressionistic complaints—

unsupported by physical evidence or corroborating testimony—to supersede the legal rights of her appointed guardian."

Seething silently, Sebastian fixed his gaze on Helliwell, waiting for him to confer with Sewell and guide him in a rebuttal, feeling as though the chances of victory were slipping away like a scent on the wind.

Chapter Twenty-Seven
Selina

Selina had come to love the time at the breakfast table with the Hollis children. It was earlier than she generally liked to take the first meal of the day, but the reward of being with them more than compensated for this. The conversation was always enlivening and never predictable.

Yesterday, the topic of discussion had been whether a sword or a hot air balloon would be a better purchase if they came into unexpected wealth. Today, Felix insisted on arguing that Pip was indeed able to pull a small cart, provided it was not loaded with too many heavy items.

He was finally forced by Hugo to admit that it would only be possible on the most manicured of roads, and the debate came to a begrudging end.

"Did your brother mention what time we can expect him today?" Selina tried to make the question sound offhand—a mere passing curiosity—but she doubted anyone was fooled.

Margaret's gaze flicked over as she buttered another piece of toast, only to drop swiftly again.

Selina's brows drew together at the strange reaction. "What is it?"

"I do not believe we shall see him until later," Margaret said, even less successful than Selina in sounding nonchalant.

"Oh." She considered whether to pursue the subject and ended in deciding to abandon any pretense of disinterest. "Why is that?"

"He is at court," Hugo said, shoveling an enormous mouthful of eggs into his mouth.

Selina's heart stuttered.

"Hugo," Margaret chided.

"What?" he asked, mouth full. "I heard you talking to him yesterday."

"At court," Selina repeated. "Do you mean he is at the guardianship hearing, Margaret?" Selina's chest was tight, her pulse racing.

Margaret nodded, but Selina could only assume from the chagrin on her face that Sebastian had asked her not to divulge the information.

Why would he keep such a thing from her?

She grabbed the napkin on her lap and set it on the table as she stood. "I must go, but Phoebe will be down shortly, I imagine."

Margaret nodded, while Hugo and Felix gave only the most cursory of acknowledgements, their focus taken up by more important things like raspberry preserves and adding more sugar to their tea.

Selina had no true plan, for there had not been time for formal arrangements with her solicitor, but she had to reach the court before the matter was decided.

The thought sent a flash of nerves through her. George had been a magistrate, and she had attended the Quarter Sessions when one of their servants had stood judgment for poaching. When she had suggested offering a reference of the tenant's character, George had read her a scathing lecture on the place of women.

For her to march into the Court of Chancery and speak unbidden...he would be rolling over in his grave.

But she could not stand idly by.

It would take too long for her own carriage to be prepared, so one of the footmen helped her hail a hackney carriage. With coins to grease the driver's fist, Selina was conveyed with all haste to Lincoln's Inn Hall, praying she would not be too late.

She was recognized by a surprised acquaintance when she reached the building but was obliged to do away with politeness when he attempted to speak with her. She offered him a quick, apologetic smile and hoped he would understand she was not at liberty to stop for conversation.

A clerk stood by the door to the chamber, and while he looked at her curiously, he made no move to stop her. The hearings were public, but she doubted he would have allowed her to pass if he had known what she intended.

Her gaze raked over the room and settled upon Sebastian, whose grim face was turned toward the imposing figure presiding over the proceedings. He wore forbidding black robes and a long, curled, white wig.

Selina's nerves sprang to life again as she pictured George in his place.

"The guardianship of minors is not a matter the Court considers lightly," the master's deep voice intoned, echoing in the large hall. "The welfare of the children must, of course, be paramount, and yet the Court is constrained by precedent and by the legal rights of the guardian. The evidence presented by the petitioner, Mr. Drake, suggests concern for the children's well-being, but the petition lacks sufficient demonstration of financial capacity and long-term provision."

Body trembling, Selina hurried forward. "My Lord," she called out. "I beg your forbearance, but I must speak for the sake of the children."

There was a collective gasp as all the bodies in the room turned toward her, their eyes wide with shock.

Sebastian's head whipped around, a look of utter disbelief on his face.

She held his gaze for a moment, then forced it back to the Master of Rolls.

He regarded her with a pinched look over the top of his wiry spectacles. "Madam, you are not a party to this petition. This is most irregular. Who are you to make such an audacious request?"

Chapter Twenty-Eight
Sebastian

Sebastian was not imagining things. Selina truly was there, standing a dozen feet from him, facing the Master of Rolls with the calm of someone accustomed to interrupting formal proceedings.

"I am Selina Lawrence, my Lord," she said. "The Hollis children have been in my care since they fled Mr. Hollis's household fearing for their safety. I believe I hold information that will aid the Court in its deliberations."

The Master of Rolls frowned, and a thick silence fell over the chamber.

"My Lord," said Mr. Hollis's barrister, "this is *highly* irregular. The lady is not represented by counsel—nor has she any standing at all in the matter."

The Master of Rolls put up a hand to stop him, then looked at Sebastian. "Is what this woman says true, Mr. Drake?"

Sebastian stood. "The children have been staying with Mrs. Lawrence at my request. We believed it the safest arrangement, given the circumstances."

The Master of Rolls regarded him for a moment, then gave a stiff nod and turned back to Selina. "Madam, you tread a very fine line. This Court does not receive interventions from parties without legal standing—least of all unrepresented gentlewomen. I might have you removed for your interruption—or worse, held in contempt."

Sebastian's every muscle was taut. What would he do if he lost the petition *and* Selina was held in contempt of the court?

But Selina met the Master of Rolls' gaze. "I quite understand, my Lord. I beg the Court's indulgence and assure you I will be brief. I have no wish to flout the Court's authority—only to assist its judgment."

There was a long pause.

The Master of the Rolls tapped a finger against the bench, then finally gave a reluctant nod. "You may proceed, but be concise. And be warned, madam: any deviation from the matter at hand, and you will be silenced."

"Thank you, my Lord," she said, and Sebastian noted for the first time the trembling of her hands, which she clasped before her tightly. "I understand the Court's concern lies in Mr. Drake's capacity to provide for the children's material welfare."

Sebastian could not have sat any closer to the edge of his seat. What was she about?

"That is correct," the Master of Rolls conceded briskly.

"I have this very week instructed my solicitor to begin the legal transfer of funds to be held in trust for Margaret, Hugo, and Felix —enough to ensure the children's welfare, clothing, and education for many years to come."

A rush of whispers ran through the gallery of spectators and petitioners, but Sebastian was entirely still.

"The condition of this offer," Selina continued, her voice stronger to ensure that she could be heard, "is that the children remain in Mr. Drake's care. The offer is made solely on that basis."

"My Lord," Hollis's barrister complained, "the lady presents no affidavit—no legal evidence of this clai—"

"Had I been aware of the hearing's timing," Selina said, turning toward the man, "I would have brought the relevant documentation. My solicitor may easily confirm the particulars."

There was another silence as the Master of Rolls considered her words, lips pursed. "And what is your interest in the children's welfare, madam? Have you some relation to them?"

Her eyes flitted to Sebastian, then away just as quickly. "No relation, my lord. I have nephews and nieces of my own, however, and when I discovered the plight of the Hollis children, I was moved to help them. Every child deserves to be protected."

Sebastian was riveted to his seat, unable to so much as blink.

"And what makes you so certain that Mr. Drake is the most fitting guardian for the children?"

Selina's eyes turned to Sebastian, and their gazes locked. Only the deepest clutches on his willpower kept him in his seat when every other part of him wanted to rush over to her and pull her into his arms—or stand by her side, at the very least.

She returned her focus to the Master of Rolls. "I have come to know Mr. Drake, my lord, and there is nothing he would not do for these children."

Sebastian swallowed, for there was both compliment and shame in those words. Selina knew better than anyone what he had done in his efforts to help them.

"Whatever Mr. Hollis's barrister has claimed," she continued, "Mr. Drake is both capable and caring. There is no one with whom I would more readily trust my own nieces and nephews if the situation ever required it. He has my utmost respect and admiration and is by far the most logical choice as a guardian."

Sebastian's eyes prickled. Those words meant more, even, than the money she was offering. He did not deserve it—not her defense, not her trust.

"Thank you, Mrs. Lawrence," said the Master of Rolls. "You may take a seat."

Selina obediently shifted to the edge of the gallery of spectators, where space was made for her.

The Master of Rolls shuffled the papers in front of him. "The information that has come to light—unorthodox though the manner may be—alters the nature of the petition significantly, as I am certain you can see." He glanced at both barristers. "In light of this—admittedly irregular—occurrence, and pending formal documentation of the trust described by Mrs. Lawrence, this court provisionally grants guardianship of the minors in question to Mr. Sebastian Drake."

A rustle moved through the courtroom, and Hollis shot to his feet. "This is outrageous!"

His barrister reached for his arm, but Hollis shook him off and looked at Sebastian, his face turning mottled. "You will regret this, Drake! Mark my words!"

"Mr. Hollis," the Master of Rolls said in a loud, authoritative voice, "you will conduct yourself with restraint in this court, or you will be removed from it. The ruling stands. Let it be recorded. The matter is concluded."

Hollis pushed past his barrister, who stumbled before regaining his balance, but Hollis was rushing across the courtroom.

Every person stood, gasping as he hurtled toward the spectator gallery—toward Selina.

"You!" Hollis bellowed.

Sebastian sprang to his feet, vaulted the gallery rail, then leaped in front of Hollis, intercepting him in a crushing tackle. They hit the floor with a thud, a tangle of limbs and fury.

Hollis twisted to break free as chairs scraped and shouts rose.

Sebastian's fist connected with Hollis's jaw just as the court officers reached them and pulled Hollis away.

The Master of Rolls banged his gavel as the officers pulled Hollis to his feet. "Order!"

Sebastian was on his knees, breathing hard, his fist still clenched and burning.

"This is a court of law, not a boxing yard! Mr. Drake, your intervention may have been warranted under the circumstances, but the handling of Mr. Hollis is now the court's concern."

"Yes, my lord," Sebastian said, rising to his feet.

The Master of Rolls looked to the tipstaffs, who held the squirming Hollis firmly. "Take him away."

Hollis was forcibly removed from the courtroom, and a few spectators clapped, bringing the gavel into use yet again.

Sebastian's gaze searched for Selina, but the gallery of spectators had grown chaotic and disorganized.

"Well," Helliwell said, blocking his view, "that went well, did it not? I was worried for a moment there—several moments, in fact—but it resolved very satisfactorily. Had I known Mrs. Lawrence meant to make such a generous offer—"

"We need those papers," said Sewell, who had come up beside Helliwell. "Who is her solicitor?"

But Sebastian was not thinking about papers or solicitors.

"Excuse me." He pushed past them and made his way through the gallery as the clerk called the next matter for the court's consideration.

Selina was not in the gallery, and Sebastian searched the room, finally spotting her walking toward the door.

"Mr. Drake," said Lord Blackstone, who stepped in front of him, preventing his progress, supremely unaware that Sebastian had a destination in mind. "I must say, I have never been at a more enlivening session of this court!"

"Forgive me, sir," Sebastian said, trying to move around him. "I must—"

"Tongues will be wagging for some time, and I would wager the gallery will be crowded for weeks to come."

"I must speak with Mrs. Lawrence, my lord," Sebastian said, his patience wearing thin as Blackstone walked backward, remaining an obstacle.

"To make her an offer of marriage, I trust! After that display, Society will certainly expect it."

Sebastian stopped and squared Blackstone with his gaze. "I don't give a damn what Society expects."

The viscount's eyes widened slightly. "You do not intend to marry her, then?"

"Oh, I most certainly do," Sebastian said, setting a hand on Blackstone's shoulder to prevent him from moving. Sebastian darted around him and toward the door, pushing through it.

It had grown even busier since his arrival, and his eyes searched frantically amongst the hordes of men.

Selina was nowhere to be found.

Chapter Twenty-Nine
Selina

Selina hailed the first hackney she saw, her heart beating at a strangely steady pace given the circumstances. She had just given Sebastian Drake the very thing she'd sworn she never would.

Now, he had no need of her.

She had done it on her own terms, though. She had given it willingly, and a strange sense of liberation filled her.

For so long, she had let the weight of her wealth guide her decisions. She had been afraid of being wanted for it, afraid of trusting anyone because of it.

No longer.

As for Sebastian...

Her heart fluttered as she remembered the way he had looked at her in the courtroom.

She loved him. She would not deny that any longer.

She wanted *him*, though, not his gratitude or his sense of obligation toward her after her scandalous appearance in court. That was why she had left the chamber as quickly as possible after the decision by the Master of Rolls.

She did not regret what she had done, even if it did lead to scandal. Now that she was free of the hold of money upon her, she would not trade it for the stranglehold of reputation.

In allowing her to end the engagement on her terms, Sebastian had released her from any obligation toward him. She would do the same for him now. He owed her nothing. She had not done it for him. She had done it for the children and for herself.

Yes, she hoped that Sebastian loved her, but she would not assume anything. There was the real possibility that, now that he had what had drawn him to her in the first place, he would fail to see the purpose of her in his life.

If that was the case, well...she had survived heartbreak and adversity before, and she would manage to do so again.

She paused at the door of Number 14. The children would be there, of course, and they would be eager for news.

But it was not her news to give. Sebastian should be the one to tell them what their future held.

She opened the door quietly and put a finger to her lips to silence the footman who stood in the entry hall.

He nodded his comprehension, his gaze darting to the corridor behind him, where the muffled sounds of the children's voices came from the sitting room.

"What are they doing?" Selina asked in a whisper.

"They are...uh...eating, ma'am," said the footman.

Selina laughed softly. "Of course they are. I do not wish for them to know I have returned just yet. I shall go upstairs, but I expect Mr. Drake will call in the next hour or two."

"Very good, ma'am."

She picked up her skirts and took the stairs, wondering what she should do with her time. Write to her solicitor, certainly.

A muffled squeaking slowed her progress, however, and she stopped to listen.

A smile crept over her face as she located its origin—the closed door to her right.

She opened it slowly, and the squeaking stopped.

Pip appeared near the base of the door.

"Hullo, Pip," she said. "Have you been relegated here while the children eat all the delicious food without you?"

He slipped through the opening and jumped onto her arm.

She looked at him with a cocked brow. "You take a great deal for granted, don't you?"

His large, curious eyes stared back at her, and she thought back on when she had seen him at the pet shop. She had been so charmed at first. She had shortly realized, though, that however endearing his appearance, he was a creature of chaos, hell-bent on upending her life.

He and Sebastian had that in common.

She let out a resigned sigh, smiling slightly. "Very well. I could use the company, I suppose."

She took him with her to her bedchamber, a thing she had never before done. "It has been quite a day, Pip." She let him crawl from her arm onto the escritoire. "And it is not even midday." She took a seat and moved to pick up the quill. Her diamond ring caught on the light from the window, sparkling.

She stared at it, tilting it and watching it catch the light. Then, she removed it and set it on the desk.

Pip snatched it up, and Selina did not stop him.

"What do you think, Pip? Do I belong at Bedlam?"

He bit the ring, then seemed to decide against consuming it.

"If *you* are not at Bedlam," she said, "*I* do not belong there."

"A matter for debate, I think."

Selina swung around and found Sebastian leaning against the door. She could have sworn she had closed it.

Heart beating fit to burst through her chest, she stood and faced him. "You might have knocked."

"I might have." Using his shoulder, he pushed himself off the door and walked toward her. "But I did not. I am feeling impatient today."

She recognized the same words she had used when she had unceremoniously burst into his bedchamber. It felt like a lifetime ago, but in reality, it had not even been a fortnight.

"What are you doing here, Sebastian?"

"What do you *think* I am doing here, Selina?" There was a light in his eyes that made her heart race.

She tried to step backward, but the chair was in her way. She gripped the top of it with her hands, glad for something to steady her.

"I think," she said, "that you have come to thank me."

He gave a little nod. "And?"

"And," she continued, annoyed to find her voice breathless, "because you are concerned that my actions today have made me a target for Society gossip."

"Ah," he said, his gaze still fixed on hers from less than a foot away. "You believe I have come to save your reputation."

"My reputation does not require saving, but yes, I imagine that is why you are here." Before he could respond, she hurried on. "Before you say anything else, you should know that providing for your siblings is only part of the plan that has been set into action. I mean to donate a large portion of my fortune to various charities."

Sebastian's eyes bored into her, making her entire body warm. He took a step even closer. He looked at her for a long second, taking her in like a man who hadn't dared hope he'd see her again.

A sudden movement startled them both as Pip scrambled up the fabric of Sebastian's arm until he found his perch on his shoulder.

Sebastian turned his head to look at the marmoset. "Impeccable timing, Pip."

The monkey reached his small hands to Sebastian's hair and began his usual grooming.

"I am sorry, old boy, but that will have to wait." He strode toward the door, took the monkey from his shoulder, tossed him outside, and shut the door.

"Sebastian!" Selina cried. "You cannot let him loose in the house."

"I can, and I did. Now"—he turned back to her—"where

were we?" A mischievous light sparkled in his eyes as he took slow but purposeful steps toward her again, reminding her of that night in the music room. "Ah, yes. I think I remember."

He returned to the place he had left, making her heart beat faster with every inch he drew closer, until she was obliged to lift her chin to meet his gaze.

"You were warning me," he said, "that in coming here to save you, I would be attaching myself to a woman with a damaged reputation and little fortune to offer."

"I also mentioned that I do not require saving—"

"Perfect." His hand stole around her waist and his body pressed against hers until the only thing within her view was his eyes. "I have no intention of saving you from Society gossip, Selina, nor am I in a position to do so. My own reputation is hardly spotless, you may recall." His other hand rose to her cheek, his eyes devouring hers. "As for your money, you may donate every last penny of it, as far as I am concerned. Your wealth is by far the least interesting thing about you. I came here for one reason and one reason only."

Her hands grasped the chair back within an inch of its life. "And what reason is that?" she managed.

"I came," he said, "because, be we paupers or kings, I have no intention of living as much as a second of my life without you. You may send me home with a hundred Pips and a thousand dead pigeons to test the barriers of my love, but I swear to you, Selina, you will come away empty-handed, for those limits do not exist." His eyes raked over her face for a moment, then found hers again, nearer than ever. "You are more beautiful than any diamond."

Selina's chest tightened.

"But I have no wish for diamonds," he said. "I want a wife who will sit with me in the evenings and care for the children with me when they are unwell. I want a wife who will laugh with me and tell me when I am being pigheaded. I want a wife who knows how to shoot me with a double-barreled musketoon but chooses not to. In short..." He brought her hand to his mouth and kissed it. When it came away, his eyes fixed on the finger, bare but ringed with red where the diamond had been. His eyes met hers. "I want *you*, Selina Lawrence. Every bit of you. Have I made myself clear?"

She nodded. It was all she *could* do.

The space between their lips diminished as he whispered one final word. "Good."

His lips covered hers, and her body sank into his, her fingers leaving the chair and finding his coat instead. They clutched at his lapels in ways no amount of ironing would ever fix.

It was not the tender, soft kiss of that night in the corridor. It was the kiss of a man determined to make her understand he was not here because anyone or anything demanded it of him. He was here to ensure she knew that he wanted her—and meant to keep her. He was here to claim every part of her she was willing to give him.

Selina thought she had learned what it was to be truly kissed in that dark corridor, but she knew better now. Sebastian was intent to show her that there were as many ways to kiss her as there were beats of her heart, and she was more than willing to be shown.

His hand slipped from her cheek into her hair, threading through the curls at the nape of her neck, and her body trembled.

She pulled back, embarrassed at the reaction. "Forgive me."

"For what?" he whispered, his lips just out of reach while his breath teased her.

She searched in vain to describe what she was feeling. Words were insufficient. "Tell me it is not only me—that I am not alone in what I am feeling."

He drew back until his gaze found hers, intent and searching. He took one of her hands from its place curled up in the lapel and placed it over his heart. "Can you feel that?"

Beneath her palm, his heart pulsed quick and strong as he stared into her eyes, willing her to understand.

She closed her eyes, feeling each blessed beat.

"You undo me, Selina," he said softly. "I love you now, and I promise I always will."

Eyes still closed and heart aflame, she lifted her lips to his again.

"Who let Pip out of my room?" The muffled words were followed by a knock on the door.

"Ignore it," Sebastian mumbled, taking her lips with his again.

But there was another, more insistent knock, and they pulled apart just as the door opened.

Felix stared at them, Pip in his arms. "Pip was wandering the house. Who let him out of my room?"

Selina, whose face must have resembled a cherry, tried to step away from Sebastian.

He did not allow it, keeping his arms securely around her waist.

"Your brother did it," she said.

"I did no such thing," Sebastian protested. "I let him out of *this* room, not yours. The culprit you are looking for is Selina."

Felix regarded her for a moment, a frown passing over his brow. "What are the two of you doing?"

Selina pulled her raw lips between her teeth and looked at Sebastian expectantly. Felix was *his* brother, after all. He should be the one to explain.

Sebastian thought for a moment. "We are...betrothing."

"Betrothing?" Felix repeated with a bunched brow. "What does that mean?"

"Yes, what *does* it mean?" Selina looked at him with amused curiosity, eager to see how he would extricate himself from this tangle.

"If you must know, we were kissing," Sebastian said.

Selina's eyes widened, and Felix's face contorted as if he had been told tonight's dinner would be pigeon feet.

"And I have every intention of kissing her again, so you had better—"

Felix ran, shouting at the top of his lungs. "No one go in Mrs. Lawrence's room! She and Sebastian are kissing!"

"There," Sebastian said with satisfaction, pulling Selina by the waist until he could shut the door with his boot. "That ought to give us a bit of time."

"You," she said, "are..."

"What?" he asked with ill-concealed delight, his hands spanning her waist firmly. "What am I?"

The door opened again, and Sebastian cast his eyes to the heavens.

Hugo stared at them, and Margaret and Phoebe came up behind him, breathless.

"Hugo!" Margaret called at him, but her eyes flicked to Selina and Sebastian. Her brows rose.

Phoebe, on the other hand, grinned widely at the sight of them. "Are you—"

"Engaged," Sebastian said abruptly.

"Again?" Hugo asked.

"Again," Sebastian confirmed. "And anxious for a moment to enjoy it properly this time. Privately."

"Sebastian," Selina said, unable to keep from grinning with overflowing joy. "You should tell them."

"I just did." His frown transformed suddenly as realization struck. "Oh! Yes."

"Tell us what?" Hugo asked.

Sebastian stepped away from Selina and peeked his head into the hall. "Felix!" he called.

A few moments later, footsteps came down the corridor, and Felix's head appeared, tentative, as though he feared he might see something unwelcome that would be forever branded upon his memory. Pip was nibbling on something, unconcerned with the news Sebastian was about to deliver.

Apparently satisfied that the scene was safe for the time being, Felix brought his full body into view. "What is it?"

"*It*," Sebastian said, "is that you are looking at"—he put out his hands to display himself—"your new official guardian."

Selina cleared her throat softly.

Sebastian reached over and snatched her by the waist, pulling her up against him. "And your *other* new soon-to-be-official guardian."

Margaret's hands covered her mouth, the corners of her eyes wrinkling with joy.

Hugo stayed still for a moment, then rushed toward the two of them and wrapped his arms around them in an innocent gesture at odds with his wizened twelve years.

"Does this mean we can stay here forever?" Felix asked, his eyes alight.

"That is precisely what it means," Selina said.

It was Felix's turn to be demonstrative, and he pushed Hugo out of the way to do so. This naturally turned into a tussle between the two of them, their gratitude and joy instantaneously forgotten in the need for victory.

Sebastian shared an amused look with Selina before Margaret and Phoebe came over to embrace them.

"Are you certain you are prepared for this?" Margaret asked Selina, glancing at her bickering brothers, whose argument had abruptly shifted to which one of them Pip belonged to.

Selina's eyes moved from the boys to Sebastian, who was laughing with Phoebe. Her heart fluttered at the sight of him and the knowledge that, whatever she faced in life, she would have him beside her.

She had never felt so well-equipped for anything in her life.

"Yes," Selina replied, pulling Margaret into an embrace. "Decidedly, yes."

"Selina may have welcomed you to stay here forever," Sebastian said, pulling the boys apart before the argument devolved to fisticuffs, "but you are *not* welcome to stay in this room even one more minute. You may tear one another limb from limb elsewhere." He guided them firmly out of the room.

Phoebe came over to Selina and threw her arms around her, holding her tightly. "You cannot imagine how utterly overcome with joy I am."

Selina squeezed her. "Oh, but I can! Thank you for seeing him properly when I could not." She pulled back and looked at Phoebe, who dashed a smiling tear away.

"It is hard to see others properly when you cannot see yourself properly," she replied. "You deserve every happiness life can provide, Selina." She kissed Selina on the cheek.

"I owe you an apology, Phoebe."

Phoebe's brows rose.

"I influenced you against Mr. Evenden, and I regret it. You have a keen mind, Phoebe. You should trust yourself with it. He deserves a chance."

Phoebe blinked quickly and embraced her again. "I intend to give him one."

Something between a growl and a yell came from the corridor, and Phoebe gave a watery laugh, then hurried out behind Margaret.

Sebastian let out a satisfied sigh, shut the door, and turned the privacy lock. "Now, where were we...again?" He came over, and Selina slipped her arms around his neck.

He ran his hands from her wrists all the way up to her shoulders, leaving tingling in their wake.

"I love you, Sebastian," she said simply.

His eyes fixed on hers, losing a bit of their funning in favor of earnestness. "You cannot imagine how I have longed to hear those words from your lips."

"You will tire of them, I fear."

He shook his head. "Never."

Felix would have been horrified by what happened next.

Epilogue
Sebastian

Sebastian picked up the fowling piece and situated it how he thought it should be held. "See? A natural."

"There is nothing natural about the way you are holding that, my love." Selina approached him from behind his back, her arms wrapping around him to show him the way.

He smiled at the feel of his wife against him and made his arms and hands clay in her capable hands. The sounds of London were present but not all-encompassing in the seclusion of the townhouse garden.

"Elbows in," she said, squeezing his arms inside hers to force his obedience. "Cheek to the stock, not the trigger. And keep your stance steady, else you will knock yourself flat when you pull the trigger."

Her breath brushed the back of his ear, and he turned his head toward her, his cheek decidedly not against the stock.

He shifted his body enough to steal a kiss.

She smiled but quickly pressed her lips together severely. "Focus, Sebastian."

"You are distracting me," he complained, then stole another kiss.

She nudged him away from her, but her cheeks were pink

with delight. "Have you any wish to learn, or is this simply a joke to you?"

"I am to concentrate my mind on holding this weapon of destruction when my wife is fairly throwing herself at me?"

Her head tilted to the side, and she pegged him with an impatient look, though her eyes danced.

True to her word, Selina had donated hefty sums to various charities, along with selling Chesleigh House. The London townhouse had been kept and a modest estate purchased in Surrey. In short, they had kept enough to lead a comfortable life and provide the children with robust educations. With the help of Silas Yorke, their investments continued to grow what they had to draw upon.

It had been a happy year indeed—by far the happiest of Sebastian's life.

The door opened, and a flurry of voices sounded. Margaret, Felix, Hugo, and Pip emerged, and behind them, Phoebe and Mr. Evenden.

"We have some news," Phoebe said, looking at Mr. Evenden with a glow about her.

He met her gaze with an expression that was better suited to the privacy of the bedroom than a garden full of children.

"They are engaged!" Felix yelled, beating them to the news.

"Felix," Margaret said, horrified.

"It is the truth," Mr. Evenden said. "Phoebe has done me the honor of accepting my presumptuous offer of marriage."

Selina's arms dropped from around Sebastian, and she ran to Phoebe, pulling her into her arms. "The happiest news possible! Oh, Phoebe!"

Sebastian strode to Evenden and put out his hand, smiling broadly. "My felicitations, Evenden."

The garden was full of laughter and animated voices for the next few minutes, until Pip managed to grab hold of the fowling piece in Sebastian's grasp. Only after a fair amount of careful grappling did he and Selina manage to extricate the gun.

. . .

"Perhaps you had all better go inside," Selina said significantly.

"I am making marked improvements, I'll have you know," Sebastian called out as Phoebe, Mr. Evenden, and the children disappeared into the house with Pip.

"Your form is as bad as your poetry," Selina teased, giving the gun to him again.

"Which has *also* improved markedly," he defended.

Nothing brought him greater pleasure than leaving terrible poems around the house for her.

"I am well on my way to becoming a crack shot," he said, running a hand over the length of the fowling piece in the manner of someone accustomed to handling firearms. There was a smudge, and he frowned, then thumbed it.

A sharp crack rang through the air, making them both jump as a flock of birds tore away from one of the trees.

Sebastian looked at his wife, whose eyes were closed, as though she was praying for serenity.

"Entirely on purpose," he said. "A true hunter always maintains the element of surprise."

Selina suppressed a smile and removed the gun from his care, setting it aside. "Shall we see whether the tree will survive this element of surprise?"

They walked hand in hand to the tree and found a few marks in the tree where the shot had scattered.

"Oh dear," Sebastian said.

Upon the ground lay a dead pigeon.

Selina's hand flew to her mouth.

Sebastian's expression grew solemn. "This must be Montfort, Montague's brother. An aspiring messenger pigeon cut down in his prime."

Selina's eyes wrinkled at the sides, and her shoulders shook with laughter. "Oh, Sebastian. What shall we do with the poor creature?"

"He must join Montague in the study, of course." He regarded the bird pensively. "Quite a good shot, don't you think?"

"Oh, yes! If only it had been on purpose."

He tried and failed to suppress a chuckle. "I *will* learn, my love. One day, I will ride to hounds with you, and I will only discharge weapons on purpose—and at intended targets."

She stepped up to him and grasped his braces with her hands, smiling up at him. "I know it, and I look forward to it. But I do enjoy having the upper hand in at least one area."

Sebastian's mouth quirked up at the edge, and he trailed a finger along her hairline tenderly. "Well, then, my dearest sharpshooter." He brought his mouth just shy of hers. "The pigeons of England had better watch out."

She laughed in delight, but the sound was stopped when his lips covered hers.

The warmth of the kiss spread through Sebastian like fire through dry brush, and he held her more closely, still hardly able to fathom that after everything, she was his. Pigeons, Pips, pretense. None of those had kept them from one another.

And nothing in the future would, either.

Bachelors of Blackstone's

A Bachelor's Lessons in Love by Sally Britton
A Trial of His Affections by Mindy Burbidge Strunk
A Gentleman's Reckoning by Jennie Goutet
To Hunt an Heiress by Martha Keyes
Love is for the Birds by Deborah M. Hathaway
Forever Engaged by Ashtyn Newbold
A Match of Misfortune by Jess Heileman

Other Titles by Martha Keyes

A Chronicle of Misadventures

Reputation at Risk (Book 1)

Secrets of a Duke (Book 2)

A Reckless Courtship (Book 3)

The Donovans

Unrequited (Book 1)

The Art of Victory (Book 2)

A Confirmed Rake (Book 3)

Battling the Bluestocking (Book 4)

Matchify

No Match Found (Book 1)

Sheppards in Love

Kissing for Keeps (Book 1)

Just Friends Forever (Book 2)

Selling Out (Book 3)

Hail Marry (Book 4)

Sheppards in Love-Adjacent Titles

Host for the Holidays (Christmas Escape Series)

Solo for the Season (Gift-Wrapped Christmas Series)

Summer Tease (Falling for Summer Series)

Tales from the Highlands Series

The Widow and the Highlander (Book 1)

The Enemy and Miss Innes (Book 2)

The Innkeeper and the Fugitive (Book 3)

The Gentleman and the Maid (Book 4)

Families of Dorset Series

Wyndcross (Book 1)

Isabel (Book 2)

Cecilia (Book 3)

Hazelhurst (Book 4)

Romance Retold Series

Redeeming Miss Marcotte (Book 1)

A Conspiratorial Courting (Book 2)

A Matchmaking Mismatch (Book 3)

Standalone Titles

To Hunt an Heiress (Bachelors of Blackstone's Series)

A Suitable Arrangement (Castles & Courtship Series)

Goodwill for the Gentleman (Belles of Christmas Book 2)

The Christmas Foundling (Belles of Christmas: Frost Fair Book 5)

The Highwayman's Letter (Sons of Somerset Book 5)

Of Lands High and Low

Mishaps and Memories (Timeless Regency Collection)

The Road through Rushbury (Seasons of Change Book 1)

Eleanor: A Regency Romance

Acknowledgments

It's been six years since I published my first book, and now, more than ever, I realize how vital my community is to each book I write.

My husband, Brandon, is the number one essential person I rely upon, and I'm so grateful for his support and patience!

Thank you to my critique partners and dear friends, Kasey, Deborah, and Jess. Couldn't do this gig without you, and I certainly wouldn't want to.

I love every one of the women who wrote books in this series—there's a reason we've continued to work together all these years!

Thank you to my beta readers: Brooke, Emily, Heidi, Karen, Heidi, Jamie, and Nan. Your feedback was instrumental in getting this story into shape, as always.

Thank you to my editors, Jacque, Emily, and Carolyn, for helping make sure this book was fit for public consumption!

Thank you to all my readers who make it possible for me to continue writing stories. I will forever be grateful to you for spending your precious hours on my books!

About the Author

Whitney Award-winning Martha Keyes was born, raised, and educated in Utah—a home she loves dearly but also loves to leave for stints of world travel. She received a BA in French Studies and a Master of Public Health from Brigham Young University.

Her route to becoming an author was full of twists and turns, but she's finally settled into something she loves. Research, daydreaming, and snacking have become full-time jobs, and she couldn't be happier about it. When she isn't writing, she is honing her photography skills, looking for travel deals, and spending time with her family.

Printed in Dunstable, United Kingdom